# THE
# GODDESS
## OF
# SHIPWRECKED
# SAILORS

# THE
# GODDESS
## OF
# SHIPWRECKED
# SAILORS

*A
Lizzie Crane
Mystery*

# Skye Alexander

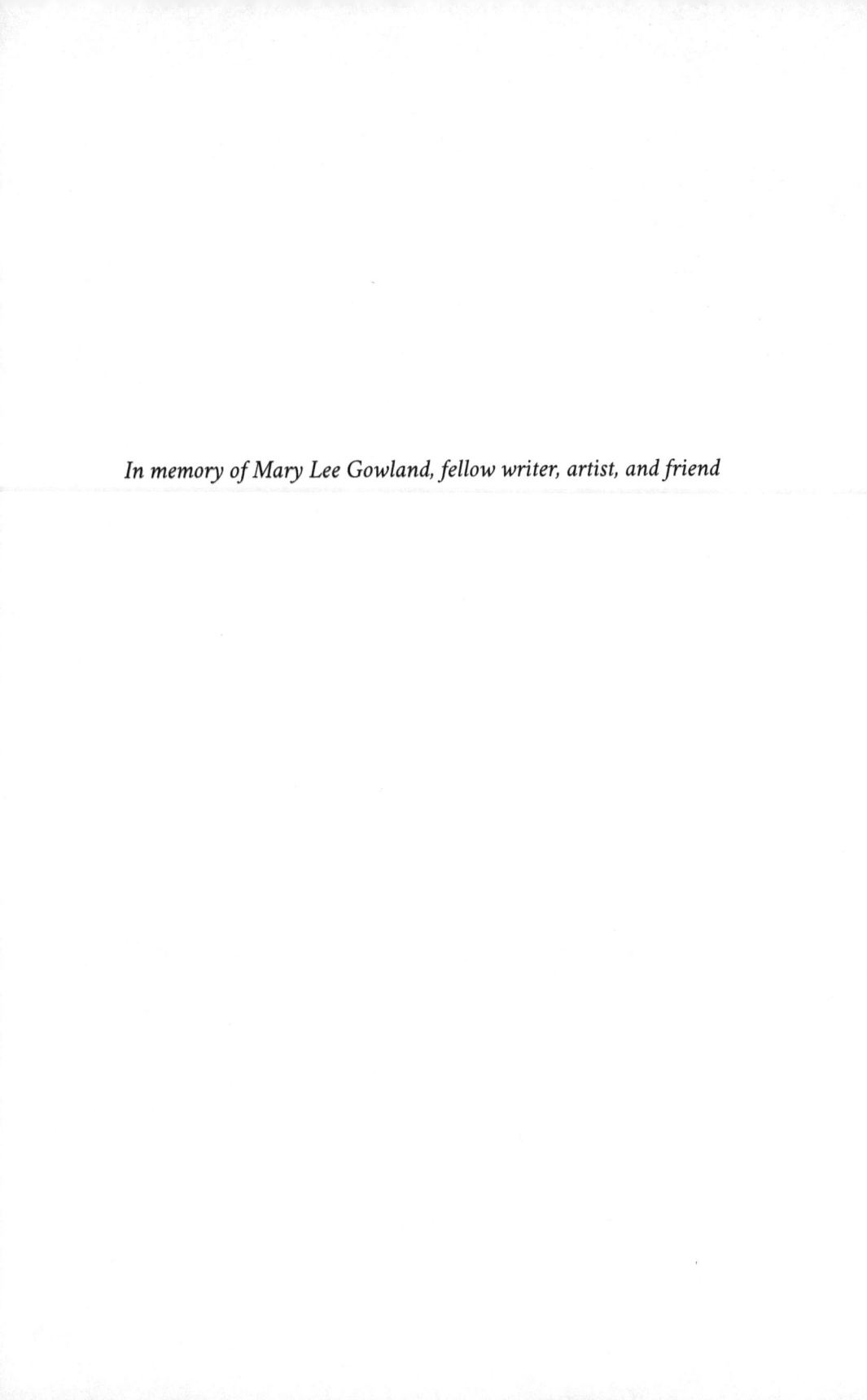

*In memory of Mary Lee Gowland, fellow writer, artist, and friend*

# Praise for the Lizzie Crane Mysteries

"Skye Alexander's characters are realistic, intriguing, and filled with adventure. *The Goddess of Shipwrecked Sailors* is the perfect historical mystery, steeped in the Jazz Age, and filled with plot twists and turns. Fortunately for readers, it's only the beginning of more thrills for Lizzie Crane and her admirers as the series continues."—Susan Van Kirk, author of the Art Center Mystery Series and the Endurance Mystery Series

"Skye Alexander takes her readers on an exhilarating ride that will keep them turning the pages all the way to the exciting and altogether unexpected climax. This is a great read, filled from beginning to end with accurate historical references, and unforgettable characters."—Gregory Stout, author of *Lost Little Girl* and *Gideon's Ghost*

"The Golden Age of Mystery is alive and well in Skye Alexander's clever and charming Lizzie Crane novels.... Agatha Christie fans: You've found your next great read."—Lori Robbins, author of the On Pointe and Master Class mystery series

# Chapter One

"On the second day of Christmas

my true love sent to me:

Two Turtle Doves

and a Partridge in a Pear Tree."

— *Frederic Austin, "The Twelve Days of Christmas"*

After driving for seven hours, the four musicians arrived at Matthew Gardner's home on the most fashionable street in Salem, Massachusetts, a three-hundred-year-old town known for its seafaring history, Nathanial Hawthorne, and hanging women suspected of witchcraft. Lizzie eyed the grand boulevard and the elegant eighteenth- and nineteenth-century mansions that lined both sides of it.

"How very pretty," she said.

Candles burned in the windows of the Gardners' handsome three-story Georgian house. An electrified Moravian star illuminated the front portico. In the yard, an evergreen tree strung with chains of popcorn and cranberries offered food for the birds. Despite temperatures in the low teens, a group of carolers, bundled up against the cold, strolled from house to house, celebrating the holiday with joyful voices.

Sidney parked his new Buick convertible at the curb. "Not as swanky as some of our other venues."

Lizzie sensed a hint of pique in her longtime friend's voice. She knew he'd wanted to stay in New York through the holidays, performing at a few private parties and clubs. Easy, relaxed. Nothing fancy. He'd hoped to unwind after two recent traumatic engagements that had tested the group's mettle in ways they could never have expected and left them wary of coming to Massachusetts again. But Lizzie urged him to accept this last-minute invitation, citing the generous fee Mr. Gardner had offered. Reluctantly, Sid had agreed.

"At least it's not creepy like the last place we played," Melody grumbled from the backseat. She yawned and stretched her arms overhead, pressing her gloved palms against the Buick's cloth top. "We can be thankful for that, I guess."

"Look, I know you'd rather be home with your family and your new beau, but this will be fun," Lizzie told her nineteen-year-old colleague.

"If you say so," Melody answered, but she didn't sound convinced.

Unlike her friends, Lizzie was glad to get away. For her, Christmas was fraught with unrealistic expectations, stress, and guilt at a time when peace and happiness should prevail. Yesterday—Christmas day—she'd visited her parents in their fourth-floor walk-up flat in the Bronx and handed her father an envelope stuffed with cash, so he could buy presents for her six younger siblings and keep the heat on through the holidays.

"I think it's pretty too. I'm glad we came," Bert said, and Lizzie knew he relished a temporary escape from the city that held so many unpleasant memories for him. This time last year, he'd been living on the street, playing for change in the subway and parks.

"Hand me my hat, will you, Bearcat? I'll just see what's what," Sidney said. Leaving the auto running, he grabbed his fedora and stepped out into the frightful cold.

Lizzie pulled her cloche hat over her dark, bobbed hair and threw off her lap blanket. "I'm coming with you." She followed him through the mansion's wrought iron gate and up its brick sidewalk to a heavy wooden

2

door decorated with a balsam wreath.

Sidney knocked, and a balding butler wearing a morning coat and gray-striped trousers greeted them in a tone almost as frosty as the air. "Good afternoon. May I help you?"

"Good afternoon. I'm Sidney Somerset, and this is my colleague Elizabeth Crane, with The Troubadours. We're the New York musicians Mr. Gardner hired to entertain his guests during the holiday."

"Mr. Gardner is expecting you. I was told there would be four performers."

"The others are waiting in my motorcar. I'll go fetch them, now that we know we've arrived at the right address."

"You may park your automobile around back, in one of the empty bays in the carriage house."

Lizzie pulled her coat tight against the chill and smiled at the butler. His close-shaven reddish jowls reminded her of the barber who owned the shop where her father worked. "You know my name, sir. May I know yours?"

"Robert Townsend, at your service, miss."

"I hope you enjoyed a merry Christmas, Mr. Townsend."

His head dipped in the slightest of nods. "And you as well, Miss Crane."

Melody and Bert climbed out of the Buick, shivering in the fierce cold. While Sidney parked the car, the carolers approached the Gardner mansion and launched into a lively rendition of "The Twelve Days of Christmas." Before they'd finished the second verse, a short, middle-aged man with a full head of wavy graying hair pushed past the butler. He stood in the open doorway and joined in the singing.

*He's a first-rate baritone,* Lizzie noted with surprise. Inspired by the revelers' high spirits, she added her professional voice to the others.

After the final "partridge in a pear tree," the short man invited everyone into the mansion. "Come in, come in one and all. Warm yourselves with a cup of wassail."

The Troubadours and the carolers streamed into a central entry hall decorated with winter greenery. Holly swags hung on the balustrade of a sweeping staircase. Festive aromas of balsam, bayberry candles, and hot wassail laced with cinnamon welcomed them.

A housemaid approached the entertainers and asked, "May I take your wraps?"

"Thank you," Lizzie said, shrugging out of her silver-gray cashmere coat with its curly lamb collar.

Melody, Sidney, and Bert handed their overcoats to the maid, too, and then followed the carolers into a formal dining room lit by both candles and electric fixtures. Hand-painted wallpaper hung on the walls. Ornate Chinese porcelain filled a handsome breakfront. On a mahogany sideboard sat a silver tray of cookies and a crystal punchbowl full of purple liquid on which orange slices floated. Two serving girls, wearing starched white aprons over their prim gray dresses, stood ready to assist the sudden influx of visitors.

Lizzie hung back, watching the others partake of the traditional holiday treats. She looked around, expecting to see her host's wife, but no woman who fit the "wife" description appeared. The short man with the lovely voice hung back too.

"I'm Matthew Gardner," he said, tilting his face up to smile at Lizzie, who stood a good six inches taller than him. "You must be the acclaimed New York diva who's come to entertain my family and guests. None of my acquaintances can sing so exquisitely."

She held out her hand. "Elizabeth Crane. I'm pleased to meet you, Mr. Gardner. Thank you for this opportunity to celebrate the holiday season with you, your family, and your friends."

"Thank *you* for agreeing to come on such short notice," he said, steering her into the elegant dining room.

She knew his first-choice entertainers had cancelled at the last minute, leaving him in the lurch. One of Gardner's neighbors, a woman Lizzie had met during The Troubadours' previous engagement in nearby Gloucester, had recommended them and encouraged them to charge a hefty fee due to the late scheduling.

Lizzie reached for a cookie as the butler approached Gardner. In a hushed voice he said, "Pardon me, sir, but there's a policeman here to speak with you."

"If he's looking for a donation, tell him I'll contribute next week," Gardner said.

"I think it's something more urgent than that, sir."

"Very well. Miss Crane, will you please excuse me?"

"Of course, Mr. Gardner."

As her host accompanied his butler into the mansion's entry hall, Lizzie followed at a discreet distance. Two deaths during two of the troupe's recent stints had made her jittery around policemen. Most likely, the nervousness she felt now was unfounded, and she was overreacting, but if anything suspicious were afoot, she wanted to know about it sooner than later. She ducked behind a lacquered Oriental screen and eavesdropped on the conversation between her host and a uniformed officer who seemed to be suffering from a winter cold.

The policeman blew his nose and said in a nasal voice, "I apologize for bothering you, sir, but a man has just been found dead near the harbor. He had a letter addressed to you in his pocket."

"I'm sorry to hear of his passing, at Christmastime no less," Gardner said, his jovial mood plummeting. "Who is the man? Do you know how he died?"

"We don't know much yet, sir. No identification on him. But the letter said 'The lady is not so easily won.' It wasn't signed. Does it mean anything to you?"

Gardner shook his head. "No, nothing. May I see the letter?"

"Sorry, sir, but it's at the station. Evidence, you know. You can come downtown and read it there if you like."

"I understand. I wish I could be of more help."

"If you think of anything that might be useful, Mr. Gardner, I trust you'll be in touch." The officer sniffed loudly, then blew his nose again. "All right, then. I'll leave you to your guests. A good evening, sir."

\* \* \*

The carolers apparently hadn't noticed the wheezy policeman's presence—or if they had, they paid no attention to it. The man's visit had lasted only a few minutes. As soon as she could, Lizzie sneaked back into the dining room where people cheerfully clustered around the wassail and cookies.

Among them, she spotted a woman in her middle years whose delicate figure and ivory skin made her seem younger. She reminded Lizzie of a porcelain doll. The woman's burgundy-colored afternoon dress, although conservative in cut, spoke of quality, and Lizzie guessed those were real rubies in her choker. *Could this be Mrs. Gardner?*

Two girls who looked to be in their mid-teens stood at the far end of the room, avoiding the visitors. From the sullen looks on their faces, they wished to be anywhere but here. The older one's dreamy beauty made Lizzie think of the ladies in John Waterhouse's paintings. She wore a lovely rose-pink frock of the finest wool and a jeweled comb in her glossy chestnut hair. The younger girl resembled her, but with her plainer face and thicker torso, she seemed a poor imitation of the other, whom Lizzie guessed was her sister.

Lizzie's colleagues stood apart from the rest of the guests, awaiting instructions from their host. After helping herself to a cup of wassail, she joined them.

"What was that about?" Sidney asked her.

"Just a policeman making a holiday visit."

He narrowed his eyes. "Is that a fact-ski?"

"Not exact-ski. I'll tell you later," she said and took a sip of her drink. "This wassail isn't half bad, considering it's made with plain old grape juice, not proper mulled wine."

"Maybe the Gardners are teetotalers," Bert suggested.

"Or they don't want to serve the real thing to a bunch of people who've just wandered in off the street," Sidney said.

Melody interrupted. "Look, a lady's coming this way."

The four Troubadours turned their attention to the petite woman in the burgundy velvet frock. She wound her way through the group of carolers, who called out good wishes as they merrily prepared to depart and head back outside into the bitter cold.

The winter sun had set half an hour ago, and tonight's temperature would drop into the single digits. Lizzie tried not to think about the poor who'd suffer in this harsh weather. Suddenly an idea popped into her mind: perhaps the dead man the policeman asked about had frozen to death. Nothing sinister. But what did the cryptic note to Matthew Gardner mean? Before she could consider the possibility further, the doll-like woman reached them.

"Welcome to our home. I'm Abigail Gardner. My husband and I are pleased to have you as our guests." She held out her hand to Sidney, who gently grasped her fingers. He dipped his head in a graceful bow, revealing the balding spot Lizzie knew he was sensitive about.

"Thank you for allowing us to take part in this festive occasion and to entertain your family and guests as we greet the New Year," he said in the voice he used with clients. "I'm Sidney Somerset, The Troubadours' pianist and business manager. This lovely lady is Elizabeth Crane, our songbird and choreographer. Melody Fitzgerald, as you'll soon see, is a virtuoso on flute and violin. And our newest member, Bert Halley, plays saxophone, clarinet, and trumpet, though if a coronet or trombone came his way, he'd manage to play it too."

Mrs. Gardner smiled and nodded at each member of the group. "My neighbor, Cora Delaney, has spoken highly of you. She says she met you at a birthday party in October."

Mention of that ill-fated gathering stirred up unpleasant memories, but Lizzie forced herself to keep a polite expression on her face. How much had Cora told the Gardners? Did they know about the lady who died there? Or that Cora read tarot cards?

"We're grateful to Miss Delaney for her recommendation," Lizzie said. "I hope I'll have a chance to visit with her while we're here."

The diminutive woman looked up at Lizzie and answered, "I'm certain you will. She's agreed to attend a few of the events we have planned for the holiday."

"Wonderful," Lizzie said.

"I expect you must be tired from your long journey," Mrs. Gardner said. "Our housekeeper, Mrs. Platt, will show you ladies to your room. Our butler will have one of the lads take the gentlemen to their quarters. Mr. Townsend will arrange for your luggage to be brought in."

"Thank you, Mrs. Gardner."

"After you've had time to settle in and freshen up," she continued, "our cook will send supper to your chambers. If there's anything else you need this evening, please don't hesitate to ask."

Sidney rubbed his right thumb and fingertips together, and Lizzie knew he longed for a cigarette but didn't know if it was proper to light one here. "When Mr. Gardner and I agreed to this commitment, we discussed a performance schedule," he said. "Miss Crane and I would like to go over that with him in the morning."

"Yes, of course. My husband and I will meet with you after breakfast to address the details. Shall we say ten o'clock, in the double parlor across the hall?"

"I'll need to see the space where we'll be playing as well," Lizzie said.

"The front half of the parlor can be closed off for intimate and casual gatherings. The pocket doors can be opened to accommodate larger events." Mrs. Gardner smiled at Sidney. "I think you'll find the acoustics quite satisfactory and the Steinway Grand exemplary."

# Chapter Two

"Three things cannot long be hidden: the sun, the moon, and the truth."

— *Confucius*

While climbing the stairs to the mansion's third floor, Lizzie fretted about being housed with the servants. Although the terms of their contract stipulated that their employer must provide room and board for the entertainers during their stay, the specifics of those terms could be defined broadly. Having come from a poor family herself, she didn't look down on girls trying to earn their way in the world—quite the opposite. But servants' quarters, minimal as they usually were, didn't provide the amenities two New York entertainers required for their extensive wardrobes, grooming, and other necessities. They also tended to be poorly heated, and she couldn't afford to catch a cold when twelve days of singing lay ahead of her.

However, when the plain, stocky housekeeper—whose drab appearance mocked her colorful name, Violet Platt—unlocked the door to the room Lizzie and Melody would share, the singer was pleasantly surprised. The chamber's windows afforded a fine view of the city. Twin brass bedsteads, a wardrobe so large Lizzie wondered how someone had managed to muscle it up the stairs, a pretty vanity with a marble top, a six-drawer bureau, and two armchairs upholstered in green velvet furnished the room. *Surely the maids who occupy the rest of this floor don't enjoy such finery,* she thought. *Maybe this is where the Gardners put visiting relatives who don't rate accommodations on the second story with the rest of the family.*

"The bathroom is through that door." Mrs. Platt pointed and handed Lizzie a key. "A button on the wall, just there, will summon a maid if you need anything. I hope you'll be comfortable during your stay."

Radiators hissed welcome heat into the room, and a fireplace laid with oak logs waited for someone to light them. The entertainers' suitcases and steamer trunk, as well as Melody's instrument cases, had been delivered and now sat piled on a floral hooked rug in front of the fireplace.

"Thank you, Mrs. Platt. I'm sure we shall be."

After the housekeeper left, Melody said, "This is nice, don't you think?"

"I do," Lizzie agreed. "I wonder where they put Sidney and Bert."

"I heard something about a carriage house."

Lizzie cringed. She could almost hear Sidney grousing. At one of their earlier venues, he'd been quartered in a barn with the stable hands, which sparked no end of complaints. Some patrons viewed the entertainers as honored celebrities; others considered them hired help. The latter always threw Sid into a state of righteous indignation. *We need to establish better guidelines,* she decided.

"Why don't you unpack and relax while I find out where the men are," Lizzie told her younger colleague. "You might even have time to write a letter to your parents to let them know you've arrived safe and sound."

Downstairs she found a housemaid, a girl almost as tall as Lizzie though not so curvaceous, whose prettiness was marred by a port wine birthmark that covered most of her left cheek. "Good evening. I'm Elizabeth Crane, one of the Gardners' guests for the holidays. And who are you, may I ask?"

The girl rubbed at her apron nervously, as if brushing off crumbs. "I'm called Fanny, ma'am."

"Well, Fanny, I wonder if you could direct me to where the men in my troupe are staying."

The girl glanced around, apparently searching for somebody to sanction or forbid her actions before she complied with this outsider's request. Seeing no one, she said, "Follow me, ma'am."

Lizzie trailed the girl through a spacious, well-appointed kitchen awash in tantalizing smells, down a hallway with a larder on one side and a laundry room on the other, and out into a courtyard blanched white with winter frost. The sharp chill stunned her, and she wished she'd thought to wear her coat. A nearly full moon lit their path to a two-story carriage house where lights shown in the upstairs windows. Lizzie followed the servant to a narrow flight of stairs on the outside of the building that led up to a door. A dim electric lamp burned above it.

"They're up there, ma'am," the girl pointed.

Lizzie handed her a coin. "Thank you, Fanny."

"Shall I come later and guide you back to the big house?"

"No, I can easily find my way."

The girl looked at the coin with surprise, and Lizzie wondered if the maid thought she was up to no good, visiting the men's quarters alone.

"I'll leave the back door open for you, ma'am," Fanny said.

* * *

"Not bad," Lizzie said as she assessed the apartment in the Gardners' carriage house. "Quite pleasant, really."

The men's quarters included a bedroom, sitting room, kitchenette, and bathroom. Modestly furnished and comfortably warm. She wondered how her two colleagues would handle the single bedroom. *Does Bert even realize that Sid prefers men to women—or care?*

Although she'd expected complaints from Sidney, he pointed to a wooden cabinet in one corner. "It even has a radio."

"And a Frigidaire," Bert added, obviously pleased with the tony new appliance.

"Plus, it's private," she said. "You can sneak out unawares and enjoy Salem's nightlife without anyone knowing what you're about."

Sidney fitted a cigarette into an ornate silver holder and lit it. "You think this provincial town in the frozen hinterlands has a nightlife?"

"Don't be such a snob. It's not New York, certainly, but I bet it's not as dull as you think. More than 40,000 people live here. And seaports are known for all sorts of delights and debauchery." Lizzie dropped into a tan leather armchair and propped her feet up on an English folding campaign table. "Now, Sid, as I recall, you brought several bottles up from the City. How about opening one to celebrate our new adventure?"

"What's your preference?"

"A bit of gin-ski."

"You're in-ski."

"How about you, Bert?" Sidney asked.

The long-legged young horn player had been restlessly ambling about since Lizzie arrived, as if trying to work off the forced immobility of the long drive from Manhattan.

"Sure, pour me some too."

Sidney found ice cubes in the refrigerator, then splashed a few fingers' worth of gin into three glasses. He handed one to each of his colleagues.

"Cheers," he said as they clinked glasses. "May 1926 bring us success, wealth, and happiness beyond our wildest dreams."

"Hear, hear," Bert agreed.

*And may this engagement go off without a hitch,* Lizzie silently prayed.

Sidney settled himself into a leather armchair that matched the one Lizzie sat in, except for the cigarette burn in one arm, and blew smoke rings at the ceiling. "Want to tell me why that copper stopped by tonight? I get the feeling he wasn't simply wishing our host happy holidays."

This trip back to Massachusetts stirred up bad memories, and she knew her companions were all a bit on edge. She hesitated to reveal what little she'd overheard, knowing it might rattle Sidney. Her friend longed for a life as comfortable as a trip in a luxury Pullman car and balked at controversy, especially when it threatened to interfere with their work. Still, she decided, he had a right to know.

"A man was found dead near Salem Harbor. That's about a mile from here. He had a letter in his pocket addressed to Matthew Gardner."

Bert whistled through his gapped front teeth. "Wow. What do you make of that?"

"I don't know what to make of it," she answered. "It's probably just a coincidence."

"A man gets killed while *coincidentally* carrying a letter to our host." Sidney ran a hand through his thinning dark hair. "Sounds fishy to me. Not an auspicious way to begin this stint."

"Don't get in a lather, Sid. I'm sure there's a logical explanation. I'll try to find out more—"

"No, stay out of it, Bearcat," he cut her off. "Remember what happened the last time you went poking your pretty little nose into places you shouldn't have."

Bert stopped pacing and leaned against the refrigerator. "Maybe Lizzie's right. If our man Gardner is involved in some kind of shady business, we don't want to get dragged into it. The devil you know, and all that."

"And if it's nothing, we can scratch it off our worry list." Lizzie held out her glass for a refill. "Now, how about another drink-ski?"

Sidney pushed himself up from the armchair and plucked the glass from her hand. "You know what I think-ski? Coming here was a bad idea from the start, regardless of how ducky the dough is."

*But you don't have to worry about dough, Sid. You have a trust fund to fall back on,* she thought. *For you, getting paid good money for doing what you love is just proof that other people value your talent.* Instead she said, "We're all tired. Let's finish our drinks, eat supper, get a good night's sleep, and see what the morning brings."

* * *

When Lizzie returned to her bedchamber, Melody was just about to dig into the meal a housemaid had delivered.

"Oh, good, you're here," the petite blond flutist said. "I was afraid everything would be cold by the time you got back."

"What's for dinner? It smells good." Lizzie helped herself to two slices of roast chicken, butternut squash, mashed potatoes, and pickled beets. A

13

basket held Parker House rolls, and she slathered one with butter. "I see there's apple cobbler for dessert too. If only we had a gift of the grape to go with this."

"There's a pot of tea."

"Yes, well, I suppose that will have to do."

"How are Sid and Bert? Are they settled in?" Melody asked. "What's their place like?"

"They're fine. Their accommodations are comfortable enough, and Sid's pleased that they have a radio."

Lizzie set her plate on the vanity and began eating. *A table would be nice,* she thought. *Maybe I should ask the Gardners for one.*

"What did that policeman want?" Melody asked after a bit.

For a moment, Lizzie considered lying to her younger friend, but decided instead to soft pedal what she'd overheard. "He said a man had been found dead not far from here and asked if Mr. Gardner knew the deceased. It's possible the poor fella may have frozen to death."

"How sad to die during the holidays. I'll say a prayer for his family."

"Good idea."

"Did Mr. Gardner know the dead man?"

"He said not," Lizzie answered. *But if not, why was the man carrying a note addressed to Matthew Gardner? And what lady might their host want to win?*

# Chapter Three

"They that go down to the sea in ships, that do business in great waters;

These see the works of the Lord, and his wonders in the deep.

For he commandeth, and raiseth the stormy wind, which lifteth up the waves thereof."

— *Psalm 107, King James Bible*

After bathing and applying a bit of face powder and lipstick, Lizzie dressed in a conservative royal blue daytime frock that complemented her smoky eyes and dark hair. She ate a hearty breakfast of apple pancakes, washed down with plenty of strong black coffee, brought to her bedroom by one of the housemaids. Then she went downstairs to visit the kitchen.

"Good morning," Lizzie said to a young woman with skin the color of amber and short, curly black hair. "I'd like to offer my compliments to the cook."

"Yes, ma'am. That's my mother." She pointed to a woman with the same golden skin and a figure like an overstuffed easy chair. A bright red turban wound around her head. "Mama, there's a lady here to see you."

With a slow, rolling gait, the woman crossed the brightly lit kitchen, where a bevy of girls stirred pots, slid trays into ovens, and washed stacks of dishes. At a worktable in an out-of-the-way corner, two more girls kneaded dough. The woman wiped her forehead with the back of her hand, leaving a streak of flour above her eyebrows. Her heavy-lidded brown eyes assessed Lizzie.

"Yes'm? What can I do for you?"

"Hello, I'm Elizabeth Crane, from New York City. Mr. and Mrs. Gardner have hired my friends and me to perform during the holiday."

"Yes'm, I heard some big-time New York musicians be here."

*We're a long way from the big time,* Lizzie thought, *but I'm glad we're being touted as such.* "I wanted to thank you for the delicious meals you sent to my bedchamber last night and this morning."

"You be welcome, I'm sure, Miz Crane."

"May I know your name?"

"Pearl. And this here's my oldest girl, Ruby."

"You're named for jewels."

The cook nodded. "My other two girls be Jade an' Opal. I called 'em that so's they'd always remember they're precious."

"What a lovely idea," Lizzie said. "Well, I just wanted to make your acquaintance and express my appreciation."

"Just doin' my job, ma'am. Anythin' special you be wantin' you let me or Ruby know."

"Thanks, I will. Good day, then."

"G'day to you too, ma'am."

\* \* \*

The grandfather clock in the central hallway struck ten as Lizzie entered the double parlor where Sidney and their hosts waited. An evergreen tree, decorated with hundreds of ornaments and several strings of colored electric lights, stood in a corner near the windows facing Chestnut Street, where passersby could admire it.

Pocket doors had been opened to reveal a gracious space that stretched from the front of the mansion to the back, an expanse of perhaps fifty by

16

thirty feet. Celadon-colored silk covered the walls. Chippendale sofas and chairs, upholstered in creamy damask, flanked a fireplace in the front part of the parlor. As promised, a Steinway Grand piano, gleaming like a glossy black onyx, presided at the rear of the double room. Lizzie wondered if Sid had already made its acquaintance. As she entered the parlor, her friend and Mr. Gardner stood. Gardner's head barely came up to Sidney's shoulder, but he radiated such vitality that he seemed a more forceful presence than his modest stature would suggest.

"I trust you slept well and have settled in comfortably," her host said.

"Yes, thank you. Everything's quite copacetic," she answered, motioning for the men to sit. "A good morning to you all."

Abigail Gardner perched on the edge of a settee beside her husband, her hands folded in her lap. Lizzie noticed the diminutive woman's feet didn't quite touch the floor. "Would you care for coffee or tea?" she asked.

"No, thank you, I've had plenty," Lizzie said as she sat in an armchair next to Sidney.

Gardner got right to the point. "We've planned on a small concert this afternoon for about twenty people, beginning at two and lasting until four or thereabouts. I know we didn't discuss this in advance, and it's short notice, but can you manage it?"

"Certainly. What mood do you want us to set?" Sidney asked as he fitted a cigarette into his signature silver holder, apparently testing the waters to see if his hosts would object to him smoking.

"I understand jazz is your specialty," Mrs. Gardner said.

"Ab-so-lute-ly," Lizzie answered.

"Then shall we treat our guests to an afternoon of jazz, Matthew?" Mrs. Gardner laid her tiny white hand on her husband's arm.

He nodded. "Yes, indeed."

"Excellent. I'd like to play the piano beforehand," Sidney said. "And we'll need this space for practice an hour before your guests arrive."

"Mr. Somerset, we are at your disposal," Gardner said.

Lizzie handed Sidney a notebook in which she'd written down their proposed schedule. He studied it briefly, then said, "Tomorrow evening,

17

we've got a formal dinner party, and on Tuesday, a luncheon with gaming afterward."

"That's correct," Mrs. Gardner said.

"Excuse me, but I have a question," Lizzie interrupted. "How will your guests enjoy our music if we're playing in here and you're eating and chatting across the hall in the dining room?"

"Can't you play loud enough for us to hear?" Gardner asked.

"Yes, but you'll miss the dramatic effect of a live performance. You may as well listen to a phonograph record."

He seemed puzzled. "What do you suggest, Miss Crane?"

"What would you think of moving the dining table and chairs in here, just for the evening?"

"Oh, dear," Mrs. Gardner muttered, a note of worry in her voice. She glanced about nervously, apparently trying to imagine what sort of setup Lizzie had in mind.

"There's plenty of room, if we shift some of the furniture around." Lizzie waved her hands as if to magically move the parlor's sofas, chairs, and tables out of the way. "Plus you've got this lovely fireplace, and with the Christmas tree all lit up, well, it will be quite festive."

Gardner slapped his thigh. "You know, I think it would work. I'll have a couple lads see to it tomorrow morning. Under your direction, Miss Crane."

"Thank you, Mr. Gardner. Say, while they're at it, do you think they could bring that little dropleaf table under the window over there up to my bedchamber, so my colleague and I will have something to eat on during our stay here?"

He grinned and nodded. "Anything else?"

Lizzie smiled back. "Not at the moment, sir. Thanks ever so much."

They worked their way through the rest of the proposed schedule, discussing music preferences and making a few adjustments to the original plan. Although Abigail Gardner seemed uncertain—and perhaps peeved at the idea of having her home rearranged to suit an outsider's whim—her husband appeared delighted.

*I'll have to be careful of her,* Lizzie thought as she studied the lady of the house. Dealing with the wives at their engagements was always a challenge. Their husbands were inevitably drawn to Lizzie's sensual beauty, and she'd learned to use that attraction to her advantage. Deflecting the women's jealousy presented more of a challenge. Not for the first time, she thought how much easier it would be if Sid felt differently about her, if they were a couple. But she might as well wish for eternal youth. Pushing her regrets aside, she brought her attention back to the meeting.

By the time they'd finished ironing out the details, Gardner was calling Sidney "old chap." He even complimented the pianist's silver cigarette holder.

"I have a carved ivory one my grandfather acquired in China in 1850, although I prefer a pipe myself. He owned clippers and traded in the Orient." Gardner pointed at several intricate wooden models of ships displayed on floor-to-ceiling shelves in the rear portion of the double parlor. "Those represent some of his fleet."

Curious, Lizzie stood and crossed the golden pine floor made of King George boards to get a better look. Each model was a carefully crafted work of art about three feet long and two feet high. Linen sails and rigging graced their masts. Tiny lifeboats hung on their sides. Numerous details—flags, ropes, anchors, and even cannon—hinted at their stories. *How beautiful the real ships must have been,* she mused.

Matthew Gardner joined her as she admired a replica of a ship more delicate than the others and, to her untrained eye, more graceful. "That one, *Peregrine,* was the last in my grandfather's fleet," he said. "He named her that because she was the swiftest of all."

"What happened to her?"

"She sank in a storm in 1868, a few miles from Salem Harbor. The captain and all but one member of the crew died."

"How very sad."

"Yes, but by then, the clipper ship era was over. The opening of the Suez Canal the following year hammered the final nail in the coffin."

# Chapter Four

"Life is a lot like jazz...it's best when you improvise."

— *George Gershwin*

After talking with the Gardners, Lizzie felt reasonably content with their performance schedule. Melody had gone downstairs to meet with Bert—she'd decided to give him flute lessons, and in return, he'd offered to teach her the clarinet. Sidney was making friends with the Steinway Grand. Finally, she had a sliver of peace and quiet all to herself. She kicked off her shoes, then fluffed up the pillows on her single bed, leaned them against the brass headboard, and settled in to write two letters.

The first was a thank-you to Cora Delaney, who'd recommended The Troubadours for this engagement. On stationery she'd found in the vanity drawer, Lizzie expressed her gratitude and asked if she could visit. Two months ago, under troubled circumstances, she and the Salem heiress had met and established a tentative friendship. According to Lizzie's tourist map of the city, Cora lived within easy walking distance of the Gardners' home.

The second letter required more thought. Since The Troubadours' first trip to Massachusetts four months ago, Lizzie had indulged romantic fantasies about a handsome, wealthy, and prominent Boston socialite she'd met while performing at the Ipswich estate of a noted industrialist. A man who stirred her blood and starred in her dreams. They'd exchanged a few letters since that time and met on two occasions when he came to New

York on business. Although he seemed interested in her, the social and economic disparity between his standing and hers made her wary of getting emotionally involved. Still, she couldn't stop thinking about him.

After several false starts, she crumpled the letter into a ball. It probably wouldn't reach him in time anyway if she mailed it by general post. She could telephone him, if the Gardners allowed her to use their phone. Or, she could send a telegram from the newly opened Hawthorne Hotel next to Salem Common, where she and her friends had spent a night during their last visit to Massachusetts.

A clock on the bedside table read half past eleven. If she hurried, she could walk to the Hawthorne in twenty minutes and be back in time to practice for this afternoon's concert. Lizzie stepped into her shoes again. She buttoned up her coat, wrapped a scarf around her neck, and pulled a cloche hat over her fashionably bobbed dark hair. A phone call would be easier, she realized. But the possibility of missing him—or worse yet, hearing his secretary say, "Mr. Peabody isn't available to receive calls"—led her to choose this alternate route.

On the way out, she encountered a plump housemaid with blond braids wrapped around her head. "Pardon me," Lizzie asked, "Could you arrange for a letter to be delivered to a neighbor?"

"Yes, ma'am," the girl answered.

Lizzie handed her the envelope addressed to Cora Delaney, along with a coin. "Thank you. And would you please bring back a response?"

"Yes, ma'am," the girl said again.

Lizzie pulled on her kidskin gloves and stepped out into the biting cold. All along the broad boulevard, she saw grand houses of beautiful proportions boasting architectural details that defined two centuries of style. Some of the mansions had been built by the captains of clipper ships or merchants who'd dared to invest in the risky, yet profitable, China trade. Trade that brought tea, porcelain, silk, spices, and opium to America. Men like Matthew Gardner's grandfather.

Puffing out clouds of smoky breath, she walked the length of Chestnut Street, then on toward the Common. By the time she reached the new brick hotel, Lizzie's nose was bright red, and her cheeks stung from the cold. Her toes had started going numb, despite her woolen stockings. Inside, at the front desk, she asked a young man in a dark blue uniform if she could send a telegram.

"Yes, ma'am," he said and handed her a form to fill out.

After writing down Alan Peabody's address for the clerk, she succinctly composed her invitation.

> Dear Alan,
>     I'm in Salem for twelve days at the home of Matthew Gardner on Chestnut Street. If you have time to meet, I'd welcome your company.
>     Lizzie.

She passed the form back to the young man and paid for the telegram's delivery. Then she pushed through the hotel's heavy glass door into the sub-freezing morning, thankful that at least it wasn't snowing.

A weak sun struggled to shed a hint of warmth on the town as Lizzie detoured a couple blocks to a centuries-old cemetery and slipped through the wrought-iron gate that cordoned it off from Summer Street. Cemeteries had always fascinated her, despite the raised eyebrows and teasing comments from friends who considered her interest macabre. Burying grounds, especially in old cities like Salem, recorded the histories of the people who'd lived and died there—they were family albums etched in stone. They told of diseases like the influenza of 1918 that ravished whole communities, young mothers who perished in childbirth along with their infants, and seafarers who managed to escape the sirens' song only to end up lying in the cold, dark earth instead of at the bottom of the ocean.

Her shoes crunched on the frozen grass as she meandered among tombstones dating back to the first half of the seventeenth century. Crude death's heads carved on gray slate stared back at her with round, vacant eyes. She also saw headstones from the Classical Revival period engraved with weeping willow branches and urns, symbols of mourning drawn from ancient Greece and Rome. Lizzie knelt and ran her gloved fingertips over some of the inscriptions. The earliest epitaphs expressed foreboding statements about the finality of death, whereas the later ones offered hope for an afterlife.

*I'll have to come back here again, when I have more time and it's not so cold,* she promised herself.

Shoving her hands into her coat pockets, she hurried through the rest of the cemetery. As she neared an exit to Pickering Street, she spotted two men standing at a gravesite. Instead of observing the headstone, however, they faced each other. The shorter of the two gesticulated in a dramatic manner while the larger man stood with his arms crossed over his chest, feet planted firmly, as if refusing to concede any ground to the other. Not wanting to interrupt them or to let them see her, Lizzie slipped behind a granite monument on which a human-sized angel stood with wings outstretched.

"She's mine, and I want her back," the shorter man demanded.

"I'm the one who's taken care of her all this time," the bigger man said.

*Are they rival lovers quarreling over a woman?* Lizzie wondered. She started to walk away, but just then, the short man turned slightly so that the morning light illuminated his face, and she realized it was Matthew Gardner.

* * *

Servants had arranged rows of chairs in the rear portion of the double parlor. While guests filled them, Sidney played low-key popular tunes, preparing the way for the livelier jazz numbers The Troubadours would perform during the afternoon. Lizzie spotted the two young ladies she'd seen in the dining room yesterday afternoon, sitting in the audience with Mr. and Mrs. Gardner. *Their daughters,* she decided. Afternoon sunlight poured through the windows. Balsam fir scented the space with an inviting aroma. Thankfully, the mansion's modern heating system and the added warmth from the fireplace made the spacious room quite comfortable, for Lizzie's skimpy flapper dress exposed more of her bare skin than might be wise on this wintry day.

The Troubadours had chosen to start with a medley of George and Ira Gershwin's well-known songs, including two of Lizzie's favorites, "Oh, Lady Be Good" and "Somebody Loves Me." They'd follow with "Rhapsody in Blue," which gave Bert a chance to impress his audience with the clarinet and Sidney to showcase his skill at the piano. Unanimously, the group voted to play "Who Stole My Heart Away" from the popular new musical *Sunny* that had opened recently on Broadway.

"I bet none of these provincial Brahmin have heard it yet," Sidney said.

Bert, a goofy grin on his face, asked, "Does that mean we're performing a public service?"

"Ab-so-lute-ly," Lizzie said as she licked her fingers and slicked down the cowlick in Bert's unruly brown hair. "All right, places everyone."

For the next hour and a half, the quartet played, sang, and danced. Although Lizzie had hoped some members of their audience would get up and launch into a Charleston, none did. Still, the expressions on their faces and their tapping toes suggested these reserved Yankees were enjoying themselves.

On impulse, she called out, "Mr. Gardner, would you join us for a song? Ladies and gentlemen, as I'm sure you know, our host has a swell voice and loves music. What do you say?"

Several guests clapped and urged him on. After a moment of feigned modesty, Matthew Gardner stood and approached her, a pleased smile on his face. Lizzie held out her hand to welcome him.

"Do you have a favorite you'd like to sing?" she asked.

"Do you know 'Yes, Sir, That's My Baby'?"

"Of course."

Bert blew a few bars of the tune, and Lizzie signaled the rest of the group to fall in. As she started singing, Gardner joined her. His face lit up, and his eyes sparkled. Melody moved to his other side, and the two women maneuvered him into an awkward, yet playful dance. When the song ended, Lizzie applauded her host and motioned for the audience to give him a hand. They did. Obviously satisfied with himself, Gardner returned, beaming, to his seat beside his wife.

# CHAPTER FOUR

*Which woman was he thinking about when he sang that song?* Lizzie wondered. *His wife or the one he spoke of in the cemetery?*

# Chapter Five

"Any woman or man who would write the truth of their lives would write a great work. But no one has dared to write the truth of their lives."

— *Isadora Duncan, My Life*

Some of the Gardners' guests stayed for tea. The Troubadours—after accepting compliments on their performance—excused themselves and escaped to their quarters. While Melody settled in to read Margaret Kennedy's new bestseller *The Constant Nymph,* Lizzie changed into velour corduroy knickers and a heavy woolen cardigan, then grabbed her coat and went around back to the carriage house to visit Sid and Bert.

"I thought we were smashing this afternoon," she said as she sank into one of their apartment's comfortable leather chairs.

Sidney poured three glasses of scotch and served his friends. "We did a damn good job, if I do say so," he agreed. "Clever move, Bearcat, getting Gardner to join us for a song. An inspired stroke of public relations."

"Always good to butter up one's host."

"Just be careful not to look like you're flirting with him. I know it's hard for a tomato like you to avoid men's advances, but we don't want Lady Gardner to get in a lather."

Lizzie sipped her scotch, letting its smoky smoothness calm the afternoon's excitement. "It's not me she needs to worry about. Ol' Matt's got his sights set on another woman."

"How do you know that?" Bert asked.

"I overheard him talking about his lady friend to a fella this morning."

Sidney lit a cigarette and threw her a disapproving look. "Stay out of it, Lizzie. It's none of your business."

"It is if it balls up our stint here." Before he could reply, she said, "Don't worry, I'm just keeping my eyes and ears open. The only drama I want to be a part of is our little play on New Year's Eve."

She recalled the letter the police found on a dead man the night they'd arrived. Addressed to Matthew Gardner, it read "The lady is not so easily won." Was this the lady Gardner claimed was his and wanted back? Whoever she was, she already had blood on her hands.

Then another thought wormed its way into her mind. Had Gardner seen Lizzie this morning in the cemetery, before she ducked behind a monument? And if so, did he realize she'd heard him discussing the other woman? Although Lizzie had no intention of carrying the tale to his wife, he didn't know that.

Bert, still keyed up from their performance, restlessly paced the length of the modest sitting room. He wiped fog from one of the apartment's windows and peered out. "I wish it wasn't so cold outside. I'd like to see some of the city."

"Say, why don't we take a drive around town?" Lizzie suggested. "That new floor heater works pretty well, and you'll be warm enough under the Buick's blanket, Bert. We could get a look at the House of the Seven Gables, the harbor, the Common."

She considered scouting out other, less savory historic sites too—Judge Corwin's house, where the Salem Witch Trials were held in 1692, and Gallows Hill, where nineteen people he'd condemned were hanged. But that could wait for another time.

"You're on-ski," Sidney said.

"Then we're gone-ski. I'll fetch Melody and meet you back here in fifteen. Oh, and by the way, it turns out I have a second cousin living in Salem. I never knew about him until I visited my mother on Christmas day and told her we were performing here. His name's Jacob Watkins. Owns a pub around here someplace. Maybe we can find it."

"Got an address?" Bert asked, eager to flee the confines of the apartment.

Sid blew smoke rings at the ceiling. "A pub…that could be a useful connection."

\* \* \*

With the temperature in the single digits, Sidney had a bit of trouble starting his Buick, even in the protection of the carriage house garage. But once it sprang to life, the four friends piled in and headed toward Salem's harbor. Sixty years ago, glorious clipper ships bearing immense wealth from the Orient sailed to and from this port. However, the city's shallow, silty harbor had been forced to relinquish its prominence to Boston and New York. Since then, Salem had shifted its attention to manufacturing and the leather industry in particular.

"Where are we going, Bearcat? You're supposed to be navigating," Sid reminded her.

Although it was only a little past five, a curtain of darkness had already dropped over the city. The Buick's headlights cut a yellowish path through the blackened streets.

Lizzie aimed a flashlight at her tourist map. "Turn here."

The harbor spread out before them. An almost-full moon spilled silver light over the water and lit up the indigo sky. Across the street from the pier, electric lights illuminated the windows of the handsome brick Custom House and other historic buildings along the waterfront. They drove a few blocks farther and turned onto a small side street that led to the fabled House of the Seven Gables. The dark, ominous-looking structure, named for the sharp peaks on its roof, overlooked the ocean. Only a single electric light burned above its front door.

"It's pretty spooky. I'd be afraid to live in it," Melody said.

"This was Hawthorne's cousin's home, and he visited here often. The house inspired his famous novel," Lizzie told her. "If you haven't read the book, you might want to give it a try. I bet the Gardners have a copy. Maybe we can come back and see the house in the daytime—it's probably not so spooky then."

"Where to next, Madame Tour Guide?" Sidney asked.

"Can we try to find my cousin's pub?"

"Okay by me. Lead on."

"Take the next left," Lizzie said.

She couldn't stop thinking about the as-yet-unidentified man who'd died somewhere around here the night before last on his way to deliver a message to Matthew Gardner. Had they unknowingly driven over the spot where he'd taken his last breath? Lizzie hoped the poor fellow had passed quickly and peacefully, perhaps from the dreadful cold, rather than as a victim of foul play. Foul play that led straight to the Gardners' door.

In the dark, she couldn't make out any street numbers, but the pub was easy enough to find. The two-story clapboard structure sat right up against the narrow street. Although she had limited knowledge of architecture, she guessed the building must be at least a hundred years old. Smoke wafted from a central chimney. Weak electric lights burned in the first-floor windows. A simple wooden sign hanging above the front door identified it as Misery Tavern.

"That's it," she said.

Sidney braked in front of the pub and idled while Lizzie contemplated whether or not to go inside. *Misery Tavern's not a very inviting name. Why would anyone slap that depressing moniker on a place of business? Surely it would chase customers away or draw in the most sorrowful down-and-out sorts.* She shone the flashlight on her map again and noticed two islands to the south of Salem's harbor called Misery Islands.

"Well?" Sid prompted her.

"It's getting late," she said, deciding not to pursue it further until she'd had time to think things through. "I'll come back in the daytime when I can see more. Besides, I'm hungry. Let's get something to eat."

"Hear, hear," Bert agreed.

\* \* \*

When Lizzie and Melody returned to their shared bedchamber, they spotted a letter lying on the floor. Apparently, a housemaid had slipped it under the door. Melody stooped and picked it up. "It's addressed to you," she said.

The paper smelled faintly of lavender, and Lizzie's name was written on the envelope in a feminine hand. She tore it open and read:

> Dear Lizzie,
> I'm glad you've arrived safely at the Gardners' home. I'd planned to catch up with you at the tea on Tuesday, but if you'd like to come by tomorrow, I'll be in all day and would welcome your visit.
> Sincerely,
> Cora

She propped the letter against the vanity mirror and took off her coat. Visiting with Cora Delaney could be a pleasant way to spend the afternoon. In the morning, she'd send a girl to Cora's home with a note accepting the card reader's invitation.

"I'm going downstairs to see if I can find a book to read. Mr. Gardner kindly gave me access to his library," she told Melody, who'd already curled up in one of the bedchamber's armchairs in front of the fireplace with her own book.

Silence blanketed the mansion as Lizzie descended the two flights of stairs to the first floor. When she switched on the electric lights, she saw that the servants had tidied the double parlor and repositioned all the furnishings in their usual places. She crossed to the back half of the spacious room, where floor-to-ceiling bookcases and cabinets lined two walls. All manner of books, it seemed, had found their way into the Gardners' collection: history, philosophy, medicine, religion, art, science, economics, poetry, and fiction, all neatly aligned and arranged by subject matter.

Lizzie chose one about Samuel McIntire. The renowned architect's stately buildings graced Chestnut Street and other parts of the town—he'd even designed the Gardners' mansion. *Since I'm here, I really should familiarize myself with his work,* she decided. *When else will I have a chance to see his actual buildings?*

From the many maritime volumes, she selected one about the shipbuilding industry in the nearby town of Essex. She climbed another rung on the library ladder and noticed a group of books about Salem's infamous witch trials. Running her fingers along their spines, she spotted a thick text with a worn cover titled *Salem Witchcraft: with an account of Salem village and a history of opinions on witchcraft and kindred subjects.* She plucked it from the shelf.

"That should hold me for a while," she said aloud as she stepped down from the ladder. She wished she had time to read everything on the shelves. *One day I'll have a library like this,* she promised herself.

# Chapter Six

"It is a truth universally acknowledged that a single man in possession of a good fortune, must be in want of a wife."

— *Jane Austen, Pride and Prejudice*

Rearranging the furniture on the mansion's first floor turned out to be a bigger job than Lizzie anticipated. Although Matthew Gardner had authorized her to oversee the transfer, his wife and the butler, Robert Townsend, kept popping in to check on things and give advice.

First, the two men Gardner assigned to the task had to move the pieces from the rear half of the double parlor into the front half—except the small dropleaf table that Lizzie had asked them to take upstairs to her bedchamber. Next, they had to disassemble the handsome Chippendale dining table, due to its size, and carry it across the hall in sections. In the process, one of the men knocked over a Chinese porcelain vase and it shattered on the floor.

When Abigail Gardner saw it, she uttered a high-pitched cry, like an animal in pain. She picked up a shard and pointed it at Lizzie, as if she meant to slash her with it. Instinctively, Lizzie backed away. Mrs. Gardner's ivory skin flushed red with anger, then she threw the porcelain fragment on the floor and scurried away from the scene, apparently afraid to witness another calamity.

*Jeepers creepers,* Lizzie thought as a housemaid rushed in to sweep up the pieces. *Now I'm officially on her hate list. That vase was probably worth more than we'll earn from this job.*

Townsend continued to hover nearby in his proper morning coat and gray-striped trousers, scowling and cautioning the movers with each step: "Watch out, lads," and "Easy does it," and "Careful going there."

After nearly two hours, the men had reassembled the dining table and positioned it at an angle, so every guest could see the piano and the corner of the rear parlor where The Troubadours would perform tonight. They arranged fourteen chairs around the table, leaving exactly the same amount of space between each chair and its neighbors. Townsend ran a white-gloved hand over its gleaming mahogany surface, and then ordered a housemaid to polish off the men's fingerprints. The parlor's squarish carpet didn't complement the table's rectangular lines and graceful rounded corners, but Lizzie wasn't about to mention that. She'd already caused enough upset for one morning. She thanked the two men and, when Townsend wasn't looking, tipped them both.

No sooner had she gotten back to her third-floor bedroom than a maid arrived with a lunch tray. "Would you set it there, please?" Lizzie asked, pointing at the newly appropriated dropleaf table.

Melody knelt to raise one of the leaves. "This table is darb, Lizzie. How'd you get the Gardners to give it to us?"

"Ask, and you shall receive," she answered. *Good thing I asked before the vase got broken.*

After the serving girl left, Lizzie lifted the lid of a tureen to reveal a hearty chicken soup with potatoes, carrots, and turnips. A basket covered with a linen napkin held corn muffins. A bowl contained halved pears baked with brown sugar and sprinkled with currants.

"Dig in," Lizzie said. "Got to keep up your strength so you can perform well this evening."

Melody ladled soup into two bowls. "Did you get the dining room furniture moved, okay?"

"After a fashion, though not without casualties." Briefly, she explained what had happened. "Say, do you remember Cora Delaney from our last event?"

"The tarot card reader? She's the one who got us this job, isn't she?"

"Right. I'm going to visit her after we finish lunch to thank her. Want to come along?"

Melody paused for a long moment, twisting a lock of golden hair around her finger. "If you want me to...."

"Poor little bunny, you don't have to go. Maintaining contacts isn't part of your job description."

"It's just, well, she seemed sort of strange to me."

"That whole lot was strange," Lizzie agreed, remembering the group of occultists they'd met two months ago at the neo-Gothic castle called Halcyon, fifteen miles north of Salem. "Cora's probably the most down-to-earth of the bunch. Anyway, I rather liked her and thought I'd stop by to say hello. She lives only a few blocks from here."

"Will you say hello for me too?"

Lizzie slathered butter on a corn muffin. "Sure, consider it done."

* * *

Lizzie flipped through her wardrobe, trying to decide what to wear for her meeting with Cora. Even though this was a casual daytime visit, not a fancy tea with a group of Cora's upper-class friends, she remembered the stylish outfits and lovely gowns the woman had worn at Halcyon Castle. She didn't want to appear over- or under-dressed, but she hadn't a clue what was considered proper for a modern, single woman in a conservative town like Salem. Finally, she slid into a calf-length, plum-colored pencil skirt, and a creamy silk blouse, added a rope of pink pearls, then rolled stockings up to just above her knees. She buttoned her gray cashmere coat with its curly lamb collar, pulled on her kidskin gloves, and tucked her purse under her arm.

"I'm off," she said to Melody, who sat at the table doing a crossword puzzle.

"What's a seven-letter word for deceit, beginning with P and ending with Y?" the blond flutist asked.

Lizzie thought for a moment. "How about perfidy?"

"Yes, that's it," Melody said and penciled it in. "You know so many more words than I do, and you never even finished high school."

"Well, I read a lot. That's the best way I know to improve one's vocabulary."

"Have a nice time with Cora."

Outside, the air still had a bite to it, but at least it was warmer than yesterday. *It might even be above freezing,* Lizzie thought as she crossed Essex Street, which ran parallel to Chestnut and then walked another block to Federal Street. Everywhere she looked, she saw handsome eighteenth- and nineteenth-century mansions. Their beautiful entrances, in particular, impressed her. Arched fanlights topped paneled doors. Pretty porticos with neo-classical columns and decorative moldings invited her to come inside. Salem, she'd read, was the most architecturally significant city in America.

Cora's house, like many of its neighbors, followed the Federal style: a central entryway and symmetrical rows of windows with wooden shutters on either side. Three stories tall with clapboards painted a bluish-gray, it had a slate roof capped by a widow's walk, although the house was probably too far from the harbor for a woman to climb up there and scan the sea for a glimpse of her husband's ship. As Lizzie recalled, the spinster Cora, who was probably a dozen years older than Lizzie's twenty-six, lived here alone. *She must get lonely, rattling around in all this space.*

She knocked on the mustard-colored door. After a few moments, a gray-haired housekeeper in a plain brown dress and a crisp white apron opened it. Her face was deeply lined, and her shoulders stooped. Purple veins stood out in her hands as she held the door open, allowing precious heat to escape into the chilly outdoors.

"Good afternoon. I'm Elizabeth Crane, here to see Miss Delaney."

"Please come in out of the cold, miss. She's expecting you."

The woman led Lizzie into a gracious parlor where a fire burned brightly in the fireplace. Cora sat at a Queen Anne secretary, writing a letter. She looked up and smiled warmly, then stood and approached Lizzie, holding out both hands to her guest in welcome. Her well-tailored tweed suit and good pearls made Lizzie glad she'd opted for a classic, understated look.

"I'm happy you could come," Cora said.

"Thank you ever so much for convincing the Gardners to hire us."

To the housekeeper, Cora said, "Would you please bring us tea?" Then she motioned Lizzie toward a sofa and pair of wingchairs positioned near the fireplace. "I hope Matthew and Abigail are treating you well."

"They've been swell," Lizzie said, avoiding the incident of the broken vase.

"Good. Abigail's nice enough most of the time, but she can be a real vixen if you cross her. Did she tell you she comes to me for card readings?"

Surprised, Lizzie said, "No, and I wouldn't have guessed someone like her—"

Cora laughed. "You'd be amazed at the people who pay me for readings."

"You mean, this is a business of yours? Not just a hobby for you and your friends?"

"It's both. I do it to help other people and to gain knowledge for myself. Plus, it brings in a little money to offset the costs of running this place." Cora waved a hand to indicate the beautiful antique house, which Lizzie assumed must be expensive to keep up. Heat alone would surely cost a bundle.

The housekeeper returned bearing a tea tray and set it on a mahogany table in front of Cora and her guest. The fragrant scent of Earl Grey wafted into the room, causing Lizzie to think about how the lucrative tea trade had influenced Salem's evolution. Cora filled two cups, and Lizzie stirred a spoonful of sugar into hers.

"Speaking of tarot readings," Cora said, interrupting her thoughts, "whatever happened with the rich man I saw in the reading I did for you back at Halcyon?"

For a moment, Lizzie hesitated, uncertain whether to share her feelings and experiences with Cora. At one time, she'd wondered if Cora, too, fancied the man Lizzie hoped to see during her stay in Salem.

"We've met up a couple times," she finally admitted and reached for a ginger cookie from the tea tray. "But I can't say anything's taken off. He's in Boston, I'm in New York, and our schedules don't exactly mesh."

"Ah," Cora said, fingering her rope of pearls. "Are we talking about the man I *think* we're talking about? Alan Peabody?"

Lizzie nodded.

"Well, then, you should know that the Gardners have their sights set on him as a husband for their elder daughter, Sarah."

"What?"

"As Jane Austen wrote in *Pride and Prejudice*, 'It is a truth universally acknowledged that a single man in possession of a good fortune, must be in want of a wife.'"

An image flashed in Lizzie's mind of the winsome young lady she'd seen in the Gardners' dining room the evening The Troubadours arrived in Salem. A young woman with all the things Lizzie lacked: money, status, family connections. Something bright and beautiful and full of hope crumbled painfully inside her. With shaking hands, she picked up her teacup and took a sip. *I always knew it was too good to be true. I shouldn't have dared to think I could hitch my cart to that star.*

"Can we talk about something else?" Lizzie asked, struggling to keep her feelings from showing on her face. "I recently learned that I have a relative here in Salem. A second cousin by the name of Jacob Watkins. He owns a pub not far from the House of the Seven Gables, with the awful name of Misery Tavern."

Tentatively, Cora asked, "What do you know about your cousin?"

"Nothing. We've never met. I only heard of him a few days ago. I'd considered popping over to the pub this afternoon to say hello."

Cora poured herself another cup of tea. "I've never met him either," she admitted, "but the place gets written up in the newspaper from time to time. Rumors of illegal alcohol, of course. Brawls and such. It's not in the best part of town."

"Still, if Watkins is a relative of mine, I'd like to meet him. Other than my parents and siblings, I don't know any of my family. The rest of them still live in Ireland."

"All right, I have an idea. If you're bent on seeing him, I'll drive you over there—you won't want to walk that far in this weather. You can spend half an hour with your cousin. You can introduce yourself, chat about family memories or what have you, then I'll come back and pick you up."

"You'd do that for me?" Lizzie asked.

"Better you visit in the daytime. And at least I'll know where you are. You can't wear that coat, though. It's much too fine and will attract attention."

"But it's freezing out."

"I've got some old things of my mother's. She died last year, and I'm still organizing her belongings to give to charity—she never threw anything out, no matter how worn or dated it was. Maybe I can find a plainer one that's out of style and a headscarf to cover your hair. Wash off that face paint too."

Lizzie laughed. "You're going to make me look like a bug-eyed Betty."

"No chance of that, but you don't want to be a target for pickpockets. Or worse."

Once again, Lizzie wondered about the man who'd died near Misery Tavern on Saturday night. Had he been killed in a robbery or a fight? The note the police found on the body mentioned a lady. Jealousy had sent many a man to his grave, but where did Matthew Gardner figure in?

After they finished their tea, Cora rummaged through some boxes stashed in a closet under the stairs and pulled out a simple brown woolen coat. It was several inches too short for Lizzie and had a moth hole in one sleeve.

"Leave your jewelry and your purse here, too," the card reader said.

"What if I want to buy a drink?"

"Nothing stronger than a Coca-Cola."

Lizzie pocketed a single dollar bill and tied a knitted scarf over her bobbed hair. "What do you think?"

"You're still going to turn heads. Oh well, it's the best we can do."

They climbed into Cora's Model T Ford and motored toward the harbor. "I'll be back to fetch you in thirty minutes. If you're not standing outside on the curb waiting for me, I'm calling the cops."

# Chapter Seven

"Only he who is without anything is without enemies."

— *Rafael Sabatini, Captain Blood Returns*

A tall, burly, barrel-chested man with a nose that looked as if it had been on the wrong side of a few too many right hooks stood behind the bar at Misery Tavern. He had dark hair combed back from his face, a brushy salt-and-pepper mustache, and long graying sideburns fifty years out of date. Even though the pub was far from warm, he wore only a chambray shirt, sleeves rolled up to his elbows, and trousers held up by suspenders.

As Cora had predicted, the customers in the dimly lit tavern—only five men and two women on this Monday afternoon—turned to stare at Lizzie as she entered. Ignoring them, she stepped up to the bar and said, "I'm looking for Jacob Watkins."

"You found him," the burly man said.

"I'm Lizzie Crane, your second cousin from New York."

"Is that a fact?" He didn't seem particularly interested.

"Polly Crane's daughter, her maiden name was Baker. You and she have the same grandparents on your mother's side. That makes us cousins."

The man folded his muscular arms over his chest. "So what do you want from me, Cousin?"

"How about a drink?" Lizzie said and slid onto a stool.

"And what sort of drink might you be wanting?"

"A pint of ale, actually, but I don't guess you'd serve me one, would you?"

"You're right there, girlie."

"A Coca-Cola then, please."

He pulled a pale-green bottle from an icebox, uncapped it, and set it on the counter along with a glass that looked none too clean. Lizzie handed him the single dollar she'd brought with her, and he made change. Something about him seemed familiar, but she couldn't imagine why—this coarse man bore no family resemblance to her pretty mother.

Now that her eyes had adjusted to the low lighting, Lizzie noticed a collection of framed black-and-white photographs hanging on the pub's walls. Several pictured sailing ships.

"Are you a sailor?" she asked.

"Nope, I'm a barkeep."

"Why do you have those photos of ships hanging around then?"

"You ask a lot of questions, Cousin."

Lizzie chose not to use the glass and drank her Coca-Cola straight from the bottle. The bubbles tickled her throat. "I'm trying to get to know you, *Cousin.* Except for my parents and siblings, I don't know any of my relatives. Until Christmas, I didn't even know you existed."

"Well, now you do."

A man seated at one of the tables called for another bottle of ginger ale, and Watkins took it to him. When he returned, he grabbed a rag and began wiping the countertop.

"I'd like to know about your parents and your grandparents," Lizzie said, still trying to engage him in conversation.

"My father was a sailor." Watkins pointed to a faded photograph of a bearded man in old-fashioned clothes standing in front of Misery Tavern. "That's him. When he quit the sea, he started this place."

"When was that?"

"Eighteen seventy."

"So you're following in the family business."

"Looks that way, doesn't it?"

"Must've been easier to make a living running a tavern in 1870. I guess Prohibition's put the squeeze on you."

"I get by," he said.

"Misery's an odd name for a tavern. I thought people came to a pub for a bit of fun. Why'd your father call it that?"

Watkins poured himself a cup of coffee from a pot kept warm on an old cast-iron stove behind the bar. "Named it for the islands. His ship ran aground there in a storm and sank. He managed to row to shore. All but him died."

"That sounds miserable indeed."

"When a ship goes down, rich men lose their investment. Poor men lose their lives," he said, a note of bitterness in his voice.

"I'm glad your father survived. What was the name of the ship?"

"*Peregrine.*"

"Say, didn't William Gardner own her?" Lizzie said, thinking of the graceful model she'd seen in Matthew Gardner's parlor. The last of his grandfather's clippers.

Watkins narrowed his eyes and tugged at his mustache. "How do you know that?"

"I'm working for his grandson, Matthew Gardner." She started to tell him about The Troubadours and their holiday stint at the Gardners' home, but decided it might be better to let him think she was in service there as a housemaid.

A buxom woman about Lizzie's age wearing a too-tight dress with a too-low neckline edged behind the bar. She balanced a tray of dirty dishes on her shoulder.

"Who's she?" the woman asked Watkins.

"My cousin up from New York."

Lizzie smiled, trying to appear friendly. "Hi, I'm Lizzie Crane."

The woman slid the tray of dishes into a pass-through to the kitchen. "Didn't know Jacob had a cousin in New York."

"I didn't know about him either, until Christmas day," Lizzie said.

"Get on with your work; 'tis none of your business," Watkins told the woman, who tossed her head defiantly before sauntering back to check on her customers.

"Your wife?" Lizzie asked.

"My wife's dead. The influenza."

"I'm sorry."

Dozens of Lizzie's neighbors and friends she'd known in school died in the flu epidemic of 1918. By some miracle, she and her family had been spared when so many, especially in the poor neighborhoods, had perished.

"You want another one of those?" he asked, nodding at her empty Coca-Cola bottle.

"Oh, no thanks. A lady's coming to collect me soon. I only wanted to make your acquaintance. Do you mind if I stop in again sometime?"

"It's a public place. That's what 'pub' means, y'know."

"Yes, I realize that," Lizzie said. "Say, Cousin, you wouldn't happen to know where I could get a *real* drink, would you?"

Watkins leaned his elbows on the bar and stared hard at her. "How do I know you're not a cop?"

"Do I look like a cop?"

"Do I look like a fool?"

Lizzie laughed and shook her head. "Okay, it was worth a try. So long, then."

Only after she'd left the tavern did Lizzie realize why its owner looked familiar. *He's the man I saw talking with Matthew Gardner in the cemetery yesterday.*

\* \* \*

"Not the friendliest fella I've ever met," Lizzie said as she slid into the passenger seat of Cora's Model T Ford. She recounted their conversation as Cora motored along Derby Street. "He seemed to think I was an undercover cop."

"I don't think Salem has any policewomen," Cora said. "But maybe they hire ladies as lures, to trap men they suspect of trafficking in alcohol. Or other crimes."

"Anyway, thanks for driving me there and back. And thanks for the disguise. At least he didn't figure me for a showgirl, and I didn't tell him."

"Keep the coat and scarf. I have a feeling you'll be seeing Jacob Watkins again."

"Did you read that in the cards?" Lizzie asked.

"No, but you're the curious type. I can't imagine you abandoning your 'quest' after a single brief and unsatisfactory meeting."

"I do want to learn more about my family, my grandparents in particular. I never met them," Lizzie admitted. "He didn't even ask about my mother. Really, he was rather rude."

Cora pulled into her driveway. "Well, if he thought you were a cop...."

"There's another thing. I'd hoped he might be a source of booze, but that's a dead end. Sid brought a few bottles up from the City, but they won't last, and I haven't seen anything flowing through the Gardners' house."

"I've got a few extras in my cellar I can let you have. When I knew Prohibition was coming, I stocked up. A lot of us who could afford to put plenty aside."

"Really, Cora? Thanks. You're a peach."

While Lizzie collected her belongings, Cora wrapped three bottles in newspaper and slipped them into a canvas bag.

"Please let me pay you for these," Lizzie said.

Cora waved away her offer. "Consider it an investment. I expect to hear some good music while you're in town, and a little libation may help lubricate your pipes."

Both women laughed, and Lizzie thanked the card reader again. "I wish you were coming for supper tonight."

"I doubt I'd be an asset tonight, but I'll see you tomorrow at tea."

While she walked back to the Gardners' home, Lizzie mulled over her disappointing meeting with Jacob Watkins. She'd expected a warmer welcome from her cousin, a little congeniality at least. Was her sentimental longing for a family connection with this man causing her to behave foolishly? Maybe she should consider his off-putting manner as a sign to end her "quest," as Cora put it. Misery Tavern certainly looked like a rough place and no doubt it got rougher at night. If Watkins were engaged in selling alcohol illegally, pursuing a relationship with him might even be dangerous.

She opened the wrought-iron gate and walked around to the carriage house behind the Gardners' mansion. As she started climbing the stairs to the second floor, another troubling idea hit her. *What if Watkins saw me in the cemetery? What if both he and Gardner know I heard them arguing about a lady? A lady they must meet in secret to discuss?*

* * *

"Make a wish-ski," Lizzie said when Sidney opened the door to the carriage house apartment and let her in.

"A bottle of whis-key."

She pulled a bottle of Kentucky bourbon from the canvas bag and sang, "Ta-da!"

"Where'd you get that, Bearcat?"

"From Cora Delaney. I had tea with her this afternoon. I went to thank her for getting us this job with the Gardners. When I asked if she knew where I might lay my hands on some hooch, she gave me these." Lizzie unwrapped the other two bottles, one of gin, one Highland scotch. "I think she might be my fairy godmother."

"Let's see what may have inspired Stephen Foster's music, shall we?" Sidney asked as he uncapped the bourbon. "I can always use a little inspiration."

Lizzie sat in one of the apartment's comfortably worn leather chairs. "What's Bert up to?"

"He and Melody are giving each other music lessons," Sidney said as he handed a glass to Lizzie. "Bearcat, you don't think there's anything more going on between them, do you? They know our policy against getting emotionally involved with colleagues. It could be disastrous for us."

Lizzie patted his hand. "Relax. Melody has a sugar daddy in Connecticut who's sweet on her, and she's goofy about him. Besides, she'd never take up with someone like Bert. In case you haven't noticed, our innocent-looking flutist is a gold-digger." She took a sip of her bourbon and then continued, "I think they're both lonely. She's a nineteen-year-old, pampered only child, separated from her home and doting parents during the holidays. He's a castoff kid who lived on the streets of New York before he came on board with us. They're surrogate siblings to one another."

Sid lit a cigarette, inhaled, and let out a lungful of smoke. "I hope you're right, Bearcat."

"I am. Now, about tonight. What do you think of the redecorating I did in the parlor?"

"It works strategically," he said. "I heard about the broken vase, though."

"I hope it wasn't Ming or Ching or Ding-dong. They can't hold me responsible, can they?"

"Why? You're not the one who broke it."

Sidney passed her a list of songs they planned to play that evening and she spread out the piece of paper on her thigh. Abigail Gardner had requested they play chamber music tonight at supper—not their usual fare, but the group had performed Baroque numbers at their last job and enjoyed it. The diversion had stretched their abilities and increased their appreciation for another period in musical history. She intended to add her voice to Pachebel's Canon in D and sing one of Bach's duets with Melody. But "Der Holle Rache Kocht in Meinem Herzen" from *The Magic Flute,* one of her favorite pieces, was too dramatic for this setting. And Bach's cantata for the third day of Christmas—which would've given her a chance to sing with both Melody and Sid—called for more instruments than they had at their disposal.

It only took them two drinks and thirty minutes to iron out the evening's lineup. "Meet you in the parlor at five for a quick run-through before the guests arrive," Lizzie said as she rose to go back to her bedchamber to bathe and change clothes.

She took the back route through the kitchen, where a medley of succulent smells greeted her. Cookware clanged in a discordant symphony. Kitchen

45

maids scurried about toting mixing bowls, glassware, and platters laden with food. Cook's helpers stirred pots on the huge cast iron stove and slid pans into ovens. At the center of it all stood Pearl—solid, confident, and commanding in her red turban and gold hoop earrings—directing the girls like an orchestra conductor.

In the entry hall, Lizzie noticed a copy of *The Salem Evening News* lying on a table and grabbed it, promising herself she'd return it later. Before going upstairs, she veered into the double parlor. Since this morning, several arrangements of candles in silver holders had been placed on the mahogany dining table. A candelabrum now sat on the piano. A centerpiece of balsam, holly, and pinecones tied with golden ribbon ran the length of the table. The room smelled of cloves and cinnamon. As she circled the Chippendale table with its fourteen chairs, she wondered what sort of people the Gardners had invited for the evening's event. Family friends? Society notables? Business associates? For some reason, Cora Delaney hadn't made the cut.

Satisfied that the setting would give the guests a good view of the area where The Troubadours would perform, Lizzie climbed the stairs to the mansion's third floor and let herself into her bedchamber. Melody sat at the vanity, arranging her blond curls and pinning them in place with rhinestone-encrusted combs.

"How was your visit with Cora?" the flutist asked.

"Good. I enjoyed seeing her. She'll be here for tea tomorrow," Lizzie answered without going into details.

She didn't want to talk about her encounter with her cousin until she could make some sense of it all. Even more than Watkins' unfriendly behavior toward her, his angry conversation with Matthew Gardner in the cemetery perplexed her. She had trouble imagining her prosperous, socialite host fancying a woman who'd take up with a barkeep. Upper-class men sometimes sought out trollops for favors their wives refused, she reminded herself, and the doll-like Mrs. Gardner didn't seem the type to go in for anything risqué. Could Misery's waitress be the woman the two men argued about? *Good heavens, she's young enough to be either man's daughter.* Then a new possibility lit up Lizzie's thoughts. What if the "lady" Watkins had taken care of all these years was an illegitimate daughter, not a mistress?

Melody interrupted her thoughts. "I'd like to play violin on Pachebel's Canon and let Bert play flute tonight. What do you think?"

"You really feel he's up to it?" Tonight's formal supper was an important part of their twelve-day stint, and Lizzie wanted to be sure everything went smoothly.

"We've been studying together as you know and, well, he's very talented. It's not a big stretch from clarinet to flute anyway."

Lizzie contemplated the idea for a moment, then said, "Okay, if you think he can handle it."

"I do."

"You're on then."

Lizzie excused herself and went into the bathroom to run a tub of hot water. She brushed her dark hair and studied her unadorned face in the mirror. When she returned to the bedchamber, her pretty young friend was trying on gowns for the evening's performance.

"Wear the green one," Lizzie said.

"You think so?" Melody asked. "You don't think it's too strong?"

"We're going for strong tonight. I'll wear my red one. I know, red and green, it's a cliché, but this is the fourth day of Christmas." She reached into her jewel chest, pulled out an emerald necklace, and handed it to Melody. "Here, wear this with it."

Melody stared at her, surprised. She knew the complicated story behind the necklace and the man who'd given it to Lizzie. "Are you sure?"

"I'm sure. Now, I'm off to take a bath. If the maid shows up with food while I'm indisposed, save some for me, will you?"

# Chapter Eight

"Don't you dare marry him! I won't let you marry him! Do you hear?"

— *Alice Gerstenberg, Fourteen*

Lizzie read on the newspaper's front page that the man who'd died Saturday near the harbor had been identified as Nickolas Owens, a thief known to police. A blow to his head caused his death, the article said, but whether the injury resulted from a fall or had been inflicted beforehand remained unclear.

Questions raced through her mind. *Has Gardner read the paper yet? Why would a thief have a letter for Matthew Gardner in his pocket? Surely the police will dig more deeply into the connection, won't they?* And finally, *how might this affect The Troubadours?*

She didn't have long to ponder the situation, however. She finished painting her face and slipped into a red gown on which a field of rhinestone flowers bloomed.

"You look smashing in that gown. Red's your best color," Melody said.

"It stands out in a crowd anyway," Lizzie said. "You look smashing too. We're going to knock 'em dead tonight."

Instantly, her choice of words brought her thoughts back to the thief named Owens. Shaking off the unwanted images, she hooked a gold necklace set with a single two-carat ruby around her neck—another gift from another admirer—then gave her dark hair a final pat. "Okay, let's get a wiggle on."

Melody picked up her violin and flute cases, and the two entertainers went downstairs to meet their colleagues in the double parlor. Sidney, sleek as a Siamese cat and movie-star handsome in a black tuxedo with a red carnation pinned to his lapel, sat at the Steinway "warming up the ivories," as he called it. Bert, also wearing a tuxedo but awkwardly so, shot the women a gap-toothed grin when they entered. Lizzie noticed he'd slicked his cowlick into place with petroleum jelly.

"Melody says you're going to make your debut on the flute tonight," she said to the skinny young man with the big ears and uneven smile.

Bert cracked his knuckles. "Yep. I'm kinda nervous, though."

"You can back out and let Mel take over if you want. We won't think less of you."

"Nope, I really want to do it."

"I always feel a bit nervous before a performance too. Especially when I'm trying something new. But a little edginess keeps you sharp. Don't worry, you'll be darb. Once you start playing, the music will take over, and that self-consciousness will melt away," she assured him. "Okay, everybody. We've got an hour before the Gardners' guests start arriving. Supper's at seven. Let's start with the Canon so Bert can work out his jitters, then follow with Bach's duet so Melody and I can tune up our pipes."

They ended up playing Pachebel's beautiful piece twice because Bert flubbed it in a few places.

"Maybe I'm not ready yet," he said, a chagrined expression on his face.

"Third time's a charm," Lizzie said and patted his arm. "You'll play it perfectly when you've got an audience."

Before the hour was up, they'd worked through the kinks and felt comfortable going into the evening's repertoire. As per Lizzie's instructions, the doors between the two sections of the double parlor would remain closed until it was time to seat the Gardners' guests for supper.

Yesterday morning, she'd convinced her hosts that this would offer maximum impact. "You can socialize in the comfort of the front room with your friends as they arrive," she'd explained. "Then, a few minutes before seven, the servants will light the candles and throw open the doors, and we'll welcome everyone in with beautiful music. It will be quite dramatic, you'll see."

Abigail Gardner had seemed uncertain. Lizzie couldn't decide if the woman was merely nervous or didn't like relinquishing control of this important event to a hired showgirl. "But what will we listen to between six and seven?"

They'd agreed that Sidney would play a medley of piano pieces, although he complained the closed doors would muffle the sound. "Why don't they just turn on the Victrola?" he grumbled when she laid out the plan.

"The alternative is to have a lot of chattering people mulling about drinking punch and eating canapés and not paying proper attention to us anyway," Lizzie pointed out. "This way, we'll get off to a strong start and capitalize on it throughout the rest of the evening. You want to make a splash, don't you?"

He'd sighed melodramatically. "You're right, Bearcat."

Now it was showtime. At seven o'clock sharp, two housemaids pulled the pocket doors aside, and The Troubadours launched into the Canon. The Gardners and their guests did, indeed, appear suitably impressed. As Lizzie scanned the crowd, however, her heart skipped a beat. She had to struggle to keep her voice steady. Amid the other men and women in the audience stood a tall, handsome, red-haired man whose dark eyes and broad smile sent a flush through her body.

The butler and the housekeeper directed the guests to their places at the table, set with a heavy damask cloth, gleaming silver, and sparkling crystal. Housemaids stood against the wall, awaiting instructions from Townsend. Matthew and Abigail Gardner took their seats at the table's head and foot, respectively. In the place of honor at their host's right sat their beautiful elder daughter, Sarah, elegantly dressed in a russet silk gown that showed off her lovely shoulders. Beside her sat the red-haired man, wearing the latest midnight blue tuxedo made famous by the Prince of Wales. Alan Peabody.

Lizzie wanted to scream. Is this why he hadn't answered the telegram she'd walked a mile to the Hawthorne Hotel, braving bitterly cold temperatures to send? Although she never expected he might make any sort of lasting commitment to her, she'd still hoped he cared for her a little and that at least a fleeting romance between them was possible. Cora had warned her that the Gardners planned to marry their eighteen-year-old daughter to him. *So it's true,* she thought, fighting back tears.

With effort, she pulled herself together. *I'm a professional. I can't let personal matters interfere with my work. I have a show to do.* When he caught her eye, she smiled back at him in a cordial, but uninviting way.

She vowed to give the best performance of her life for the next two hours. *I won't give him the satisfaction of seeing he's upset me.* Focusing on her music, Lizzie managed to push aside thoughts of the man who'd starred in her fantasies the past four months. She poured her emotions into the musical compositions of the masters and sung her heart out until the housemaids gathered up the dessert plates and the dinner guests rose to make their departures. While the room emptied, Sidney played a piece Lizzie didn't recognize, and she wondered if he'd composed it himself.

\* \* \*

Alan Peabody approached Lizzie. "You sang exquisitely tonight. I couldn't help but think of Erik's line from the *Phantom of the Opera:* 'Behold, she is singing to bring down the chandelier!' "

"Thank you, Alan. What an unexpected pleasure it is to see you here. How do you know the Gardners?"

"Matthew is a client. His family has a long-standing relationship with my firm."

"Was tonight a business dinner, then?" Lizzie asked.

"Part business, part personal." Golden sparks flashed in his dark eyes. "I got your telegram. I didn't reply because I wanted to surprise you."

"You succeeded."

"How long will you be in town?"

"We're booked through January 6," she answered. "We contracted for the twelve days of Christmas."

"Will you have time to see me while you're here?"

Still unsure of his intentions—toward her *and* Sarah Gardner—she struggled to sheathe the double-edged sword of desire and anger that lodged in her chest. "What do you have in mind?"

"I've been invited to the Gardners' New Year's Eve festivities, but I must admit I accepted on the condition that you'd be performing that night." He brushed the backs of his fingers lightly against her cheek. "Tonight, I've taken a room at the Hawthorne Hotel. If you'd care to join me there, I'd be honored."

The idea sent erotic feelings coursing through her veins. However, his audacity to proposition her after he'd accompanied Sarah Gardner tonight—and perhaps meant to marry her—ignited a different sort of fire in her. *I might only be a showgirl, but I'm not a cheap harlot.*

Reining in her emotions, she summoned her skill as an actress and said, "I apologize, Alan, but I'm too tired after my performance this evening to be good company. I'll look forward to seeing you on New Year's Eve. If you find yourself free for lunch or tea one afternoon before then, I'd enjoy visiting with you. By the way, I read the book of Mr. Rumi's poetry that you gave me. Perhaps we could discuss it?"

"Of course. I hope you enjoyed his poems." He lifted her hand to his lips and kissed each of her fingertips individually. "I'll leave you to your rest now. Thank you for an inspired evening."

With every cell in her body, she longed to go with him to the hotel, to lie beside him through the cold dark night, to dissolve all her worries in the warmth of his embrace. Instead, she said, "Thank you for coming tonight, Alan. It's lovely to see you again."

\* \* \*

Angrily, Lizzie stripped off her red evening gown and hung it in the wardrobe, then yanked on a pair of tweed trousers and an Irish fisherman's sweater. "I'm going to see Sid," she told Melody.

"Did you know Alan Peabody was coming to supper tonight?" her friend asked.

"No, it was a bit of a shock."

"He came to see you, didn't he?"

"I don't know. It's very confusing."

"Love always is," Melody said, and Lizzie wondered what her sheltered young colleague knew of such things.

"I'll be back in a while. By the way, you were darb tonight, Mel. And Bert did a fine job on the flute. You've taught him well."

The electric light burned above the door to Sidney and Bert's quarters. Eager for the company of her longtime friend Lizzie knocked, although she knew Sid usually liked to spend time alone after a performance to review all the things that had gone right and those that needed improvement. Tonight, virtually everything had been perfect—except Alan's presence in the company of Sarah Gardner.

"I need a drink-ski," she said when Sid opened the door.

"I'm on the brink-ski. What's your pleasure?"

"Got any of that brown plaid left?"

He poured golden liquor into two glasses and handed one to her. For several minutes they sat together, sipping their Lagavulin without talking. Finally, Sidney asked, "Why was Peabody here tonight?"

"He and Gardner are business associates."

"Why was he seated next to Gardner's daughter?'

Lizzie let out a long sigh. "Gardner wants to marry Sarah to him."

"And what does Peabody want?"

"Haven't the foggiest."

Sidney lit a cigarette and blew out a lungful of smoke. He stood up and paced the length of the small apartment. He tapped his fingertips along the kitchenette's counter top, as if it were a keyboard.

"Lizzie, you have to end this infatuation. It will be the ruin of you. Of The Troubadours too."

She waved him off. "You're exaggerating. He's just a fleeting fantasy. A pretty fantasy, admittedly, but nothing serious."

"Bushwa, I know you better than that."

"He asked me to come to his hotel room tonight," she said. "I refused."

"Good decision, Bearcat. He's a rich, powerful man who can have any woman he wants. You're only one dish on the smorgasbord."

Lizzie stared into her drink, knowing her friend spoke the truth even though it hurt. "You seem so cynical about his intentions."

"I'm a man, and I know men's ways. Yet I also have the unfortunate ability to understand a woman's position in matters of the heart." He stubbed out his cigarette and lit another. "I don't want you to get hurt, Bearcat, and I don't want personal problems to interfere with The Troubadours."

"What should I do? I feel so discombobulated."

"Focus on work. That's the only solace and salvation there is. The only thing you can rely on to carry you through. Lovers come and go, but your work, what you create with your heart and soul and mind, lives forever."

# Chapter Nine

"What we play is life."

— *Louis Armstrong, Louis Armstrong, in His Own Words*

After breakfast, Lizzie supervised the reinstatement of the Chippendale dining table and chairs to their original location. This time, to her relief, nothing got broken in the process, and the transfer took place without incident. Next, she oversaw the placement of numerous gaming tables around the room so the Gardners' visitors could play bridge, dominoes, mahjong, backgammon, and chess this afternoon.

*What fun all this must be,* Lizzie thought, as she meandered through the improvised game room, studying the pieces the housemaids laid out on the various tables. She wondered what the red and green designs on the ivory mahjong tiles meant and delighted in the jade and cinnabar chessmen standing ready to do battle on the checkered board. *Had these pretty amusements come from the Orient on one of William Gardner's ships?*

She picked up a tiny horse carved from pale green stone and traced its delicate features with her fingertips. She'd never learned to play these games that were the province of the wealthy, who had leisure time to while away at such casual pleasures. *Who invented these practices? What inspired them?* she wondered, and decided to learn more. She eyed the built-in floor-to-ceiling shelves that lined the Gardners' back parlor. Surely they held books that described the games' histories and meanings. Perhaps she'd even learn how to play them.

Cora Delaney had told Lizzie that the tarot might have begun as a game during the Renaissance and later evolved into a tool for predicting the future. Although Cora had been invited to the afternoon's activities, Lizzie doubted the card reader would ply her trade among the Gardners' guests. *I wonder if Abigail Gardner's husband knows she goes to Cora for readings?* And then, *Does Abigail ask about her daughter's prospects for marriage to Alan?* Lizzie shook her head, casting out fears she couldn't afford to dwell on now, and brought her attention back to work.

According to the schedule she and Sidney had ironed out with the Gardners, lunch would be served in the dining room at one. After that, their guests would repair to the double parlor to engage in their favorite entertainments while The Troubadours played light jazz numbers. Matthew Gardner had hinted at a sing-along, but both Lizzie and Sidney discouraged it.

"Your guests might not wish to be distracted from a hand of cards or a chess match, especially if they're winning," Sidney pointed out.

Until then, however, Lizzie had a couple hours to herself, and decided to use the opportunity to visit some of Salem's tourist attractions. She'd invited Melody to join her, but the flutist had just finished washing her blond hair and tying it up in rags to curl it, and was busy composing a letter to her beau in Connecticut. Bert, she discovered, had borrowed a bicycle from one of the Gardners' workers and gone tooling about the city on his own.

She slipped through the kitchen, where the staff was busily preparing lunch under the watchful eye of Pearl, the cook. A tray of deviled eggs sat on a counter, and Lizzie grabbed one.

"Take two," Pearl said without turning around.

Lizzie laughed. "How did you see me filch that egg? You were looking the other way."

The cook grinned, exposing a gold molar. "Got eyes in the back of my head. Yes'm, when you got three daughters, you gotta see what can't be seen."

"Thanks, Pearl," she said and darted out the back door, across the parking area to the carriage house.

She climbed the outside stairway and knocked on the door to the upstairs apartment. Shivering in the cold, she waited for what seemed an excessively long period of time before Sidney answered. His blanched face and sullen expression took her aback.

"Sid, what's wrong?"

"I'm not feeling well."

"Oh dear, is it serious? Should I telephone for a doctor?"

"No, no." He stepped aside to let her in. "Probably something I ate. Digestive problems. It will pass."

"How can I help?"

"You can't." He dropped into one of the leather armchairs and drew his bathrobe tight around him. "What do you want, Lizzie?"

"I came to see if you'd like to go sightseeing with me for a bit before we perform. But I gather that's out of the picture."

"Obviously."

"Will you be able to play this afternoon? Would you rather rest? We can revise the repertoire…"

"Stop fussing over me. I'll be fine. I just—" Suddenly, he jumped up and dashed for the bathroom. When he returned, his face looked even more ashen. "Bearcat, please leave me alone for a while. I'll be okay. If you want to take the Buick, the keys are in a bowl on the table near the door."

"I don't want to leave you like this."

"Frankly, I wish you would. I just need to rest for a bit. Now skedaddle, will you please?"

Lizzie scooped up the car keys and stuffed them in her coat pocket. "All right, but I'll be back soon to check on you, and if you're not better, I'm calling a doctor."

He waved her away. "Go."

She closed the door and hurried back to the bedchamber she shared with Melody. Her friend was curled up in one of the green velvet armchairs, sipping a cup of tea and reading *Pride and Prejudice*.

"Sid's sick," Lizzie said.

"What's wrong?"

"He says it's nothing serious, a digestive complaint. Something he ate."

"Well, then, he'll be okay soon."

"But we've all eaten the same things, and the rest of us aren't sick."

Melody laid her book aside. "Lizzie, people get tummy aches all the time. Stop fretting; he'll feel better after a rest."

"I suppose you're right."

"If it will make *you* feel better, I'll take him some Pepto-Bismol."

Lizzie started to unbutton her coat, but Melody stopped her. "You can't hang around here all afternoon. You'll just pace back and forth and worry and drive me batty, and I really want to finish this book. Go out and see the sights like you planned. I'll be here if he needs me." She shook the tangle of knotted rags in her hair and laughed. "And you call Sid our 'mother hen.'"

\* \* \*

Lizzie motored down Derby Street along Salem's harbor and turned off toward the House of the Seven Gables. When she got there, however, she discovered the historic home was closed due to a broken water pipe. Disappointed, she drove to the Custom House, but found it closed too.

"Drat," she muttered as she shifted the Buick into gear and headed for the Peabody Museum in the center of town.

As she drove, she wondered if the museum had any connection to Alan Peabody. But her musings stirred up unpleasant thoughts of last night and the possibility that he might be romantically involved with the Gardners' daughter Sarah. *Well, why wouldn't he be interested in her?* she asked herself. *The girl is more than pretty and comes from a prominent, wealthy family. Men like him only dabble with women like me, they don't marry us.*

She pulled up in front of the museum and, to her dismay, discovered it wouldn't open until noon. "Is the whole of Salem under wraps?" she said aloud. "My one chance to witness the town's history, and it's all gone bust."

Frustrated, she parked the auto and got out. Even though the temperature hovered around freezing, she chose to walk off her annoyance. Few people dotted the usually busy street, and only a smattering of stores appeared to be open for business. *Now that Christmas has passed, I suppose everyone's tired of shopping,* she decided.

After a few blocks, she came to an antiquarian shop where three electric lights illuminated a display window filled with curiosities. As she pushed the door open, a tinkling of Tibetan temple bells announced her entrance.

"Good day," she said to the elderly proprietor whose white beard, spectacles, and twinkling blue eyes reminded her of Old Saint Nick.

He looked up from the newspaper he'd been reading. "Good day to you too, miss. Are you seeking anything in particular?"

"It seems you're one of the only places open today."

"I'm not sure that speaks well of me," he said with a smile. "Perhaps it's an indication that I have nothing else to do."

"May I just look around?" she asked.

"Of course. If I can be of assistance, you have only to say the word."

Despite its electric lights, the shop's interior felt shadowy and claustrophobic. A musty odor permeated the space. Still, it boasted all sorts of beguiling treasures. Dark wooden bookshelves displayed not only leatherbound books with gilt-edged pages, but also decorative items made of porcelain and glass, silver, and bronze. Cabinets held intriguing art objects and statuary. In one case, Lizzie spotted an array of walnut-sized objects carved from yellowed ivory. Upon closer examination, she realized the intricately wrought pieces depicted erotic acts. She blushed and turned away, embarrassed that the old shopkeeper might see her looking at them.

In a nearby vitrine, she saw a gracefully carved jade statue of a woman about six inches tall. Despite her size, the statue's fingers and toes were beautifully rendered, her facial features defined with great delicacy. In one hand, the statue held a vial from which she poured water onto the ground; in the other, she clasped what might have been a willow branch or a sheaf of wheat. Her countenance conveyed the most perfect sense of peace Lizzie had ever seen.

She stood so long, looking at the exquisitely formed pale green statue, that the shopkeeper took notice. "She's known as Quan Yin," he said. "The Chinese goddess of mercy and compassion. Some people say she's the female counterpart of the Buddha."

When Lizzie didn't respond, he continued. "That statue was brought here during the China trade. I don't know how old she is, seventy-five years anyway, perhaps much more."

"What do you want for her?"

The man named a price beyond Lizzie's means. Still, she couldn't bear the thought of leaving without taking the statue with her.

"I can't afford that much," she said. "Is there any leeway in your price?"

They bargained back and forth for several minutes, but the gap between his asking price and her ability to pay seemed insurmountable.

"I'm from New York, doing a job here. I'll get paid at the end of next week," she said. "Could I give you a down payment on the statue and retrieve her later?"

The old man smiled, the wrinkles in his face deepening. His watery blue eyes glistened behind his spectacles. "Certainly. She will wait for you."

Lizzie fished in her purse for the deposit as the shopkeeper wrote out a receipt. After pocketing her money, he ran his finger along the spines of a row of shelved books. He pulled down a thin, leather-bound volume and handed it to her. "Here, this will tell you what you need to know about the goddess."

"How much?"

"Please accept it as a gift."

\* \* \*

Lizzie parked the Buick in a bay at the Gardners' carriage house and climbed the stairs to the upstairs apartment. She knocked on the door and, after a bit, Sid opened the door. Though still pale, he looked better than he had two hours ago. As she entered, he held up a hand to fend off her questions.

"Before you ask, I'm well enough to perform this afternoon. I've been drinking ginger tea, and it's helped. Melody made me down some disgusting pink gunk too."

"Whew, you had me scared," Lizzie said, drawing her hand across her forehead in an exaggerated display of relief. "Can I do anything for you?"

"You can stop fussing over me," he said, lighting a cigarette.

"Do you think you should be smoking when you're ill?"

Sidney exhaled a lungful of smoke. "I'm not *ill,* I just ate something that didn't agree with me."

"At least we can perform this afternoon's numbers in our sleep, so we don't have to rehearse."

"Yes, that's a plus," he said, sinking into a leather armchair. "So, what did you see and do today in the historic city of Salem?"

"I bought a statue of a Chinese goddess."

He rolled his eyes. "What, pray tell, are you going to do with a statue of a Chinese goddess? I hope it's not too big to fit in the breezer."

"She's only as big as my hand," Lizzie said. "And honestly, I don't know what I'll do with her or why I bought her, except I simply couldn't resist. She *spoke* to me, almost like a piece of music does. It's as if she and I have a connection, strange as that may seem."

After leaving Sidney to his rest, Lizzie checked the double parlor one last time to make sure everything was ready for the afternoon's performance. For several moments, she stood in front of the wooden model of William Gardner's China clipper *Peregrine.* What treasures had she brought to Salem? What marvels had her captain and crew witnessed during their voyages to the Orient before a storm sank their ship? Once again, she thought about the thousands of men who, in pursuit of wealth and adventure, had lost their lives at sea.

She heard footsteps and turned to see Matthew Gardner crossing the room toward her. "Good day, Mr. Gardner," she greeted him.

"Good day to you, too, Miss Crane. My family and I are eagerly looking forward to this afternoon."

"So are my colleagues and I."

"You seem interested in my grandfather's ships."

"I'm intrigued by Salem's clipper ship trade. I didn't know anything about it before coming here. Such an important time in our country's history." Lizzie wanted to touch the graceful model, but it seemed too delicate, and she feared she might accidentally damage it. "It's so sad the *Peregrine* and her crew perished."

"Yes, it is," Gardner said. "But that's the risk sailors take. As Vincent van Gogh said, 'The fishermen know that the sea is dangerous and the storm terrible, but they have never found these dangers sufficient reason for remaining ashore.'"

"What happened to the man who survived?" She wanted to hear if Gardner would confirm Jacob Watkins's story.

"He established a tavern here in Salem. Of course, that was more than fifty years ago. I don't know if it still exists."

She thought about the beautiful porcelain dishes, vases, carpets, and *objets d'art* she'd seen displayed in the Gardners' mansion and the elegant wallcoverings in the dining room that depicted Oriental scenes. They must have been transported from the East by William Gardner's clippers.

"What happened to *Peregrine*'s cargo when she sank?"

"Much of it was destroyed—spices, tea, and such—although some items were salvaged. Wooden and metal goods mostly." Gardner touched the bow of the model ship almost reverently.

"How unfortunate," Lizzie said. "I understand the clipper ships carried opium among their other goods."

"Yes. Until eleven years ago, opium was a common, legal painkiller. Doctors prescribed it for all sorts of ailments. A very valuable commodity. Of course, people used it for other purposes too. No doubt *Peregrine*'s cache included opium, but when she sank, it was lost to the sea," Gardner said, then changed the subject. "Miss Crane, I have a request. I know it's last minute, but I've been listening to that new sensation Louis Armstrong on the radio. Do you know any of his tunes?"

"Do we ever! Our horn player, Bert Halley, does a swell rendition of Armstrong's songs. Would you like us to play some for your guests?"

"Yes, I'd like that very much."

"Consider it done."

\* \* \*

When Lizzie returned to the bedchamber she shared with Melody, the housemaid with the port wine birthmark on her cheek was setting out lunch on the dropleaf table.

"What have we here?" Lizzie asked as she lifted the lid of a pottery crock to reveal a hearty beef and barley soup. A basket contained a loaf of fresh-baked bread. A bowl held peaches with a hint of mint, no doubt canned by the kitchen staff at summer's end.

The servant poured hot tea into blue-and-white porcelain cups and asked, "Is there anything else you'd like, ma'am?"

Lizzie dismissed the girl. "No, thank you, Fanny, this will do."

"How's Sid?" Melody asked after the maid left.

"Better. Still not up to snuff, but he's well enough to perform this afternoon. Oh, and Gardner wants us to play some Louis Armstrong songs."

"Bert will be glad to hear that."

"Where is Bert anyway?" Lizzie asked as she slathered butter onto a thick slice of oatmeal bread.

Melody hesitated for a few moments before answering, "He's taken a fancy to one of the housemaids. They've been spending time together."

"Oh, no. Sid will have kittens if he finds out!"

"I think you should talk to Bert."

"You're on the trolley there. The last thing we need is to have him knock up one of Gardners' servants."

The blond flutist winced at her friend's implication, but then Lizzie often shocked her more innocent colleague.

"He doesn't mean any harm," Melody said.

"I know, but men never consider the ramifications of their actions. They're not the ones left to deal with the consequences."

"You may be jumping to conclusions. They've only just met," Melody pointed out.

"Let's hope so."

Lizzie ate several spoonfuls of soup, willing herself to stay calm. As she considered what she'd say to Bert, she recalled Sidney's warnings about her infatuation with Alan Peabody. The irony wasn't lost on her.

"Wear your blue beaded frock this afternoon, and I'll wear my rose one," Lizzie said, changing the subject. "And tap shoes. I think dancing may be in order."

"Promise you won't be too hard on Bert?" Melody asked.

"I promise I won't tell him I heard about it from you, but that's all."

# Chapter Ten

"Life without music would be a mistake."

— *Friedrich Nietzsche, Twilight of the Idols*

L izzie strolled through the Gardners' kitchen, where luncheon preparations were underway. By now, the kitchen staff had gotten used to seeing her and barely looked up from their tasks when she breezed through their workspace. She spotted Pearl's eldest daughter stirring a pot of soup on the stove. Another girl arranged smoked oysters on crackers, a treat that hadn't been delivered to Lizzie and Melody with their lunch. For Lizzie, who liked to eat but shunned cooking, The Troubadours' forays into the homes of wealthy patrons offered a surprising smorgasbord of culinary delights.

Pearl, wearing an emerald-green turban and a dress the color of new oak leaves under her apron, spotted Lizzie and raised an index finger in greeting. "Grab you one of them oysters, ma'am. I see you eyein' 'em."

"Thanks, Pearl." Lizzie reached for one and popped it into her mouth. When she'd finished chewing, she said, "These are delicious! Say, do you think you could stop calling me 'ma'am'? I'm not your boss; I'm a working woman like you."

The cook crossed the kitchen, her undulating movements resembling a slow, easy dance. "What I'm gonna call you then?"

"My name's Lizzie."

"Can't call you only by your given name. It's not proper." Pearl thought a moment. "How 'bout Miz Liz?"

Lizzie laughed. "That'll do."

"An' take some more oysters with you. You an' that lil' blond girl, what's her name again?"

"Melody."

The cook patted her ample belly. "You an' Miz Melody could both use some fattenin' up."

\* \* \*

Half an hour before the Gardners' guests were due to arrive for lunch and gaming, Lizzie found Sidney seated at the piano in the back parlor, warming up. To her relief, he looked well, and the color had returned to his cheeks. Beside him stood the Gardners' younger daughter, Emma. The fifteen-year-old girl, shorter, plumper, and plainer than her older sister was engaged in a lively discussion with Sid. As Lizzie approached, their conversation ceased abruptly.

"Hello, I'm Lizzie Crane," she said, extending her hand. "Am I finally able to make the acquaintance of Miss Emma Gardner?"

The girl shyly took Lizzie's hand. "Yes, I am Emma. Pleased to meet you, Miss Crane."

"Emma's a pianist, too," Sidney said. "She hopes to attend the Juilliard School after she graduates from high school."

"Wonderful. It's a terrific school. I wish you the best," Lizzie said.

The girl frowned. "Unfortunately, my parents don't believe that music, for a lady, should be considered more than pleasant window dressing. Like being able to speak French or do fancy embroidery. They want me to play piano for them and their friends, not make a career of it. My sister isn't any help—all she thinks about are men and clothes."

"What do *you* think?" Lizzie asked.

"Music means everything to me!"

"Then you must follow your calling. I agree with Nietzsche when he said

66

'Life without music would be a mistake.' "

Before Emma could reply, Sidney started playing a Brahms duet and motioned for her to accompany him. Without hesitation, the girl slid onto the bench beside him and placed her fingers on the piano's keys. Occasionally she stumbled as they worked through the piece, but she didn't let that stop her.

When they'd finished, Lizzie clapped enthusiastically. "Brava!"

Emma blushed and cast her eyes down at the keyboard. "I made some mistakes."

"Don't be afraid to make mistakes," Lizzie told her. "Mistakes are the bridges that lead to greater heights. Risking failure is part of the quest. You'll never know what you can do if you don't give it a try."

Emma seemed to consider Lizzie's statement for a moment before speaking. "My parents have hired other professional musicians to perform here, but they never had any time for me. And my piano teacher, well, she isn't someone I can talk to. May I talk to you again?"

"Of course," Lizzie said. "Now, skedaddle so we can get ready for the party."

While Sidney ran through a few jazz numbers, Lizzie turned her attention to the housemaid who had begun assembling a jigsaw puzzle that the Gardners' guests would have an opportunity to complete while they socialized. The idea intrigued her, although she'd never put one together herself. Hand-cut wooden puzzles were expensive and required a good deal of time to finish, and Lizzie had neither money nor time to spare.

She approached the table where the girl, whose white-blond hair and pale skin suggested Scandinavian lineage, was configuring a border.

"Was this puzzle made by Salem's own Parker Brothers?" Lizzie asked.

"Yes, ma'am," the girl said. "Isn't it beautiful?"

"Well, I can't tell much about it yet, but I'm sure it will be when it's finished."

"Mr. Gardner had it made specially. It's one of a kind. A picture of his grandfather's ships in the harbor."

"So you've already put it together and know how it comes out?"

"Mr. and Mrs. Gardner wanted me to make certain all the pieces were here before their guests tried to work it."

"It looks like fun. I've never done a jigsaw puzzle." Lizzie picked up a piece from the unassembled lot laid out on the table. "Oh, it's shaped like a horse."

The girl's pale blue eyes lit up. "Yes, ma'am, that's part of the fun. In the old puzzles, all the pieces had square sides. They didn't hold together very well, though. If you accidentally bumped the table, the pieces fell apart, and you had to start again. The interlocking animal shapes cling together better, and they're prettier. Plus, they help you figure out what goes where."

"You sound like a puzzle expert."

"Oh, no, ma'am. I just like them, that's all."

Lizzie fingered another piece, this one shaped like a dog. "Maybe Mr. Gardner will let me try it while I'm here."

"If you like, I'll be glad to show you how it's done," the maid offered. "A puzzle is a mystery that comes together one piece at a time. You have to be patient and clever to solve it."

\* \* \*

On her way upstairs to change clothes for the afternoon's event, Lizzie spotted a newspaper lying on a table in the entrance hall. She picked it up and scanned the front page, then opened it. Gardner had given her permission to read the books in his library; she hoped that might include the daily newspaper as well.

At the bottom of the third page, she noticed a short article updating what she'd read yesterday about the thief who died the night The Troubadours arrived in Salem.

> *...Eyewitnesses claim to have seen Nicholas Owens in Misery Tavern, engaged in an altercation with the owner, Jacob Watkins, shortly before Owens was found dead on December 26. His death is being investigated by police...*

Footsteps in the dining room interrupted her. Quickly she folded the newspaper and placed it back on the table as Mrs. Platt entered the hallway.

"Good afternoon, Miss Crane," the housekeeper said coolly.

"And to you, Mrs. Platt," Lizzie replied.

*Holy moly*, she thought as she mounted the stairs. *Did my cousin have a hand in Owens' death?*

\* \* \*

While the Gardners' guests lunched at the Chippendale dining table that servants had expanded to its full length, The Troubadours played what Sidney disparagingly called "background music" in the double parlor. At 2:30, twenty men and women plus the Gardner family strolled across the hall, chatting and laughing, and took their places at the various game tables. Lizzie spotted Cora, dressed in a handsome two-piece tweed ensemble, and waved. The card reader smiled and waved back as she sat at a table, readied for a game of mahjong. Other guests, fashionably attired in well-cut suits or stylish afternoon frocks, arranged themselves for hands of bridge or at chessboards. Matthew Gardner seated himself across from a short man with a pleasant face who looked very much like him, a backgammon board between them. *That must be his brother*, Lizzie surmised.

Emma Gardner joined an elderly couple at a table on which the latest books of crossword puzzles had been laid out. Her older sister, Sarah, claimed a place at the table where the jigsaw puzzle waited to be filled in. Lizzie couldn't help admiring Sarah's smart red dress with a line of tiny pearl buttons that ran down the front from its black velvet collar to the calf-length hem. Two young men hurried to join her, trying to outdo each other as they vied for her attention. Sarah flirted shamelessly with them both.

For an hour, The Troubadours played a variety of jazz favorites while the guests enjoyed their amusements. Housemaids circled the room, pouring cups of coffee, tea, and hot chocolate. Then, in keeping with Matthew Gardner's request, the musicians launched into a medley of Louis Armstrong's popular songs. Bert, given the opportunity to perform his favorite artist's pieces, took over the show, belting out tunes that made the audience interrupt their games and tap their feet.

"Time to warm up your dancing shoes," Lizzie said to Melody.

The two women in their glittery flapper dresses sparkled like tropical fish as their flying feet beat out exciting rhythms in time to Bert's horn. Sidney abandoned the piano and joined them in a three-person Charleston. Several of the younger guests—including Sarah Gardner—got up to dance too. Although Lizzie noticed a few raised eyebrows among the older members of the audience, Matthew Gardner's face beamed with delight. He even took a spin around the dance floor with his elder daughter.

As the winter sun set and purple shadows descended on Chestnut Street, the guests began to take their leave. Men and women paid their respects to their hosts while they donned their warm outer garments. Salem's gentry strolled happily down the brick sidewalk and through the wrought-iron gate to their waiting automobiles. Chauffeurs opened doors for them.

Cora stopped by to congratulate the musicians on their "lively" performance, as she put it. "You must all come by for a visit while you're here."

"I will, for sure," Lizzie said, then lowered her voice. "Thanks again for the drink. I owe you."

"Don't mention it." Cora waved her hand dismissively. "See you soon."

Melody and Bert snapped their instruments into their cases, as Lizzie strolled among the now-empty game tables. She stopped at the one where Sarah Gardner and her admirers had fitted together part of the custom-made jigsaw puzzle. Pieces cut in the shapes of lions, storks, camels, and whales melded to depict a colorful waterfront scene. Although the puzzlers hadn't finished the picture, Lizzie could make out sections of clipper ships moored at Salem Harbor and teams of men unloading precious cargo brought from the Orient. Two stevedores carried what looked like a rolled-up carpet on their shoulders. Several more bore crates of exotic tea and spices. Teak, cinnabar, sandalwood, jade, and ivory were transported to shore on the backs of muscular men. Some of those bags and chests, she suspected, held caches of opium.

The Gardners' housemaids scurried about, collecting dishes and cleaning up in the wake of the afternoon's activities. Footsteps on the wooden floor caused Lizzie to look up from the intriguing puzzle.

"Your performance this afternoon was most inspired, Miss Crane. Especially your young chap's rendition of Louis Armstrong's songs," Matthew Gardner said. "I feel certain our guests will be talking about it for days to come."

"I'm glad you enjoyed it. We aim to please," she said.

His gaze fell on the partially completed jigsaw puzzle. "I commissioned this puzzle to mark my family's history of trade in the Orient. It's not the equivalent of a painting, of course, but I thought it might be a pleasant way to engage people's curiosity about our illustrious past."

"It's striking," she said, trailing her fingertips over the colorful image. "Not only the waterfront scene, but the pieces cut in the shapes of animals, well, it's most amusing. I've never seen anything like it before. What a delightful entertainment."

"Would you like to try your hand at it, Miss Crane? I'll ask the staff to leave it as is, so you can finish what my daughter and her friends have begun."

"I'd like that ever so much," Lizzie said. "Thank you."

# Chapter Eleven

"A problem is a chance for you to do your best."

— *Duke Ellington, Music is My Mistress*

A fter changing out of her flapper dress, Lizzie wrapped herself in a silk robe embroidered with a bright red Chinese dragon. Then she settled into one of the bedroom's armchairs, opened the slim volume the antique dealer had given her about Quan Yin, and read:

"The goddess of compassion, tranquility, and mercy, Quan Yin is sometimes considered the feminine face of the Buddha. Although a popular figure in Chinese religion and mythology, the goddess is also revered in other Asian countries, including Korea and Japan. Taoists, as well as Buddhists, hold her to be sacred. It is said that instead of entering the peace and enlightenment of Nirvana, she chose to remain in the world of human beings because she heard their cries of suffering and vowed to aid all who were in need of mercy.

Quan Yin is believed to live on the mountainous island of P'u-t'o Shan, south of Shanghai, where she rescues and cares for shipwrecked sailors. Thus, she is considered the patroness of seafarers. Often the goddess is depicted holding a vial of water, which represents her role in purifying the body and mind, and a willow branch, which she uses to heal illnesses."

The book's drawings showed a serene-faced goddess seated cross-legged on a lotus flower, upending her vial to pour healing water onto a troubled world. *Maybe that's why I feel drawn to her,* Lizzie thought. *I've had too much trouble and sadness these past few months. I need to wash away all that and get on with my life.*

A knock interrupted her reading, and she opened the door to admit the plump housemaid with blond braids wrapped around her head.

"Your supper, ma'am."

"Thank you," Lizzie said and directed the girl to set the tray on the dropleaf table.

Lizzie hadn't seen Melody since the end of The Troubadours' afternoon performance. As she lifted the lids of the various dishes sent up from the kitchen, she wondered where her friend might be. A porcelain tureen contained tomato soup with a fragrant hint of basil. A casserole dish held a chicken potpie with a lightly browned crust, and a linen cloth covered a basket of fresh rye bread. A glass bowl offered a steamed pudding of apples and plums flavored with what smelled like a touch of brandy.

While she ate her meal, Lizzie sipped a cup of tea and wished she had a glass of wine instead. The Troubadours had the bottles of hard liquor Cora gave them plus the ones they'd brought with them from New York, defying the National Prohibition Act that made transporting alcohol a crime. But Lizzie didn't know where to get her hands on some decent wine.

When she finished eating, and Melody still hadn't shown up, Lizzie changed out of her robe into a pair of woolen trousers and a cable-knit sweater. She wanted to check on Sid anyway to see how he felt. Maybe he knew where Melody might be. She hurried through the Gardners' kitchen and out the back door toward the carriage house. The electric light burned at the top of the outdoor stairway, and she rapped on the apartment door.

Sidney opened it. "About time you showed up, Bearcat."

"I wanted to see how you're doing." She peered around him into the brightly lit space. "I don't recall getting an invitation to a party. What have I missed?"

"Nothing so glamorous as a party," he said, motioning her in out of the cold.

Melody and Bert stood in the guest apartment's modest living room, Bert playing one of the blond musician's flutes. Between them, Emma Gardner watched raptly.

Horrified, Lizzie thought, *What in the world will Matthew Gardner think if he discovers his fifteen-year-old daughter in the private chambers of two male musicians in his employ?* The Troubadours would be lucky to escape without a charge of corrupting a minor. At the very least, they'd be dismissed and tarred with a black mark that would damage their rising career.

Her first impulse was to scream at the lot of them. Choking back angry words, she grabbed Emma's wrist. "Come with me. *Now,*" she ordered.

"But Melody and Bert are teaching me to play the flute," the girl protested.

"Do you have any idea how this 'teaching' session might be misconstrued? If your parents knew they'd have our scalps and yours too!" Lizzie dragged the unwitting girl toward the door. "If you have any hopes of going to Julliard, you'll scurry back to your bedroom as quiet as a mouse and say *nothing* to *anyone*—least of all your sister—about being here."

Apparently convinced by Lizzie's fervor, Emma grabbed her coat and hurried across the parking area and into her parents' house. Lizzie watched until she saw the kitchen door open to admit the girl before turning on her colleagues. She crossed her arms over her chest and paced the length of the room, then spun around and retraced her steps, trying to get her temper under control. Her ire fell on Sidney. As the manager and senior member of the troupe, he should have realized the potential risk involved in allowing a young girl—the daughter of their host, no less—to visit the private quarters of two single men. Even Melody's presence as a chaperone wouldn't count for much.

She glared at Sid, whose handsome face paled under her angry glare. "What in the world were you thinking? Do you want us to get tossed out of here, or worse yet, in the hoosegow? Mel and Bert, I can understand. They're young and idealistic. But *you...you* should have known better!"

Lizzie stalked to the kitchenette and opened one cabinet after another, until she found the bottles Cora Delaney had given her. "And this. You didn't give Emma any, did you? How many years in prison do you think that might bring?"

Melody's blue eyes opened wide with anxiety. "Are we in trouble, Lizzie?"

"Not yet, but we're teetering on the edge. It all depends on Emma—and anyone else who knew she was here tonight."

"I didn't mean any harm. It was only about the music," Bert said, his long legs jiggling as if he wanted to run away, to be anyplace but here. He attempted a smile, but his lopsided grin looked more like a grimace.

Obviously chagrined, Sidney admitted, "It was my mistake. You're right. I should've known better. I don't know what to say or how to undo it."

"I don't know either," Lizzie said. "All we can hope is that this incident doesn't go any further than this room."

\* \* \*

Still furious with Sidney, Lizzie pushed through the wrought-iron gate at the entrance to the Gardners' property and walked briskly down Chestnut Street toward the center of town. *Maybe a walk will help me get my thoughts together.* The sub-freezing air stung her cheeks and made her eyes water. Shoving her gloved hands into her jacket pockets, she huffed out clouds of smoky breath. Her lungs burned with each chilly inhalation.

The almost-full moon lit her way as she stomped along the boulevard, her steps sounding her fury. All manner of *what-ifs* flooded her mind. An automobile drove past, its yellow headlights cutting through the deep-blue evening, but she saw no one else on the dark, cold street.

She'd almost reached the train station at the intersection of Washington Street when she heard footsteps behind her. At first, she thought nothing about it—passengers regularly caught the Boston & Maine here to travel to the state's capital fifteen miles south or to Portland a hundred miles north. But after she'd passed the railway station's entrance and the footsteps still echoed behind her, Lizzie turned to get a look at the person to whom they belonged. In the deepening night, she could only discern the form of a large man wearing a greatcoat and a green plaid cap.

He paused when she did. Lighting a cigarette that illuminated only his mouth and chin, he waited for her to make the next move.

A chill that had nothing to do with the temperature ran up her spine. Glancing around, she spotted a broken piece of a wooden branch as thick as her wrist, lying beside the street, and picked it up. She didn't expect it would be of much use if the man attacked her, but it was better than nothing. She squared her shoulders and continued walking around the plaza. The man trailing her did the same. Now she noticed an irregular beat to his footsteps, a limp perhaps.

If he had malice on his mind, the train station offered her the best protection. Safety in numbers. Lizzie circled the fortress-like building until she came to the boarding platform. Electric lights illuminated the area where a couple with two adolescent children waited in the evening cold. A well-dressed man stood beside a stack of luggage, smoking a cigar. A young sailor in a pea coat paced back and forth, slapping his hands together, trying to keep warm. Porters pushed trolleys laden with all manner of goods. Lizzie stepped into the light and stood ready, daring the big man in the green cap to approach her.

He didn't.

For fifteen anxious minutes, she waited, but the man kept to the shadows, making it impossible for her to see his face. Trying to calm her nerves, she asked herself why someone would trail her? She didn't even know anybody in Salem except the Gardners and Cora Delaney. Most likely, the man simply planned to catch a train, and she'd jumped to the conclusion that he was following her, and for some nefarious reason.

*I'm overreacting,* Lizzie realized. Perilous situations over the past few months had made her more suspicious and fearful than she used to be. These days sudden noises startled her. She questioned the intentions of well-meaning people. She often worried about her own perceptions, just as she was doing now. *But what if he really is following me?* She considered confronting the man and asking what he was up to, but that didn't seem like a smart move. If he *was* dogging her, she didn't want to let him know she was on to him. *What am I going to do?*

She could gather her wits and walk stoically back to the Gardners' mansion. After all, houses lined both sides of Chestnut Street, and people would hear her if she screamed. *I don't even know if he's really following me,* she reminded herself. *I may be imagining the whole thing.*

Or she could telephone Cora Delaney and ask for a ride back to the Gardners' home. Cora, she felt, wouldn't judge her and could be trusted to remain silent about the matter. They'd gone through difficult times together before, which made them comrades in arms, so to speak.

Lizzie opened the heavy wooden door and entered the station house. In stark contrast to the cold outside, the lobby, with its scent of damp wool and stale cigarettes, was oppressively warm. She located a payphone, but a sign on it said "Out of Order."

"Is there another telephone I can use?" she asked a uniformed young man at the ticket counter.

"No, ma'am, not a public one."

Lizzie explained her situation. "Would you kindly telephone my friend and ask her to come collect me?"

"One moment, please. I'll inquire." He disappeared into the station's nether regions, but returned after only a few minutes. "I've been instructed to see you safely home. Will you come with me, please?"

Although she liked to think of herself as an independent woman who'd grown up in the rough neighborhoods of the Bronx—certainly not a Nervous Nellie—Lizzie was glad tonight for the escort. The young man opened the door of an old Royal Motor Company sedan enclosed by a canvas-type cover and helped her climb in. As he started the engine, she glanced back at the railway plaza. The man in the greatcoat and green plaid cap was gone.

# Chapter Twelve

"There is no such thing as moral phenomena, but only a moral interpretation of phenomena."

— *Friedrich Nietzsche, Beyond Good and Evil*

Having arrived safely back at the Gardners' mansion, Lizzie went around to the kitchen and asked if she might have a pot of hot chocolate to chase the wintry chill that lingered in her bones. She would have liked a spot of brandy to go with that, but all the liquor The Troubadours had brought with them from New York and the bottles Cora Delaney had given her were stashed in Sidney and Bert's apartment. *I'll have to remedy that situation,* she promised herself. Still nursing her grievance at Sid, she had no intention of confronting him again this evening, even if it meant eschewing a glass of spirits that she would have dearly enjoyed on this cold, disconcerting eve.

A kitchen maid—one Lizzie hadn't seen before, a hefty young woman with broad shoulders who wore an incongruently delicate gold cross at her throat—brought the singer a pot of steaming hot chocolate on a tray, along with a cup and saucer, a stick of cinnamon, a small ceramic pitcher of milk, and a plate of oatmeal-raisin cookies.

"Shall I bring it to your room, ma'am?" the girl asked.

Lizzie reached for the tray and thanked her. "No need. I can take it myself."

However, carrying the tray up the stairs to the mansion's third floor turned out to be more of a challenge than she'd expected. Lizzie had worked in a series of restaurants after dropping out of high school, waiting tables for tips while dodging the advances of chefs, managers, and male customers. Seven years ago, when she was nineteen, she landed a job at a fashionable Greenwich Village nightspot where Sidney played piano. They struck up a friendship and began performing together in venues around the Village. Soon they started getting invitations to entertain at private parties for people who paid good money to hear their music. Lizzie gladly put her waitressing days behind her, and although she knew Sid sometimes missed those nights of playing in smoky, booze-drenched hangouts, she never looked back.

*I'm out of practice,* she thought, balancing the tray on her hip as she pushed open the bedroom door with her foot. A quick glance around assured her that Melody wasn't in. Was the flutist still playing music in Sidney and Bert's guest apartment? She set the tray on the dropleaf table, then took off her woolen jacket and hung it in the wardrobe.

They still had a week's worth of entertainments to perform. Their contract ran through the Feast of the Epiphany on January 6. New Year's Eve, the day after tomorrow, would be the highlight of their engagement and the most festive occasion on the Gardners' calendar of events. They had planned to not only perform music and dance routines, but to give a play that night too.

Usually, The Troubadours functioned like a well-oiled machine, and she was loath to throw a monkey wrench into the congenial arrangement. They couldn't afford to be at odds now. *I'll just have to get over my fit of pique,* she decided. Hopefully, she'd scared Emma enough to make the girl keep her mouth shut.

Lizzie poured hot chocolate into the china cup and sipped it slowly. Little by little, its warmth soothed her. She contemplated the man in the green plaid cap and once again questioned what now seemed to be unfounded fears. The man hadn't actually said or done anything suspicious, she had to admit. *Women are taught from the time we're children to be afraid. It's a way of controlling us,* she thought with annoyance. *A man wouldn't think twice about taking a walk alone at night or get all jittery if he saw another man on the street.*

She drank some more hot chocolate to calm her sense of injustice and shifted her attention to Alan Peabody. She'd hoped to hear from him today, but no word had come after she'd refused to go to his hotel room with him last night. *Of course, he must be busy during the holidays,* she told herself, knowing full well her refusal might have pushed him into the arms of a more willing woman.

From one of her suitcases, she pulled the book of poetry by the thirteenth-century Persian Sufi poet Jalaluddin Rumi that Alan had given her during her last visit to Massachusetts. She ran her fingers over its exquisite leather cover adorned with semi-precious gemstones and silver fastenings. She'd finished reading it and wanted to talk with him about it. More than that, however, she yearned for his touch, to have him hold her in his arms and kiss her again with the ardor she remembered.

The Gardners had invited him to their New Year's Eve festivities. Although Alan said he'd accepted only because she would be performing that night, Lizzie worried about his intentions. And the Gardners'. Cora Delaney's warning echoed in her head: "The Gardners have their sights set on him as a husband for their elder daughter, Sarah." *Does he truly have affectionate feelings for me, or is it all a sham?*

"Lizzie Crane, you're certainly in a dither tonight," she scolded herself.

She'd just finished washing off her face paint and brushing her teeth when the bedchamber door opened, and Melody entered. Usually, the shy flutist was the one who retreated to their bedroom immediately after a performance, while Lizzie stayed up late socializing or reading.

Melody shut the door and slipped off her coat. "Sid didn't mean any harm. He's sorry. We all are."

"Regardless, allowing Emma Gardner into the men's quarters—for whatever reason, innocent as it may seem—could cause a furor, disgracing her and us as well. Sid knows that."

"Emma's wild about music," the flutist said, attempting an excuse.

"Ish kabibble."

Melody hung her coat in the wardrobe, grabbed her flannel nightgown from the chest of drawers, and headed for the bathroom. "You're right. But you can't stay mad forever. What's done is done. You're the one who always says we're professionals, and we can't let our emotions and personal problems get in the way."

Her friend's frankness amused Lizzie. They all agreed that Lizzie's vision and determination kept The Troubadours on track through good times and bad. Like the matriarch of a clan, she ruled at their center. She was the rudder that guided the troupe, especially during stormy seas. Tonight, though, it felt funny taking advice from her younger colleague, and she almost laughed aloud.

With her ire waning, Lizzie said, "I reserve the right to stay mad until dawn."

"Good night, then. Sweet dreams, and wake up in the morning on the right side of the bed."

\* \* \*

Still too keyed up to sleep, Lizzie pulled on her plaid woolen jacket and climbed a narrow staircase that led to the widow's walk on the roof. Four floors above the street, the icy wind whipped at her hair and stung her cheeks. She turned up the collar of her jacket, wishing she'd worn a scarf and a hat.

She rested her elbows on the wooden railing that bordered the widow's walk and gazed out over the city. A crescent moon hung in the inky sky. Below, a handful of electric lights sparkled like land-bound stars.

"Miss? Are you all right?"

Lizzie turned and saw the Gardners' housekeeper step onto the roof. "Good evening, Mrs. Platt. Yes, I'm fine. I just came up here for a bit of fresh air."

"It's well below freezing, miss. Don't stay out here too long; you'll catch a death of a cold," the housekeeper cautioned.

"I wonder about the women who stood on these rooftops night after night, watching for their husbands' ships to come home. Never knowing if they'd return or be lost to the sea. Do you think Mrs. William Gardner came up here and looked out over the harbor, like we're doing now?"

81

"I expect she did," Mrs. Platt said. "Mr. Gardner too. Surely he would've wanted to keep an eye on his ships and to mark their entry into the harbor. In those days, a ship's arrival was a big event."

Remembering the jigsaw puzzle, Matthew Gardner had commissioned of his grandfather's ship, Lizzie asked, "On the night *Peregrine* sank, could the Gardners have seen it from here?"

Mrs. Platt clutched her woolen shawl tight around her shoulders. "I doubt they would've stood out here in the dead of night in a storm."

"How did a lone seaman manage to row a lifeboat to shore in such rough water?"

"Mr. Watkins, you mean?"

"Yes. He must've been awfully strong. And lucky, considering he's the only one who survived."

"I suppose so. Those who didn't drown would have died of the cold or been bashed on the rocks."

"So sad," Lizzie said, shivering at the thought.

After a moment's pause, the housekeeper said, "I believe you're acquainted with Mr. Watkins' son; is that correct?"

*How does she know about that?* Lizzie wondered, then answered her own question. *The help always know everything that goes on under their roof.*

"I met him briefly yesterday."

"Of course, it's none of my business, miss, but Mr. Watkins isn't the sort of man a young lady would want to associate with. I only mention it because Mr. Gardner might find such an association unseemly for someone in his employ."

Lizzie bristled at the woman's implied threat. *After Abigail Gardner, Platt's the queen bee around here. But I'm not one of her housemaids.* Checking her temper, she replied, "Thank you for your advice, Mrs. Platt."

"Well, then, I'll say good night, Miss Crane. I hope you'll be careful up here; it's a long way down. Last year we lost a girl who fell from this very spot."

"I will. A good night to you, too."

# Chapter Thirteen

"I haven't got the gift for that mental sleight of hand you people call manners."

— *Margaret Kennedy, The Constant Nymph*

After breakfast, Lizzie met with Sidney and their hosts in the front parlor to go over details for tomorrow's New Year's Eve celebration. She'd shelved her anger in the interest of business. *I've made my point,* she'd conceded while she brushed her bobbed hair and applied lipstick in preparation for their meeting. *Now on with the show.*

The Gardners had already okayed the performance of Louise Bryant's one-act play *The Game,* a tame little tale of Life and Death gambling for the lives of two young lovers. Lizzie and Sid would play Life and Death, Melody and Bert, the lovers. Unlike some of the more risqué skits The Troubadours occasionally performed, Lizzie had chosen this one because it seemed safe and had a light tone despite its theme. Plus, it didn't require any props, special staging, or scene changes.

Housemaids cleared away balsam boughs and holly swags that had dried out and replaced them with fresh greenery. They fit new bayberry candles into holders on the mantel and windowsills. The Scandinavian-blond girl set a candelabrum with six perfect white tapers on the piano. Two girls draped strings of colored electric lights above the windows, along the bookcases, and above the opening that separated the front and back parlors.

"I think the jazz has been most successful," Matthew Gardner said and turned to his wife. "Don't you agree, Abigail?"

"I do," she said. "I know how much you enjoy it too."

"Yes, I admit it gives me a lift." He smiled at Lizzie and Sidney with anticipation, like a child about to embark on a special outing. "And it's a pleasure to hear it performed so well."

For the next half-hour, the four of them decided on songs they liked and thought guests might enjoy as well. Lizzie longed to ask her hosts if Alan Peabody would attend the event tomorrow night, but resisted. *It wouldn't do for them to know I have a personal interest in him.*

"Are we copacetic?" Lizzie asked after she'd finished reading through the handwritten list of entertainments they'd agreed to.

"We are," Matthew Gardner nodded and rose, holding out his hand to assist his wife. "I have the highest expectations for a magnificent evening."

*Oh no,* Lizzie thought. *One's highest expectations can rarely be fulfilled.* She stood, looking down at the Gardners whose heads barely reached her chin, and said, "We'll do our very best, sir."

In his silken voice that sometimes made her roll her eyes at such obsequiousness, Sid offered words of assurance. "My colleagues and I look forward to providing you and your guests with an entertaining and ebullient evening. If there's anything we can do to enrich your experience, you have only to ask. We are at your disposal."

\* \* \*

Due to the demands of the New Year's Eve event, The Troubadours had requested the rest of the day and evening off to prepare. Bert, although a superb musician, was new to acting. Melody had only performed *The Game* twice before, and the entire group needed a refresher. Fortunately, it was a short piece and not a complicated one.

Lizzie corralled her colleagues in the Gardners' back parlor after lunch, and for two hours, they worked through the skit again and again. It didn't take Melody long to master her lines, and her role as a dancer in the play gave her a chance to showcase her abilities beyond those of a musician. Bert, however, flubbed his lines, spoke too softly, and fidgeted as if he didn't know what to do with his hands when he wasn't holding a musical instrument.

"You don't have to remember the words exactly. Nobody's going to care if you make a few mistakes—they've probably never seen the play before anyway," Lizzie told him. "Just put yourself in the shoes of that young man. Try to feel what he's feeling. We've all suffered rejection and heartbreak. Ad-lib if you forget the script. Just speak your feelings—pretend you *are* that confused and distraught fella."

Bert grinned his goofy grin, with only the right side of his mouth turning up. "I'm confused and distraught, sure enough."

"Good, that means you've got it in you. You can relate to this young man. I know you can do it." Lizzie patted him on the shoulder. "All right, let's run through it again."

Finally, they managed a nearly flawless effort, and Bert seemed buoyed by his success. His hands still fluttered about of their own accord, and he had trouble standing still for more than a few moments, but he remembered his lines and delivered them convincingly.

"Okay, I think we've got it," Lizzie said. "Let's take a break and meet back here at 4:30 to run through the music and dance part of our repertoire. Bert, would you mind sticking around for a few minutes?"

She waited until Sidney and Melody were out of earshot before addressing her young colleague. "I hear you've taken a fancy to one of the Gardners' maids."

He blushed, cast his eyes down, and cracked his knuckles. "Well, kind of..."

"What does 'kind of' entail?"

"I like her, and she likes me."

"How much do you *like* each other? Holding hands or carnal knowledge?"

Bert's cheeks and ears turned a deeper shade of red. "Oh no, nothing like that."

"Good. Keep it that way." She sat on a Chippendale sofa upholstered in cream-colored damask and patted the seat beside her. "Look, Bert.

I'm only a few years older than you, and I know what it's like to desire someone." Images of Alan Peabody rose in her mind, but she pushed them aside temporarily. "First of all, what are your intentions toward this girl? Are you serious about establishing a lasting relationship with her? Or are you just after a bit of fun? Remember, she's going to be the recipient of whatever happens between you, which could affect her employment here, or worse. You can walk away, go back to New York next week, with no concerns to dog you. But she can't. If you care about her, you have to keep that in mind, even when—especially when—your heart and body say otherwise."

She studied his face, his posture, and gestures, trying to ascertain his reactions to her "big sister" sermon. At least he'd stopped jiggling his legs, and she took this as a sign that he realized the seriousness of her words.

"Second, think about The Troubadours. You've made a commitment to us, and I expect you to uphold that commitment. We've taken you into our family and given you a chance. Damn it, Bert, you've got great talent. This is your opportunity to shine. Don't spoil it."

"I know." He cracked his knuckles again and studied his big hands. "You're my friend, Lizzie. You got me off the streets. I'm grateful, don't think I'm not."

"All right, then. See you back here at 4:30. In the meantime, think about what a future with a wife and baby might entail and how you'd make a living for them playing your music. You might even have to give up music altogether and go to work in a factory to support them."

"Don't be mad at me, Lizzie."

"I'm not mad at you. I care about you—and The Troubadours need you." Lizzie gave him a quick hug and tousled his unruly brown hair to let him know she wasn't dressing him down. "Just keep it in your pants, okay?"

As she climbed the stairs to her bedchamber to take a bath and get ready for their afternoon rehearsal, she lamented the fact that despite Bert's apparent chagrin, in a moment of passion, he wouldn't remember a thing she'd said.

* * *

Lizzie laid down the copy of *The House of the Seven Gables* she'd found in the Gardners' library—she still hoped to visit the places where Hawthorne had lived and worked—and answered the knock on her bedchamber door. Emma Gardner stood there. The girl held her head high and stared up at Lizzie. However, she clutched at her skirt, thumbing the fabric nervously.

"Emma," Lizzie said, stepping back to admit her hosts' younger daughter. "Please come in. To what do I owe this surprise visit?"

Emma slipped into the singer's quarters—almost furtively, Lizzie thought as she shut the door. Quickly the girl scanned the room, as if making sure no one else was present. Satisfied that they were alone, Emma crossed to one of the green velvet armchairs and sat down. She tucked her hands under her thighs, trying to keep them still, while Lizzie waited for Emma to find her tongue.

"Don't tell my parents I was discussing music with your friends. Please."

"Of course not. Why do you think I would?"

"Sarah would tattle on me if she knew."

"Well, I'm not your sister."

Lizzie sat in the companion armchair and studied the girl, who seemed alternately defiant and scared. *She's calculating how she can best win my allegiance, demand or cajole,* Lizzie decided. *Moreover, she's beginning to grasp the rules, power, and limitations that come with her status.*

"You took a careless and stupid risk," Lizzie said. "A girl—especially one in your position—can't give gossips food for their prattle. Do you understand what people in this town would say if they knew you were in the private quarters of two single men, employed guests of your parents no less? Unchaperoned? Melody's presence doesn't count."

"But you're an independent woman," Emma protested. "Surely you don't believe those old-fashioned ideas."

"I don't agree with them, but people who do can ruin a young girl's reputation or destroy her chance of achieving the future she dreams for herself. This incident, innocent as it may seem, could hurt your hopes of going to Julliard."

"You're a woman *and* a musician. You've succeeded despite all that," Emma said.

Lizzie shook her head slowly, thinking of the struggles she'd encountered along the way and those that still dogged her every step. *If only you knew how tenuous my hold on success is. What a tightrope of deference, seduction, and daring I walk.*

"I live in New York City—that's a world away from this one. Besides, I come from a poor family. I didn't have a reputation to uphold, as you do. I had nothing to lose and no one but myself to please when I chose this path. Emma, the world's your oyster. You can be and have whatever you want." She stood, dismissing the girl. "Now I have to get ready for practice, so skedaddle. But if you ever have questions about, well, music or men or other conundrums, I'm all ears. That doesn't mean I'll have the answers, but I promise I'll listen."

After Emma left, Lizzie applied fresh lipstick, ran a comb through her hair, and went downstairs to meet her colleagues for practice. *I feel like a Mother Superior, lecturing everyone on morals. If they only knew what fantasies fill my mind.*

# Chapter Fourteen

"Sometimes the very tinkle of the ice in my champagne glass nearly drives me mad."

*— O. Henry, While the Auto Waits*

"Let's go out for supper," Lizzie said when Sidney opened the door to the carriage house apartment and invited her in. She slipped off her silver-gray cashmere coat and draped it over a chair. "We'll be wrapped up tight here tomorrow, and I need a break. Maybe we can find something going on in town tonight, a prelude to New Year's Eve."

"Getting a jump on the festivities, eh?" he asked, eyeing her poison-green silk dress with its swath of rhinestones sprinkled like stars down the bodice and around her hips.

She dropped into an armchair and propped her feet up on the coffee table. "But first, a drink. By the way, I'm reclaiming those bottles Cora gave me. Sometimes a girl needs the comfort of a friend in the wee hours of the night. You've got the entire stash we brought with us from the City. It's not fair."

He laughed and slid a mirror aside to reveal a compartment where an array of bottles sat, waiting to be enjoyed. "What's your pleasure?"

"Some of that brown plaid would hit the spot," she said. "So you've found a secret hideaway. Not that any housemaid or first-day-on-the-job vice man wouldn't think to look there straight off."

"It's no crime to possess alcohol, as you well know, only to make, sell, or transport it." He poured liquid gold into two tumblers, handed one to her, and clinked his glass against hers. "Happy Eve before New Year's Eve, Bearcat."

"Cheers."

After a few sips, Lizzie asked, "Where's our favorite saxophonist tonight? Do I dare speculate?"

"He told me you read him the riot act this afternoon."

"I did. We can't risk him getting some girl in a family way, especially one of the Gardners' help."

Sidney fitted a cigarette into his silver holder and lit it. "I suppose I could forbid him to see her."

"Do you think that would work?"

"Nope."

"Maybe I should talk to the girl. Threaten to tell the Gardners if she doesn't stop seeing Bert."

Sidney sipped his scotch pensively. "I doubt that would work either."

"We could warn Bert that he'll get fired if he creates a problem," Lizzie suggested.

"Except we need him."

She sighed, sipped her scotch, and changed the subject. "Do you think we can get Chinese food in this town?"

"After nearly a century of trade with the Orient, Salem must have a Chinese restaurant or two. Give me a few minutes to change clothes, then we'll go scout around." He studied her expensive dress and jewelry, frowned, then shook his head. "On second thought, why don't we go to a more fashionable place? We can grab Chinese food another time. How about the Hawthorne Hotel? Are you game-ski?"

Lizzie held out her glass. "Perfect. Top me off, and don't be tame-ski."

\* \* \*

When they entered the newly opened hotel's dining room, Lizzie spotted Cora Delaney in the company of a man dressed in a well-cut, double-breasted evening suit with a red carnation pinned to the lapel. Cora wore a handsome sapphire-blue coat with a broad band of mink at the hem and a matching boa around her shoulders. Lizzie waved to the card reader. Cora smiled, waved back, and steered her companion across the Axminster carpet toward Lizzie and Sid.

"Perfect timing," Cora said. "Another minute and we would've missed you—we're just leaving." She turned to the man beside her, whose German ancestry showed in his strong cheekbones, square jaw, and intense blue eyes behind wire-rimmed spectacles. "May I introduce Karl Blume? He's my attorney. I'll be forever indebted to him for straightening out some complicated matters after my parents died."

"Later, we discovered we're both passionate about canasta, gardening, and mystery novels," Blume added.

"Blume means flower in German," Lizzie said, pointing to the man's boutonniere. "Do you wear it as a pretty nametag?"

He smiled, but without mirth, and she guessed people must ask him that all the time. *So much for my attempt at cleverness.*

Sid held out his hand. "Pleased to meet you, Mr. Blume. I'm Sidney Somerset, and this is my colleague Lizzie Crane. We're performers from Manhattan, hired by Matthew Gardner to entertain his guests during the twelve days of Christmas."

"We owe our engagement to Cora, who was kind enough to recommend us to the Gardners," Lizzie added.

"Yes, Cora told me about you," Blume said, taking Lizzie's hand. His touch was cold and dry, though it may have been due to the room's cool temperature on this sub-freezing night.

"Considering the circumstances under which we met, that could be good or bad." *Had Cora told him about the gathering two months ago at the home of an eccentric occultist where a woman died?*

"All good," Cora assured her. "We're on our way to a party at the home of a friend. Why don't you join us?"

"We were planning to have dinner," Sidney said.

"Then come after you've finished." Cora pulled a calling card from her pearl-encrusted evening purse and jotted a name and address on the back. "It's just across the Common. I think you'll find it…well, I'll let you see for yourselves."

"The lamb here is superb," Blume called over his shoulder before he and Cora exited the hotel lobby. Then they disappeared into the star-spangled night and its promised delights.

* * *

They strolled across Salem Common, past a pavilion decorated with colored lights and festive greenery, to a three-story brick mansion whose address matched the one Cora had given her. Late-model motorcars lined both sides of the street. Lizzie spotted a black sedan from the new Chrysler Corporation, a Lincoln Roadster, a Packard Phaeton convertible, and a Ford Model T Touring Car. When she was a little girl, she believed Mr. Ford had nicknamed his "Tin Lizzie" after her, and she'd loved cars ever since.

"Sure you want to crash this party?" Sidney asked.

"We're not crashing. Cora invited us. Don't be a flat tire."

Lizzie slid her arm through his and pulled her friend toward the pillared portico, where a red-nosed doorman, exhaling frosty breaths, stood ready to receive guests. She showed him Cora's calling card, and he opened the heavy paneled door with a gloved hand. Music and laughter spilled out into the chilly night.

"The band's nowhere near as good as we are," Lizzie said to Sid. "Maybe you could convince the fella who owns this place to hire us."

He laughed. "Always the opportunist."

"It never hurts to try."

"That's my girl-ski."

"Will you give it a whirl-ski?"

"Okay, I'll give it my best shot—if I get a shot," he promised.

A housemaid took their coats, and they followed the music into a domed ballroom twice the size of the Gardners' double parlor. Instead of Federal period décor in keeping with the mansion's pedigree, the ballroom was furnished with gaudy red brocade chairs and settees, along with tables, cabinets, and bombe chests in the ornate Louis XV style. Chandeliers dripping crystal teardrops hung from a ceiling painted with idyllic scenes of angels in paradise. Gilt-framed mirrors on the walls allowed guests to view themselves wherever they went.

A marble fountain supported by three human-sized nymphs in all their naked glory dominated the center of the room. Pale golden liquid—*champagne if I don't miss my guess,* Lizzie thought—spouted from the top and cascaded into several tiers of shell-shaped basins. Beautiful people in beautiful attire sauntered by the fountain, filling their glasses from the shimmering waterfall.

"I do believe we've come to the right place," Lizzie said.

A young waiter with hair so shiny and black it looked like patent leather glided by carrying a tray of champagne flutes. She grabbed two, handed one to Sidney, and clinked her glass to his.

"Happy almost New Year."

"Cheers, Bearcat. Is it too soon to toast to a bountiful 1926?"

Lizzie took a sip. "Maybe if we get a jump on it, our wishes will be answered ahead of everyone else's."

She glanced around the crowded ballroom, searching for Cora and her friend Karl Blume, but didn't see either of them among the seventy or so men and women who danced, chatted, drank, preened, and flirted in the grand hall. Although her own dress was beautifully made and showcased her hourglass figure, Lizzie felt upstaged by some of the women's gorgeous evening gowns. She wished she'd worn her most striking and risqué number instead of a lovely dinner frock. Of course, she hadn't planned on attending such a swanky party. Even so, with her dark, sensual beauty, she couldn't help attracting attention.

"At first, I thought you were Colleen Moore, but up close, I see you're much prettier. I don't believe we've met."

She turned to see a tall, formidably built man with shoulder-length white hair standing beside her. His face was lined with a spider web of wrinkles, but he exuded such vitality and physical strength that he seemed ageless.

In the sea of dark evening suits and tails, his pure white tuxedo made him stand out like a swan in a flock of crows. A stickpin with a diamond the size of a quail's egg adorned his lapel. On his left arm hung a stunningly beautiful young woman wearing an elaborate feathered headdress that gave her the appearance of an exotic bird. An equally gorgeous girl, dressed in a shimmering blue-and-green sequined gown that brought to mind a mermaid, grasped his right arm.

He extricated himself from the clutches of both women and bowed dramatically to Lizzie. "I am your delighted host, Isaac Roman. What brings you to my home?"

She held out her hand. "Cora Delaney told us about your party. I'm Lizzie Crane, a jazz singer from New York City. This is my associate Sidney Somerset, the best pianist you've ever heard or probably ever will."

"Is that so?" Roman flashed her an amused smile, exposing a span of teeth as straight and white as piano keys. "How did Salem manage to lure you away from the bright lights of the big city?"

"Matthew Gardner hired us to perform a series of entertainments during the holiday season. Perhaps you know him?"

"Yes, Matthew Gardner and I have a passing acquaintance. We don't have much in common, though. He's mired in the past, and I'm sprinting into the future." Roman fingered his diamond stickpin, which sparkled like a crystal ball, ready to reveal that future. "Well then, while the opportunity presents, might I persuade you to favor us with a song?"

"We're not—" Sidney began, but Lizzie cut him off.

"We'd love to."

"Good. The band is about to take a break." He signaled a waiter, who promptly brought a tray of canapés. "Try the scallops," Roman said, holding one wrapped in bacon out to Lizzie. "The shrimp, unfortunately, are overcooked."

Lizzie let him feed her—a gesture that seemed too familiar considering she'd only just met the man—but she didn't want to offend her host and jinx the possibility of an engagement for The Troubadours. The scallop turned out to be delicious. By the time Isaac Roman's hired musicians left the stage temporarily, she'd finished a second scallop, two crackers with pate foie gras, a lobster-stuffed hard-boiled egg, and another flute of champagne. The two beautiful young women who'd been hovering around Isaac Roman like bees on clover slid away and merged into the roiling crowd.

"If I didn't know better, I'd think you'd skipped dinner," Sidney teased her. He leaned closer and whispered in her ear. "What's your game-ski?"

"Fortune and fame-ski. You, of all people, should see the possibilities." She kissed her fingertips and pressed them to his cheek. "Trust me."

An opportunity like this, to audition for an obviously wealthy potential patron, was too good to pass up. *If only Bert were here to create a sultry mood with his sax.* They'd have to make do with the piano and her voice. Even without the ideal backup, she felt certain they could charm their audience. At least, she hoped so.

Roman crooked his arm, and Lizzie let him escort her to the stage, which occupied a corner of the ballroom where tall windows overlooked Salem's Common. Passersby could catch glimpses of the glamorous goings-on inside and eat their hearts out.

"What would you like to sing?" Roman asked.

"How about 'Sweet Georgia Brown'?"

"Capital. It's one of my favorites. Do you know 'Everybody Loves My Baby'?"

"Of course."

"Would you play that as an encore?"

Lizzie dipped a playful curtsy. "Your wish is my command."

As they mounted the stage and took their places, Roman shouted into a microphone over the boisterous partygoers. "Friends, honored guests, and freeloaders who managed to sneak past my doorman, I have an unexpected treat for you this evening. Lizzie Crane and Sidney Somerset, musicians up from New York City for the holidays, have agreed to entertain us with a song or two. Please welcome them with a round of applause."

Seventy pairs of hands came together with enthusiasm sparked by curiosity, a fondness for music, and copious amounts of champagne. As Sidney ran his fingers over the ivories, Lizzie shook off any apprehension she may have had and stepped up to the microphone.

They ended up performing three songs, and still the crowd clamored for more. Unwilling to steal any more of the hired musicians' thunder, Lizzie bowed, thanked Roman, and stepped down. She spotted Cora and Blume among the revelers and wended her way through the sea of bodies toward the pair. Before she reached them, however, four men had handed her their calling cards.

"You were great," Cora said, stroking her mink boa as if it were a lap dog.

"Yes, you made quite an impression," Blume agreed.

"Good, that was the point. I'm hoping Roman will hire us." She held up her crossed fingers. "Sid's off to make a pitch while the glow's still in the air."

"Oh, I'm sure you'll hear from him," the card reader said. "He gives lots of parties."

A waiter sidled by, and Lizzie snatched a glass of champagne from his tray. "So Cora, what's Roman's story?"

"Rumor has it he deals in stolen artwork."

"And other rare valuables sought by an elite group of collectors," Blume added. "A wealthy buyer targets an item he wants, either from a private source or a museum, and then engages a specialist to acquire it. It's quite a lucrative business."

Lizzie sipped her champagne, recalling the theft of the Mona Lisa fourteen years ago by Vincenzo Peruggia, a guard at the Louvre. Peruggia's famous heist had been hailed by his Italian compatriots as a political act—liberating the painting from France—as much as a monetary one. Apparently, he'd acted alone, not under hire.

"A specialist?" she asked.

"A highly skilled burglar, not your common pickpocket," Blume answered. "Naturally, the buyer doesn't want to be known by the thief, so he works through a discreet agent who handles the transfer of goods and other details."

"And that's what Roman does? Acts as an intermediary? I suppose he makes a hefty commission in the process."

Cora brushed imaginary lint from the sleeve of her spotless gown. "So rumor has it."

Blume's mention of a "common pickpocket" made Lizzie think of the man whose body was found near the harbor the night The Troubadours arrived in Salem.

"Speaking of thieves, do you know anything about a man called Nickolas Owens?" Lizzie asked.

Blume eyed her quizzically through his wire-rimmed spectacles. "You read about him in the newspaper, I presume?"

"Yes. I wondered if his death might have had anything to do with his criminal activities."

"Why do you want to know?"

"My friend Sidney accuses me of having a morbid curiosity about death. I enjoy strolling through graveyards too."

Blume paused for a moment before answering. "Nothing's been determined, of course, but Owens had a history. Petty theft, pickpocketing, burglary, and such. Did a few years in the pen for robbing a jewelry store and fencing the stolen gems."

"Do you think he might have been murdered?"

He shrugged. "In his line of work, he's bound to have had enemies."

Lizzie thought Cora seemed either bored or uncomfortable with the discussion—the card reader patted her hair, twisted her rope of pearls, and scanned the crowd of revelers as if she were expecting someone. When a waiter passed by carrying a tray of sweets, Cora reached for a chocolate truffle.

"Matthew Gardner knew Owens, or was about to make his acquaintance when the fella died," Lizzie told Blume.

"What makes you think that?"

She debated whether to tell him about the note addressed to Matthew Gardner that police found on Owen's body. But why not? Maybe Karl Blume could shed some light on the matter. Attorneys often had access to information about nefarious people and illicit activities that was unavailable to ordinary citizens. Whatever the connection between Gardner and Owens, she was better off knowing about it sooner rather than later. In the past, she'd been caught unawares in criminal entanglements, and her naiveté had nearly cost her her life.

Isaac Roman's hired entertainers, having reclaimed the stage after their break, struck up a lively rendition of a Louis Armstrong hit. Lizzie let her body sway to the music. The band was good, she had to admit, just not as good as The Troubadours. Couples sashayed onto the dance floor—if Sidney weren't otherwise occupied, she'd have dragged him out there and joined them.

Guests strolled past the marble fountain and dipped their glasses in the cascading champagne waterfall. Cora's gaze followed them.

"You know, I sometimes suspect Roman might be a bootlegger," she said.

"Really?" Lizzie asked, curious to learn more about the flamboyant man she hoped might hire her and her friends.

"Perhaps you've heard of the tunnels beneath the Common," Blume said. "They were built early last century by a group of wealthy men who wanted to smuggle goods into Salem and avoid paying duties. The tunnels run from the harbor into the center of town, and connect to various people's homes, stores, banks, and other businesses. In fact, one opens into the basement of this very house. They're still used for smuggling alcohol, drugs, all sorts of contraband."

Lizzie sipped her champagne, trying to imagine Isaac Roman in his spotless white tuxedo slogging through a maze of dark, muddy passageways carrying crates of illegal booze or stolen paintings.

"Surely, the police must know about the tunnels."

"Oh yes," Blume said. "City officials, congressmen, even a Supreme Court Justice were among the first investors—and the National Guard dug them."

A thickset man with a broad face and bulbous nose, standing about thirty feet away and ringed by hangers-on, caught Lizzie's eye. She was accustomed to seeing photographs of him in a baseball uniform, but he looked different in evening attire. Still, it would be hard to mistake the Yankee slugger for anyone else.

"Say, isn't that Babe Ruth?" she asked, gesturing toward one of the game's brightest stars.

Blume looked in the direction she pointed. "That's him, all right. The Sultan of Swat. He shows up around these parts from time to time. Our friend Roman's a big baseball fan. Even though the Bambino plays for the competition now, he still has a following here."

"You never know who you might run into at one of Roman's parties," Cora said. "Last month, it was Vincent."

"Vincent?" Lizzie asked, thinking *Van Gogh's long dead.*

"Edna St. Vincent Millay."

"The poet?"

"The same. And she brought a *female friend* with her."

The way Cora emphasized "female friend," Lizzie got the impression she meant the poet's companion was more than a platonic one. Millay had a reputation for romantic involvements with both women and men, and her marriage to Eugen Jan Boissevain didn't seem to interfere with those relationships.

"And last summer, I met H.P. Lovecraft here," Cora continued. "The town of Arkham he writes about is modeled after Salem, you know."

Excited, Lizzie said, "I'm going to try to get Mr. Ruth's autograph. Do you think he'll talk to me?"

"I'm sure he will," Blume said. "The Babe has a weakness for pretty women."

"Don't all men?" Cora muttered.

But as Lizzie excused herself and maneuvered through the clusters of guests in Isaac Roman's ballroom, a woman's shriek stopped her in her tracks.

# Chapter Fifteen

"[M]en and girls came and went like moths among the whisperings and the champagne and the stars."

— *F. Scott Fitzgerald, The Great Gatsby*

P eels of laughter replaced the initial shriek. Guests in varying stages of inebriation gathered around the marble fountain into which a young lady had fallen. Another woman reached to rescue her champagne-soaked friend and toppled in as well. A moment later, two more jumped into the fountain, splashing about like children in a bathtub. Finally, a group of men extricated the drunken women, giggling with reckless delight, and helped them stand. Their wet dresses, now nearly transparent, clung to their slim figures and dripped champagne on the ballroom's polished maple floor.

As the crowd parted to let housemaids mop up the mess, Lizzie realized one of the girls was Sarah Gardner. She wrapped her arms around the neck of a young man who appeared to be as unsteady on his feet as she was and allowed him to half-drag her across the room.

Sidney recognized her too. "Say, isn't that—?"

"It is," Lizzie said. "I wonder what the Gardners would think if they could see their elder daughter now."

A look of amusement lit Blume's face. "The girl's blotto."

"I hope she gets home all right," Cora said, fingering the jeweled comb in her hair.

"I expect someone will see to that," he said. "But the story's sure to make the rounds."

A thunderous *bang* exploded overhead, and a flash of light burst outside the ballroom windows. A *boom* followed seconds later.

"Fireworks!" a man shouted.

The partygoers, pulled away from their gawking by a new diversion, swarmed out the mansion's French doors and spilled onto the back porch. Lizzie took up a position at one of the windows at the rear of the ballroom and watched two men light fuses, launching sparkling rockets into the night.

"I can see well enough from here," she told Sidney. "It's too cold to stand around outside."

"Most of them are so ossified they don't even feel the cold," he said.

Brilliant starbursts of red, blue, green, and gold erupted against an inky backdrop. Each one elicited a chorus of *oohs* and *aahs* from the spectators. The deafening noise, like blasts from a cannon, must have awakened the entire inner city by now. Suddenly, Lizzie spotted flames rising from the roof of a storage shed. Apparently, a rocket had landed there, igniting the cedar shakes. Fire raced along the wooden gutters. The wind blew sparks into a nearby tree.

Lizzie called out to a housemaid who was gathering up empty glasses and plates. "Hello there, miss! Telephone the fire department, and hurry—an outbuilding is in flames!"

As the startled maid rushed to find a phone, some of the partygoers noticed the fire, too, and began screaming.

"Had enough fun for one night, Bearcat?" Sidney asked.

She grabbed his arm. "And how. Let's get out of here before the whole place goes up in smoke."

They crossed Salem Common and climbed into Sidney's Buick, parked beside the Hawthorne Hotel, as a fire truck clanged toward Washington Square.

"I sure hope the Gardners' party tomorrow night doesn't top *this* one," she said. "Do you think Cora and Karl got away okay?"

"Let's hope so. Sarah too, or there may not be a party tomorrow night." He slid the key into the ignition and started the motor. "Oh, by the way. Isaac Roman gave me his card and asked me to telephone him when we get back to New York. We're in. He wants us to play at a spring equinox bash."

"Assuming his house doesn't burn down in the meantime."

\* \* \*

Lizzie hung her dress in the wardrobe and washed off her face paint, but she was still too keyed up from the evening's excitement to sleep. Not wanting to wake Melody, she pulled on a sweater and a pair of trousers she'd bought in the men's department at Macy's and altered to fit her curves, then went downstairs to find a book to read. A grandfather clock chimed half past one as she entered the double parlor and switched on a table lamp.

Still feeling giddy from the champagne, she was debating whether to climb the library ladder when she spotted the handmade jigsaw puzzle of William Gardner's ships anchored in Salem Harbor. It still lay partly finished on the game table where Sarah Gardner and her friends had left it yesterday afternoon. Lizzie drew up a chair and sat down.

For a few minutes, she studied the picture, familiarizing herself with the colorful scene that portrayed the excitement and activity accompanying the clipper ship's arrival in the harbor. Townspeople gathered on the dock to greet the sailors. Horse-drawn carriages rolled along Derby Street. In the background rose the Custom House, where captains presented their cargo manifests and paid duties on precious goods imported from the Orient. Nathaniel Hawthorne, she recalled, had worked there in the mid-1800s. According to Karl Blume, some ship owners and captains sought to avoid tariffs by sneaking their booty past the revenuers via secret tunnels that ran beneath the city. Was William Gardner one of them?

Lizzie ran her fingertips over the puzzle's cleverly cut pieces, trying to discern which would fill in the incomplete scene. After a few moments, she spotted one that fit into a segment that showed seamen crawling along the ship's rigging and reeling in the sails. She slid it into place. A minute later she spied another piece shaped like a bird that added to a detail of men carrying a carved wooden chest to shore.

Sorting the puzzle's pieces according to color, she discovered, made it easier to locate their positions in the picture. Bit by bit, a vibrant image emerged. Piles of crates, boxes, barrels, and containers of all sorts sat stacked on the dock. Children darted among them. Buyers and sellers bartered deals shipside before tallying up with the customs agents.

She configured half a dozen pieces that revealed a man weighing indistinguishable substances—perhaps tea, spices, or opium—on a set of scales. Two more men displayed a length of flowered cloth to a prospective buyer. Captivated by the scene's intricacies, Lizzie lost track of time. When the grandfather clock struck three, she realized she had to go to bed and reluctantly pushed away from the table. She switched off the lamp and climbed the stairs to her bedchamber. But in her mind, the people in the puzzle continued going about their business, and they kept her from falling into a restful sleep.

# Chapter Sixteen

"Games lubricate the body and mind."

— *Benjamin Franklin*

A rap on the bedchamber door woke Lizzie. With some effort, she dragged herself out of bed, wrapped her silk robe with the Chinese dragon embroidered on the back over her nightgown, and answered the knock. The housemaid with the port wine birthmark on her cheek stood there, holding a vase of orange roses, calla lilies, and lavender.

"Come in, Fanny," Lizzie said, digging into her purse for a coin to tip the maid. "Set it there, on the table, please."

The girl placed the bouquet on the dropleaf table and laid an envelope beside it. After Fanny left, Lizzie slit open the envelope and read a note written in the careful hand of a florist conveying the sender's message:

> Dear Lizzie,
> Happy New Year! I will attend the Gardners' festivities tonight with the hope of hearing you perform. Perhaps you'll have some time to spend with me. Much remains unsaid. I wish you a lovely day and look forward to seeing you in a few hours.
> Fondly,
> Alan

Clutching the letter, she bent to smell the flowers. Each held a particular meaning, she knew, and their symbolic language expressed sentiments beyond written words. By artfully combining flowers in an arrangement, the sender could convey a tantalizing message. Orange roses indicated desire and enthusiasm. Calla lilies represented beauty. Lavender proclaimed devotion and virtue.

She hadn't seen or heard from Alan Peabody since Monday evening, and now it was Thursday morning. If he were truly eager to see her, wouldn't he have attempted to contact her sooner? She ran her fingertips over the perfect blossoms and wondered why he'd chosen to attend the Gardners' New Year's Eve event. Surely he must have many other, more enticing options in Boston. Handsome, rich, single men always did.

Mentally, she reviewed her last encounter with him. His place at the dining table beside Sarah Gardner. His invitation to accompany him to his room at the Hawthorne Hotel and Lizzie's refusal. Had she offended him by rejecting his request? Was he coming to Salem to see Sarah? And what did he mean by "much remains unsaid"?

"Too much to consider so early in the day," she said aloud.

Lizzie returned the letter to its envelope and tucked it in one of the vanity's drawers. Then she glanced at the clock and saw it was nearly eleven. *Holy moly, we have practice in twenty minutes. I'd better pull myself together.*

She washed her face, applied a bit of face powder, and ran a comb through her short, dark hair. After pulling on a knife-pleated skirt and a red woolen blouse, she hurried downstairs to grab some coffee and a muffin, before meeting her colleagues for rehearsal.

* * *

"We need a pair of dice," Lizzie said.

*The Game*, the short play they planned to perform this evening, featured two characters—Life and Death—gambling for the souls of a young man and woman. She opened a drawer in a cabinet, where she'd seen a housemaid store the mahjong set after the Gardners' party two days ago, but found no dice. Another drawer yielded only a dozen decks of playing cards and some crossword puzzle books. In a third drawer, she spotted a backgammon set. She lifted the lid of the hinged wooden box, revealing an inlaid game board, checkers made of walnut and maple, two pairs of ivory dice, and an envelope stamped with red Chinese characters.

Lizzie pocketed one pair of dice and picked up the unsealed envelope. She pulled out a single sheet of cheap paper, unfolded it, and read: "Another player has entered the game. Your move." The handwriting was clumsy and crooked, as if the note had been penned by a child or an elderly person with arthritic fingers. She slid the paper back into the envelope, returned it to the box, and shut the drawer.

"Okay, places, everyone," she called to her friends. "Let's do it from memory."

Sidney reclined on the floor, propped up on one elbow. She handed him the dice. In his role as Death, he tossed them idly while Lizzie began counting, " 'Fifty thousand, fifty-one, sixty-five, ninety.' " After a brief back-and-forth—during which Lizzie, portraying Life, tried humorously to barter the souls of Kaiser Wilhelm, the Czar of Russia, King George of England, and the Austrian emperor Franz Joseph in exchange for the lives of two distraught young lovers—Bert joined them. He looked nervous and confused. Lizzie knew the shy saxophonist really was nervous, and it worked. Even when he stumbled over a line, his awkwardness befit the hapless and lovesick youth in the play.

When it came time for Melody to perform her dance, Lizzie watched with admiration as the pretty blonde moved as gracefully as the soaring bird she pretended to be. Usually Lizzie choreographed their numbers, but this time she'd encouraged her colleague to design her own routine. The result was mesmerizing.

They'd nearly finished when Matthew Gardner entered the double parlor. He hung back for a moment, not wanting to interrupt. After she finished her last lines, Lizzie waved him closer.

"I didn't mean to disturb you," Gardner said.

"You didn't," she assured him. "Would you like us to run through the play one more time so you can see it from the beginning?"

Their host's face brightened. "I'd like that very much."

At the end of the performance, Gardner clapped loudly, and Lizzie felt a wave of relief wash through her. She bowed, and Bert blushed. Gardner reached out to shake Sidney's hand.

"Good show, old chap," he said to Sid.

"I'm glad you liked our little skit," Sidney replied. "If you agree, we'll present it after your guests have had time to socialize and enjoy hors d'oeuvres, but before supper is served."

Gardner nodded. "Yes, they should start arriving around five o'clock. Would you perform the play at half-past six?"

"Perfect," Lizzie said. "How many guests are you expecting?"

"Twenty-four. Plus my wife, my daughter Sarah, my younger brother, and myself."

Lizzie wondered if he knew about his daughter's escapade last night. How fast did word travel in Salem? She'd been concerned about Emma's reputation and what punishment her parents might mete out if they'd discovered her in Sid and Bert's apartment. But she felt no such anxiety over the elder sister's fate—and not only because eighteen-year-old Sarah was an adult. Again, Lizzie's thoughts turned to Alan Peabody, who would arrive in a few hours, and what interest he might have in Sarah Gardner. Was his relationship with her one of the things that "remains unsaid"?

"Mr. Gardner, would you please have your staff arrange chairs in here before the play and then remove them afterward, so there's room for dancing?" Lizzie asked. "We'll also need two housemaids to open the pocket doors between the front and back parlors just before we begin the play—like stagehands opening the curtain in a theater. Plus, someone to adjust the lights."

"Certainly, that can be arranged," Gardner agreed.

"Until this evening, then."

# Chapter Seventeen

"I don't know that I should care for a man who made life easy; I should want someone who made it interesting."

— *Edith Wharton*

After a quick lunch, Lizzie buttoned a heavy Shaker cardigan over her blouse and pulled on a matching knit hat. The temperature would likely drop into the teens tonight, but for the time being, it hovered above freezing, and the afternoon sun made the short walk to Cora Delaney's house quite pleasant. She hadn't sent word ahead, but hoped Cora would have time for a visit—perhaps a card reading. *Maybe the tarot can tell me what to do about Alan.*

Cora didn't seem surprised to see Lizzie and invited her into the handsome parlor with its Queen Anne furniture, Oriental carpet, and crackling fire. The wooden shutters were folded back from the windows, letting golden sunlight flood the room. As usual, Cora wore a stylish outfit and a string of expensive pearls. Lizzie wondered if the card reader ever relaxed in comfortable old clothes, even at home. Although Cora was only about a decade older than Lizzie, she sometimes seemed to come from another generation. Maybe it was due to her social standing and her inherited money, or because both her parents were dead and, with no other family and no husband, she had to fend for herself in the world.

Still, Cora felt like the closest thing Lizzie'd had to a female friend in a long time. Her musical career distanced her from the girls she grew up with in the Bronx, whose lives now centered on husbands and children, and her beauty incited jealousy among the women she met now. Even Melody, for whom she felt great affection, was more like a younger sibling than a peer with whom she could share her innermost thoughts.

Lizzie took off her bulky cardigan and draped it over the back of a wingchair near the fireplace. While a housemaid went to prepare tea, she made herself comfortable.

"Some party last night," she said. "How much damage did the fire do? Sid and I left before the firemen got there."

"With all these old houses built so close together, it could've been devastating," Cora said. "Eleven years ago, nearly two thousand homes and buildings were destroyed when a blaze started in a leather factory and quickly spread through the south part of Salem. Fortunately for Roman, only his shed's ruined. The fire didn't even dash the party. I dare say many of the guests stayed on until dawn."

"Do you think the Gardners know their daughter made a spectacle of herself last night? I saw Matthew briefly this morning, but he didn't mention it. Well, of course, he wouldn't."

"Word has surely gotten around by now," Cora said.

"What do you suppose her punishment will be? No new frocks for a month?"

Lizzie wished the girl's parents would lock her in her bedroom so she couldn't get near Alan. But that wasn't likely if their goal was to betroth their daughter to one of Boston society's most eligible bachelors. She wondered if the story would reach Alan and, if so, what he might think of Sarah's behavior.

"Once again, I'm indebted to you, Cora. Isaac Roman wants us to perform at a spring equinox party he's giving. He told Sid to telephone him when we get back to New York. We should hire you as our agent. Are you available?"

Cora laughed. "I knew he would. Charge him a bundle; he's fabulously rich."

The maid returned with a tray of tea and shortbread and set it on the coffee table. "Will there be anything else, ma'am?"

"No, thank you." Cora waved her servant away.

Lizzie took a sip of Assam from a delicate porcelain cup that might have been transported to Salem from the Orient nearly a century ago. "I found your friend Karl Blume interesting," she said. She couldn't help wondering if he was more than Cora's attorney and canasta partner.

"He is that, certainly."

Lizzie waited for the card reader to elaborate, but when she didn't, Lizzie changed the subject. "I wish you were coming to the Gardners' party tonight."

"Frankly, I've had enough party-going. I'm quite content to sit this one out, thank you."

They chatted amiably for a while until Lizzie noticed her friend studying her intently.

"You're puzzling over something. Shall I do a card reading for you?"

*Am I so transparent?* Lizzie wondered, although she felt certain Cora possessed intuitive skills beyond what she acknowledged. "Would you? I'm ever so curious and, I admit, confused."

Cora crossed the room to her mahogany secretary. From one of its many tiny drawers, she withdrew a deck of cards wrapped in a piece of blue silk. She motioned Lizzie to join her at a game table and sat down. For a moment, Cora held the cards close to her chest as if communing with them before handing the deck to Lizzie. "Shuffle," she said.

After Lizzie passed the deck back, Cora cut the cards and laid out ten in a pattern that resembled an H. The first time she'd read for Lizzie, she'd explained that each card had a meaning. Its position in the pattern meant something too. For several moments Cora stared at the configuration, examining its implications and complexities, before pointing to a card that showed a man wearing a red robe and a crown. He sat on a throne and held a wooden staff that sprouted leaves.

"The King of Wands," she said. "A dynamic, colorful, and powerful man."

The description fit Alan Peabody. Cora had witnessed the interaction between Lizzie and Alan during the ill-fated events that had brought all of them together in October. That he would be the subject of the reading was no surprise, and Lizzie felt certain Cora knew who the "king" symbolized, although she didn't say so. *How much does she know, or suspect, about my interest in him?*

With a thin, manicured finger, Cora pointed to another card. "The Hierophant here shows the King is limited by societal rules, traditions, and so on." She paused to sip her tea before continuing. "Your past is one of deprivation, but now," she touched another card that showed a cobbler busy at his workbench, "it's obvious you're working hard to get ahead in your career."

"But you know that about me already," Lizzie said. "What I really need is advice about the future."

However, her impatience didn't seem to influence Cora, who took her time studying the cards before speaking again. "This card, the Ten of Cups, is in the place of hopes and fears. You long for but resist a secure and comfortable romantic relationship."

*Of course I long for a romantic relationship,* Lizzie thought. Before she had time to reflect on what the card reader had suggested, though, Cora added, "You worry that marriage and a family would limit your freedom to pursue your music on a professional level."

While Lizzie contemplated her friend's words, Cora got up and fetched the porcelain teapot and refilled their cups. She proffered the plate of shortbread, and Lizzie took a piece.

"You're right," Lizzie said as Cora sat down at the game table again. "What do I do now?"

Instead of answering her question, Cora pointed to a card that depicted a man carrying five swords. He glanced over his shoulder as he hurried away, leaving two more swords embedded in the ground behind him. "You're facing a tricky situation in which nothing's clear. Deception is possible. It's important to stay alert."

"Jeepers creepers, can't you give me any more useful advice?"

The card reader shook her head. "Sorry, I don't mean to be obtuse. Sometimes when a matter is in flux, it's hard to see the future clearly. In your case, it seems that nothing is settled." Cora bit into a piece of shortbread, holding a napkin under her chin to catch crumbs. "One thing stands out, however—a need for caution."

"You mean the King of Wands might break my heart?" she said, a hint of sarcasm in her voice.

Cora shook her head. "No, something more serious than that."

*What could be more serious than a broken heart?* Lizzie asked herself.

But before she could speak, Cora indicated a card that showed a man lying face down on the ground. Ten swords were stuck in his back. "I fear you may be in physical danger. I suggest you watch your back."

\* \* \*

Still pondering Cora's warning, Lizzie strolled into the center of town. The streets and sidewalks bustled with activity as people rushed about doing last-minute errands in preparation for New Year's Eve. She passed the Daniel Low Building, with its twin towers and tall, peaked windows, then continued on toward the Peabody Museum. Known for its extensive collection of maritime materials, art, and objects from around the world, the museum had been founded by sea captains and funded by the philanthropist George Peabody, whom she'd learned was, indeed, Alan's relative. One day, when she had more time, she promised herself she'd go inside and see its treasures. *Perhaps Alan will accompany me.*

As she neared the Essex Institute in the next block, Lizzie felt the peculiar sensation of being watched. She turned around and spotted a man in a green plaid cap about twenty paces behind her. He stopped to light a cigarette. Bending his face down and away from her, he held up a hand to shield his match from the wind, then crossed the street. He walked with a limp. *That's the man who followed me two nights ago,* she realized with a start. In broad daylight, on this crowded street, however, he seemed less menacing. Maybe he wasn't following her. Seeing him now might simply be a coincidence.

She started walking again toward the Common. The man with the green plaid cap did too. She crossed Hawthorne Street, but instead of heading to Isaac Roman's mansion as she'd planned, she decided to stop by the antiquarian shop and check on the figurine of the Chinese goddess Quan Yin.

Inside, the elderly shopkeeper with the snowy-white beard looked up from a silver flask he was polishing and greeted her. "Good day, miss. Have you come for your statue?"

"Good day to you too, sir," Lizzie said. "No, I'm afraid I have to leave her with you a while longer. I just came to visit her."

The old man laid down the flask and unlocked a glass display case behind a long oak counter. He took out the delicate jade statue and handed it to Lizzie. Carefully, she fingered the pale green goddess, whose tiny hands held a bottle and a willow branch.

"She's even more exquisite than I remembered," Lizzie said. "Thank you for the book you gave me. I enjoyed learning about Quan Yin. Do you think she's still rescuing shipwrecked sailors these days?"

"I expect she is," he answered.

After a few minutes, she handed the statue back to the shopkeeper, and he locked her away in the glass case again for safekeeping.

"Do you mind if I browse around a bit?"

"Of course not. Stay as long as you like."

A well-dressed couple entered the shop, and Lizzie meandered deeper into its recesses. She admired a hand-painted porcelain tea set—prettier even than Cora's—and a vase similar to the one that had gotten broken when she insisted on moving the Gardners' dining room furniture. She didn't dare look at its price tag. Everywhere she turned, she saw something beautiful or beguiling. After poking around for about fifteen minutes, she picked up a silk fan decorated with cherry blossoms. Each pink petal was rendered in minute detail against a silvery background.

Pleased to discover the fan was within her budget, Lizzie folded it again and carried it to the front of the store. By now, she hoped the man in the green plaid cap had gone on his way. As she passed the well-dressed couple, she noticed they were admiring the collection of erotic ivory netsuke.

She handed the fan to the elderly shopkeeper. "I'd like to buy this."

"Do you know the secret language of hand fans?"

Lizzie shook her head. *Yet another secret language,* she thought. *Flowers, tarot cards, and now fans. Nothing is as simple or straightforward as it seems.*

"When I was a young man, half a century ago, ladies used fans to flirt with their suitors. It was a form of private-public communication during a more repressed era." He opened the fan and held it in his left hand. "This means 'come talk to me.'" Holding it to his right cheek, he said, "This means 'yes.'" Then he switched the fan to his left cheek, "and this means 'no.' And this," he said, closing the fan and touching its handle to his lips, "means 'kiss me.'"

Lizzie laughed, and he handed the fan to her. *What an odd duck he is,* she thought. *I must make time to come here and talk with him more.*

"It seems I could get myself in a lot of trouble by waving this thing the wrong way," she said.

His watery blue eyes sparkled behind his spectacles as he wrapped the fan in tissue paper. "Or perhaps some unexpected fun."

Lizzie paid him and pocketed the fan. "I'll see you next week. Please take good care of my goddess 'til then."

"I shall," he said. "Happy New Year."

"Same to you."

She stepped out into the bright afternoon sunshine and searched the street left and right for the man in the green plaid cap. He was nowhere to be seen.

# Chapter Eighteen

"What would the poor world do without your beautiful songs?"

— *Louise Bryant, The Game*

Two housemaids pulled open the pocket doors that separated the Gardners' front and back parlors. Another switched on the electric lights. Sidney, wearing a long black robe with a hood, reclined on the parlor floor. He tossed a pair of dice, a look of boredom on his face, while Lizzie, dressed in a strapless white gown that sparkled with sequins, tallied her losses in a ledger.

Sidney spoke his first lines of the play. "'Come, come, Life, forget your losses. It's no fun playing with a dull partner. I had hoped for a good game tonight....'"

Lizzie quickly spotted Alan Peabody in the audience, seated beside Sarah Gardner. Despite the girl's lovely evening gown and jewels, she seemed tired and ill—the gown's green color made her look as if she were seasick. Lizzie couldn't help feeling a bit smug. *A hangover's the price you pay for your shenanigans, Sarah.*

In their roles as Life and Death, Lizzie and Sidney bartered back and forth, arguing for the souls of two star-crossed lovers intent on committing suicide. Lizzie reveled in her chance to shine while her competition flagged. For twenty minutes, she stood in the spotlight with Alan's attention focused entirely on her instead of the sullen girl at his side. Several times she caught his eye, and once she was sure she saw him wink.

When the play ended on a happy note, the audience clapped enthusiastically. Matthew Gardner approached the actors and complimented them on their performance.

"I'd like to thank The Troubadours from New York City for such a cunning entertainment," he said to his guests. "And now, if you please, let's remove to the dining room where supper awaits us. Afterwards, we'll come back here to welcome the new year with music and dancing."

While the rest of the guests ambled across the hallway, Alan remained behind. "You were splendid," he told Lizzie.

"I'm glad you enjoyed the play."

"I did, very much." He paused momentarily, as if trying to find the right words to express what he wanted to say.

Sidney pushed the hood of his black robe off his head. "Damn, this thing's hot." He shook hands with Alan, then said, "Bearcat, I'm going to change clothes. See you in half an hour."

Lizzie smiled up at Alan. "Thank you for the lovely flowers. They brightened my day."

"I apologize for not contacting you sooner. My mother has been ill."

"I hope it's nothing serious."

Worry clouded his handsome face. "I'm afraid it is. Her heart is very weak—we don't expect her to be with us much longer. My sister is staying with her now."

"Oh Alan, I'm so sorry."

"Can we talk after supper?"

"Yes, of course."

He lifted her hand to his lips and kissed it. "Sing something special for me tonight."

\* \* \*

When Lizzie returned after changing into a beaded turquoise dress with a plunging neckline and fringed skirt that barely covered her knees, two young men were pushing the furniture in the parlor against the walls to make room for dancing. They'd already removed the chairs used during the play and rolled up the rugs, exposing the golden pine floor.

Sidney sat at the piano, playing a tune she knew he'd written. Sleek and graceful as a Siamese cat, he looked especially dapper in his best tuxedo with a white tie and a white rosebud pinned to his lapel. Bert hadn't gotten used to wearing formal attire yet. He still looked like a little boy dressed in his Sunday best, starched and spit-polished and afraid to move. Soon the music would overtake him, though, and he'd loosen up.

"Showing a lot of skin tonight, Bearcat," Sidney teased her. "Good thing you brought that fan along, in case you need to cover up."

She fluttered the fan in front of her face and asked, "Did you know fans can talk?"

"Is that a fact?"

"It's all in the way you hold it. Each position has a particular meaning." She folded the fan and lightly rapped him on top of the head with it. "This means mind your own business."

Melody laughed. "Well, I think you look smashing."

"Thanks, Mel." She eyed her friend's more modest dress of voile and gold silk that matched her hair. "You do too."

While the Gardners and their guests dined, The Troubadours played instrumental numbers, classical pieces, plus some more recent compositions by Claude Debussy and Edward Elgar. After supper, when the parlor began to fill again with people, they shifted to a repertoire of jazz songs and show tunes.

Trailing the others, Alan Peabody entered with Sarah Gardner on his arm, but they didn't talk or evince any sort of interest in one another. Lizzie couldn't tell whether the glum look on Sarah's face was the result of not feeling well or a bit of pique. Perhaps the girl was annoyed that Alan hadn't escorted her in to supper, remaining behind to talk to Lizzie instead. He guided Sarah to the front parlor, where six-over-six windows looked out onto Chestnut Street, and sat beside her on one of the damask-upholstered settees. Soon Matthew and Abigail Gardner, after circling the room to chat

117

with their guests, joined them.

Lizzie opened her new fan and held it in her left hand as she smiled at Alan. She didn't expect him to understand her signal, but it was fun flirting with him anyway.

Several of the younger couples took to the dance floor as Lizzie and Melody launched into a duet of the popular song "Everybody Loves My Baby," backed up by Bert's saxophone. They followed that with "Yes Sir, That's My Baby," Bix Beiderbeck's "Riverboat Shuffle," and after Bert switched to the trumpet, "The Charleston" from the Broadway show *Runnin' Wild*.

Usually, Lizzie and Sidney invited their hosts to dance with them at some point in their performances. Doing so not only recognized the people who'd funded the event, it encouraged recalcitrant folks to take part in the festivities. After four lively numbers, the Gardners still remained seated. Now seemed like the right time. Together she and Sid approached the couple.

Abigail looked surprised and uncertain. "But I don't know how to do those dances," she protested.

"Well, I do," Sidney assured her. "Just follow me."

Matthew jumped to his feet and took Lizzie's hand. *He's a bit too eager,* she thought and glanced at his wife to gauge her reaction. Abigail, however, seemed intent on trying to comprehend Sidney's instructions so as not to embarrass herself in front of her guests.

Now that their hosts had taken to the dance floor, the others followed suit. All except Alan and Sarah. Lizzie watched Sidney lead the tentative Abigail through Bert and Melody's rendition of "Dinah." The petite woman looked like a child in Sid's arms, but from the expression on her face, she seemed to be enjoying herself. Lizzie gave him a thumbs-up. When the song ended, Lizzie thanked Matthew for the dance and was about to take her place among her colleagues again when a hand on her elbow stopped her.

"Lizzie, may I have this dance?"

She turned to face Alan. Golden flecks shone in his dark eyes, and his coppery hair burned like hot coals in the bright parlor lights.

"Do you think it's appropriate?" she asked.

"I don't give a damn what's appropriate."

From the corner of her eye, Lizzie saw Bert grin. He raised his trumpet to his lips and played the first sultry notes of "Davenport Blues." Sidney took his seat on the piano bench and joined in.

She slid into Alan's arms as smoothly as tonic into gin. "What about Sarah Gardner?" she asked.

"Do you really think she matters to me?"

"I have no idea."

"The only reason I came here tonight was to see you. Otherwise, I would have politely refused the invitation. I have many other ways to spend my time."

"You honor me."

He pulled her closer and spoke into her ear so she could hear him over the music. "Lizzie, surely you know that many men marry women whose coffers will enrich their own, or whose political and social connections will enhance theirs. And vice versa. It's ever been thus. I wish it didn't sound so arrogant, but the truth is, I'm constantly the object of matchmakers' deals, the target of families who hope to elevate or solidify their positions by marrying their daughters to me. Sarah Gardner is only one in a long line of 'suitable' mates thrust at me. But I have no intention of marrying for money or prestige or political power—I have those already. If and when I marry, it will be to a woman whom I admire, respect, and believe to be my equal intellectually and in other ways. No one will maneuver me into a match I don't want."

She leaned against him, enjoying the warmth and strength that emanated from his body, as she mulled over what he'd said. Sarah Gardner was out of the picture. But Lizzie still couldn't be sure where she stood on the stairway that led to Alan's heart. He hadn't mentioned love in his list of things that mattered to him in a marriage. And with so many suitable mates vying for him, how could a mere showgirl from the Bronx compete?

"Which song did you sing for me?" he asked.

"All of them."

\* \* \*

The song ended, but Lizzie didn't move away from Alan. She longed to hold onto him and this moment of closeness that she feared might not come again.

"I'll get even with you!" a woman's voice hissed.

Startled, Lizzie turned to see Sarah Gardner standing behind her. The girl's face was flushed with anger and if looks could kill, her glare would have eviscerated the singer like a knife. Before Lizzie could gather her wits to respond, Sarah stormed out of the parlor, leaving surprised guests gaping in her wake.

In an attempt to cover up the disturbance, Bert picked up his clarinet and launched into Gershwin's "Rhapsody in Blue." Sidney joined in on the piano, followed by Melody's violin.

"Meet me in the storeroom behind the kitchen in fifteen minutes," Lizzie said as she stepped away from Alan to rejoin her colleagues.

Next, The Troubadours picked up the beat with Ben Bernie's hit "Sweet Georgia Brown." By the time Sidney told their audience, "We're going to take a short break, but don't go away—we've got a whole lot more music coming your way between now and the New Year," most people had forgotten about Sarah Gardner's huffy departure.

"What's going on, Bearcat?" he asked.

"Haven't the foggiest. Your guess is as good as mine."

Sidney frowned at her in disbelief. But before he could say anything more, Lizzie scooted around him and slipped away, down the hall and through the kitchen.

In the dim light, Alan's crisp white shirt stood out amid the shadows. Lizzie entered the storeroom, where he awaited her. He wrapped her in his arms and kissed her gently, then more deeply. He trailed kisses along her neck, collarbone, and bare shoulder.

"I have to go back to Boston tonight. How long will you be here?" he asked.

"Our contract goes through the sixth."

"Then, God willing, I'll meet you again before you return to New York. If fate intervenes, I'll see you as soon as I can." He kissed her again, though with more affection this time than passion. "Trust me, Lizzie."

Reluctantly, she freed herself from his embrace and straightened her dress. "I wish your mother and the rest of your family all the best."

# Chapter Nineteen

"The exhilarating ripple of her voice was a wild tonic in the rain."

— *F. Scott Fitzgerald, The Great Gatsby*

As midnight approached, serving girls carrying trays of champagne flutes began wending their way among the guests. It was the first time Lizzie had seen alcohol served in the Gardners' home. When the grandfather clock in the hall struck twelve, The Troubadours played "Auld Lang Syne" while men and women toasted each other and sang, welcoming in 1926.

Alan had left early to drive back to Boston to be with his ailing mother. Sarah hadn't returned after her outburst, and Lizzie began to worry about the girl's threat. What might she do to get even? Would she complain to her parents about Lizzie's flirtation with Alan? And if so, would the Gardners blame Lizzie for his lack of interest in their daughter? Would they cut short The Troubadours' engagement or refuse to pay them?

Cora's tarot reading had described a "tricky situation." Certainly, this one qualified. But was Sarah capable of causing the danger the cards had predicted? To Lizzie, she seemed like a petulant child, not someone who'd intentionally inflict physical harm. Still, she probably shouldn't underestimate Sarah. If the girl had her heart set on the money and prestige that a match with Alan would bring, only to be upstaged by a showgirl—in front of her family and friends no less—well, Lizzie decided, a bit of caution might be in order.

After officially heralding the New Year, The Troubadours played a few more jazz numbers. The serving girls made a last circuit of the parlor, refilling champagne glasses before retiring. None of the raucous excess of Isaac Roman's party, and unless some of the guests had brought along their own flasks, they'd all go home sober. Once again, Lizzie wondered if Matthew and Abigail Gardner knew about their daughter's behavior last night. Perhaps Sarah's indiscretion would count against her if she tried to cause trouble for Lizzie.

By one o'clock, all but Matthew Gardner's brother, who lived in Connecticut and planned to stay the night, had departed. Melody and Bert began packing up their instruments.

"Sensational show," Lizzie told her colleagues.

Bert grinned his lopsided grin and cracked his knuckles. "All in a night's work."

"Don't be modest," she said as she tousled his oak-brown hair. "You were the cat's meow."

"We really were darb, weren't we?" Melody said.

"And how!" Lizzie agreed. "We outdid ourselves. Happy New Year, everyone!"

"Care to come by my humble abode for a nightcap, Bearcat?" Sidney said. "The night's young. They'll be dancing in the streets of New York 'til the sun comes up."

"Ab-so-lute-ly. Let me change into warmer clothes. I'll catch up with you in fifteen. Make sure my gin's sufficiently chilled."

Servants moved in to clean up and restore the double parlor to its usual state as Lizzie and Melody gathered their paraphernalia and headed for the stairs. Before they got there, however, Matthew Gardner met them.

"Your performance tonight was most lively and inspired," he said. "I dare say you'll be the talk of the town tomorrow."

"I'm glad you enjoyed it, sir. We aim to please," Lizzie said.

Following his gaze, she opened her fan and held it in front of her chest.

The difference in their heights put his eyes level with the hollow at the base of her throat. *Sid was right, a fan makes a good cover-up.*

"I had no idea you knew Alan Peabody so well," he said.

*Uh-oh, here it comes.* "Yes, he's a good friend," she said without offering any further explanation.

"I see." Gardner ran his fingers through his thick, wavy hair and changed the subject. "We have the sing-along tomorrow afternoon. Shall we meet at nine to go over details?"

Lizzie groaned inwardly. She'd hoped to sleep late and ease into the day, but his question seemed more a demand than a suggestion. "Nine, it is."

"Goodnight then, ladies."

"Happy New Year, Mr. Gardner."

* * *

Sidney had changed out of his tuxedo and into a maroon silk smoking jacket. With his silver cigarette holder and classic good looks, he epitomized Hollywood's cliché debonair bachelor...if one didn't probe deeper into his lifestyle.

He handed her a martini, icy cold, and touched his glass to hers. "Cheers, Bearcat, and Happy New Year."

"Likewise," she said, dropping into one of the carriage house apartment's leather armchairs. Her mind and body still buzzed from the evening's performance and Alan Peabody's presence. "I assume Bert's ringing in the New Year with his girlfriend?"

"I assume so." Sidney blew smoke rings and watched as, one by one, they floated up toward the ceiling. "We really were spectacular tonight. I think this was one of our best shows ever."

"I agree. Too bad no music critics from the *Boston Globe* were in attendance. That's something I think we should pursue in the future. Invite the press to our performances and get them to write rave reviews about us."

He laughed and propped his feet on the coffee table next to hers. "Good idea. You know how I love praise. It's mother's milk to me."

"I'm serious." Lizzie sipped her martini, trying to gauge his response to her next suggestion. "I think we should consider recording too."

"You mean make a record?" He sounded surprised. *Incredulous is more like it*, she thought.

"Yes. Us. Make a record. It's the wave of the future, Sid."

"But we're not famous."

"All the more reason to record—to let people know we exist. If we make a record, radio stations can play our music. Thousands of listeners can hear us."

He flicked ash into a glass ashtray and regarded her with curiosity. "Go on."

"You know how much you enjoy listening to recordings of the Gershwins and Ben Bernie and Louis Armstrong's Hot Five," she said, referring to his extensive collection of gramophone discs. "If it weren't for those records, you might never have heard their music."

"Yes, so—"

"Well, then, don't you think people would enjoy listening to us play too? All those music lovers in Virginia and Indiana, and Colorado who can't hear us in person are just waiting for us to burst into their living rooms and bring them the excitement we brought to the Gardners' guests tonight."

Sidney's fingers drummed a staccato rhythm on the arm of the chair. "Bearcat, I think you may be on to something."

"Plus, having a recording of our music will give us more credibility. If we get airplay, we can demand higher fees."

He puffed on his cigarette as he considered her suggestion. "Where will we get the money to make this recording?"

"It seems to me we're doing pretty well. The Gardners are paying us top rate, and Isaac Roman wants to hire us for a gala in the spring. We're moving up in the world. It's time to take the next step. A record would be a good investment in our future." Lizzie finished her martini, licked her lips, and held out her glass for a refill.

He plucked the glass from her hand and carried it into the kitchenette. "Maybe we could find someone to back us. How about your 'friend' Alan

Peabody? He's rolling in dough."

Lizzie glared at him. "Do you really think that's the only reason I'm interested in Alan?"

"There's also the fact that he's handsome, charming, sexy, dances well, and has great taste in clothes—don't think I haven't noticed." Sidney poured gin into an ice-filled shaker, tossed it, and then emptied the crystal-clear liquor into Lizzie's glass. "Just a thought, Bearcat. Far be it from me to figure out what goes on in your heart or mind."

# Chapter Twenty

"Hell hath no fury like a woman scorned."

— *William Congreve, The Mourning Bride*

Instead of taking breakfast in her bedchamber, as she usually did, Lizzie sat at the worktable in the back corner of the Gardners' sunlit kitchen, watching Pearl's helpers prepare bread, pastries, and other baked goods. Between spoonfuls of oatmeal loaded with raisins, cream, and brown sugar, she sipped strong black coffee. In twenty minutes, she had to meet Matthew and Abigail Gardner to go over last-minute details for this afternoon's entertainment. Sing-alongs ranked among her least favorite ways to spend an afternoon. But as she watched a scullery maid hunched over the deep soapstone sink scrubbing pots and pans, she gave thanks that singing with a bunch of tone-deaf socialites was the most onerous task she'd have to perform today.

After shouting orders at her squadron of kitchen helpers, Pearl eased her considerable bulk onto a stool across from Lizzie. The cook held a mug of coffee laced with chicory in both hands. "What you doin' up and about so early this mornin', Miz Liz?"

"Got a meeting with the boss man," Lizzie answered.

"I hear you played good last night."

"We sure did. Mr. Gardner and his guests seemed pleased with our performance."

"I heard one gent *especially* liked it." Pearl grinned broadly, and her gold eyetooth glinted in the kitchen's bright light.

*Oh no, what tales are running wild around here?* Lizzie worried. "What don't you hear, Pearl?"

"I like to think nothin' gets by me, but I 'spect I miss a few things now and again." She motioned to one of the girls to bring them more coffee. "You hear about the troubles last night over at Misery Tavern?"

Lizzie's ears perked up at the mention of Misery Tavern. "No, what happened?"

"Police come in an' dragged a buncha folks off to jail." Pearl paused while the plump girl with blond braids wrapped around her head filled their cups, then continued. "Don't your cousin own that place?"

Certain she hadn't shared that piece of information with Pearl, Lizzie nodded. "His name's Jacob Watkins, and he's a peculiar fella, to say the least. Why did the cops raid Misery?"

"Don't know yet, Miz Liz. Sun's barely up an hour. I'll let you know what I find out, though."

* * *

Sidney and the Gardners were waiting for her on this first day of the new year when she entered the front parlor a few minutes before nine. Lizzie thought Sid looked as tired as she probably did, but their hosts appeared well-rested. Matthew Gardner seemed particularly chipper.

"Once again, Miss Crane, may I compliment you on an outstanding performance last night?" he said as Lizzie took a seat.

"Thank you, Mr. Gardner. It was an enjoyable evening for us too. Once again, I wish you both a happy New Year and good fortune in 1926."

"Indeed. I hope this afternoon's gathering will be pleasant as well, though not as rousing, naturally," he said. "We plan to receive visitors in our home from two until four, so would you begin playing at 1:30?"

Abigail Gardner smoothed the skirt of her blue daytime frock. She speared Lizzie with an icy stare that revealed her annoyance at the attention Alan

Peabody had paid to the singer last night.

"The kitchen staff will set up a modest buffet in the dining room, simple refreshments, and sweets," Gardner continued. "Undoubtedly, there will be some coming and going, milling about and such. Many of our guests will want to sing along with you, of course, even those who haven't any musical ability. I trust that won't be a distraction for you?"

"Not a bit," Sidney said. "We're accustomed to performing in all sorts of venues."

"Splendid," Gardner said, pulling a list from his pocket. "I'd like you to play these songs. I expect our visitors will also have some requests of their own."

Lizzie wrote on a notepad as he rattled off a list of familiar songs and holiday favorites, including "The Twelve Days of Christmas." *Today's the eighth day,* she counted, *eight maids a milking. Glad nobody thought to give those to me. No French hens, laying geese, or swimming swans either—and I don't even know what a partridge is. Gold rings are always appreciated, though. Maybe The Troubadours could find a use for eleven pipers and twelve drummers....*

"Lizzie," Sidney's voice pulled her wandering mind back to the present discussion. "Mr. Gardner asked you a question."

"Sorry, sir, would you repeat it, please?" she said.

"I wondered if you'd finished putting together the jigsaw puzzle."

"Not quite. It's delightful. It's just that I've been so busy with everything else these last few days. I do hope to complete it while I'm here, though."

"And so you shall," Gardner said. "By the way, do you play backgammon?"

She shook her head.

"I do," Sidney said. "In fact, I'm rather good at it, if I dare say so without sounding like a braggart."

Gardner clapped his hands together, childlike enthusiasm brightening his face. "You're on for a game, then."

He crossed to the built-in bookshelves and cabinets that lined the walls in the back parlor. Pulling out a drawer, he withdrew the backgammon set Lizzie had seen yesterday afternoon when she went looking for a pair of dice.

"Did you know backgammon is one of the oldest games on earth?" he asked. "It dates back five thousand years to ancient Mesopotamia and Persia. The Greeks and Romans played variations of it too."

He set the wooden box on a game table and motioned for Sidney to join him. When he opened the box, he spotted the envelope marked with red Chinese characters and raised an eyebrow. He withdrew the note inside and read it. While Lizzie watched, his expression shifted from curiosity to confusion to consternation.

\* \* \*

Half an hour before the Gardners opened their mansion to visitors, Lizzie and her colleagues gathered in the back parlor to warm up. For The Troubadours, 1925 had brought success as well as tragedy. On this first day of 1926, she couldn't help speculating about what the coming year held for her—pleasure or pain, or a bit of both?

Emma Gardner sat on the piano bench beside Sidney, dabbling at duets that weren't part of the afternoon's repertoire. She'd brought along her pet cat, a big orange tiger named Neptune, with an extra toe on each paw. The cat cozied himself between the girl and Sidney when he wasn't poking around in the Steinway's innards.

Lizzie reached out to stroke the cat. "What funny feet he has—he looks like he's wearing mittens."

"Sailors favored polydactyl cats," Emma explained. "They thought their big paws made them better mousers."

"Will you be joining us in the sing-along this afternoon?" Lizzie asked the girl.

"Am I invited?"

"Of course you're invited, unless your parents say otherwise."

"Sarah says I can't come."

"Why not?"

"She says I'm on your side. She's royally peeved."

"Really? About what?" Lizzie said, feigning innocence.

"That man you're both mooning over. The one with the red hair. She'd like to see you drawn and quartered, except Mother would consider that entirely too messy."

*Oh no,* Lizzie groaned inwardly. "Why does Sarah say you're on *my* side?"

"Because I told her he's too old, and she should just let you have him." She quickly caught her indiscretion and tried to backtrack. "I didn't mean he's *old,* only that he's too old for her—he's nearly twice her age. Besides, it's clear he doesn't like her." Emma stroked the tiger cat, and he began kneading her leg with his big front paws. "Mother's peeved too. She thinks Mr. Peabody was rude. And she knows about the flowers he sent you."

*Now I've got double trouble. Angering two women in the same family can't bode well.* Remembering Cora's card reading, she decided, *I'd better watch my front as well as my back.*

"Emma," Sidney interrupted, derailing the discussion, "did you know this piano has about 12,000 parts? It's not as complex an instrument as a pipe organ, but it's still an incredible work of art."

He played a few bars of the first short, light piece in Schoenberg's Op. 19, and then let Emma take over. When she finished, he played the second and slower of the six pieces.

Lizzie left them to their music and opened the drawer where the backgammon set nestled. She lifted the lid and glanced inside. The envelope with the red Chinese characters was gone.

She recalled the shifts in Gardner's expression while he read the note. Sidney had shamelessly beaten their host two out of three games, but surely the "new player" mentioned in the note couldn't refer to Sid. It had been written before Gardner knew he played backgammon. Closing the drawer, she wondered what had happened to the note, who the new player might be, and why that person would be reason for her host's concern.

\* \* \*

Lizzie felt her spirits lift as Cora Delaney entered the Gardners' double parlor to join in this New Year's Day sing-along, accompanied by her attorney friend Karl Blume. After an hour of hammering out popular tunes with a roomful of Gardners' friends and neighbors—who didn't seem to mind in the least that they couldn't stay on key—she was glad to see a familiar face. When The Troubadours finished Vaughn Deleath's "Ukulele Lady," having run through all the usual holiday tunes, Lizzie set her own ukulele aside.

"We're going to take a short break," she told the jolly group of guests. "But don't go away; we'll be right back with more swell music to welcome in 1926."

"I hope you didn't stop on our account," Cora said when Lizzie approached them.

"It was time for a break anyway. I need something to wet my whistle. Happy New Year. Glad both of you could come."

"Happy New Year to you, too," Blume said. "Can I get you ladies some punch, or whatever the Gardners are serving this afternoon?"

"Yes, thanks. I'd like some 'whatever,'" Lizzie answered. "Don't expect to find any bubbly or brown plaid among the offerings, though."

As he wended his way through the crowd toward the buffet table, Cora asked, "How did the New Year's Eve party go?"

"All in all, it was the berries...."

"Except?"

"Except it seems I've managed to make enemies of both Abigail *and* Sarah Gardner."

Cora closed her eyes and rubbed her temples, pretending to pick up psychic signals from the cosmos. "I see a debonair red-haired man...."

Lizzie laughed. "You're right on the money, Madame Delaney. So what should I do now?"

But before Cora could reply, Karl Blume returned bearing two glass cups of pink punch with paper-thin orange slices floating on top.

"You didn't get any for yourself?" Lizzie asked, accepting the cup he proffered.

"A bottle of I.W. Harper with my name on it awaits. Doctor's orders," he said with a smile. The Kentucky distillery was one of only ten in the country allowed to continue producing "medicinal liquor" under Prohibition's laws. "By the way, I heard the cops made a surprise visit to your cousin's establishment last night."

"I heard that, too, but I don't know anything more. Looking for booze, most likely. Jacob insists he's clean, but I can't figure out how he makes a living from a pub that doesn't sell anything stronger than ginger ale." Lizzie took a sip of her punch, which she noticed contained a fair amount of ginger ale. "Nor can I imagine how his father managed to establish Misery Tavern on a seaman's wages. It all sounds a bit fishy to me, excuse the pun."

"Maybe he had a financial backer," Cora suggested.

A young woman wearing too much rouge and a frock made of cheap, thin material with a low-cut bodice entirely unsuitable for this wintery afternoon elbowed her way toward them through clusters of chatting guests munching hors d'oeuvres. Lizzie thought she looked familiar, but couldn't place her. Abruptly, she stopped in front of Lizzie, firmly planted her feet, and squared her shoulders as if preparing for a fight.

"Who are you?" the woman demanded. "Not what you pretend to be, that's for sure."

"Excuse me, have we met?" Lizzie asked.

With blazing eyes, the woman assessed the singer. "You're no housemaid here. I'll wager you're no cousin to Jacob either."

Now Lizzie remembered where she'd seen her before. The waitress at Misery Tavern who'd seemed to take a proprietary interest in Jacob Watkins. A few nearby guests turned to eye the woman with curiosity.

"What's your game, coming around asking all those questions about family and such?" she asked, her voice rising until it was loud enough to be heard over the rumble of numerous polite conversations. "What's in this for you?"

Robert Townsend, the butler, hurried toward the disruption before it could burgeon into a full-fledged conflagration. Stiffly, he crooked his arm as if playing escort to the angry woman. "Miss, would you kindly come with me?"

"What, you're tossing me out? I'm not good enough to come to your hoity-toity party?"

He bent his balding head close to her ear and said, "I'm afraid you're not on the guest list, miss. Now please, let me accompany you without a fuss."

The barmaid continued glaring at Lizzie. "Was it you that brought the coppers down on us last night?"

Matthew Gardner politely extricated himself from a discussion with Salem's mayor and hastened to Townsend's side. "What seems to be the trouble here?"

"Just seeing the lady out, sir."

Gardner turned to the woman and said sternly, as if reprimanding a naughty child, "I'd appreciate it if you'd leave now, without further ado. You've made enough of a scene."

For a few moments, she seemed to be contemplating her next move. Then scowling at Gardner, the barmaid tossed her head, shaking her brown curls, and took Townsend's arm. She pointed at Lizzie. "I'm not done with *her* yet."

To divert attention from the scrap, Sidney took his place at the piano again and began playing. Gradually, the guests' interest returned to things other than a bad-mannered barmaid.

"Miss Crane, I apologize for that woman's rudeness," Gardner said. "I hope it won't upset your performance."

"Certainly, not," Lizzie assured him, though she did feel a bit rattled. "She's obviously mistaken me for someone else."

Matthew Gardner excused himself and went back to playing the gregarious host.

In a teasing voice, Cora said, "Congratulations. You've now incited the ire of *three* women in less than twenty-four hours."

"Holy moly," Lizzie said. "What do you suppose that was all about?"

Cora started to answer, but stopped when she saw Emma Gardner stroll across the parlor and sit down on the piano bench beside Sidney. The girl placed her fingers on the keys and began to play. Melody joined in on her violin, and Bert followed on the clarinet.

"Time for me to go back to work," Lizzie told her friend. "We'll talk later."

\* \* \*

Lizzie sank into one of the leather armchairs in the guest apartment in the Gardners' carriage house. While Sidney mixed gin and tonics, she propped her feet up on the coffee table.

"What the devil was that brouhaha about?" he asked as he handed her a drink.

"Haven't the foggiest," she answered.

He raised an eyebrow and passed another glass to Bert, then picked up his silver cigarette holder and sat down across from her. He fitted a cigarette into it and lit the smoke with his engraved lighter. "Bushwa. Who's the floozy?"

"A waitress at my cousin's pub. But why she turned up at the sing-along is a mystery to me."

Sidney puffed out a few smoke rings. "Evidently, she's got a beef with you."

"Ev-i-dent-ly," Lizzie said sarcastically. *But how did she sneak in without Townsend stopping her? Maybe he's acquainted with her?*

Bert took several long-legged strides across the apartment's modest living area to the kitchenette, then turned around and ambled back. "What's this about a bust last night? She seemed to think you had something to do with it."

"That's ridiculous. I only heard about it from the Gardners' kitchen staff this morning."

But as she spoke, an idea popped into her mind. Recalling the angry conversation she'd overheard between the two men in the cemetery, she wondered, *Might Matthew Gardner have had a hand in last night's raid in an attempt to harass Watkins? Was the barmaid the woman they'd argued about?*

"Why would she think you were involved?" Sidney asked.

Lizzie sipped her gin and tonic, trying to decide how much to tell her friends. "You know, this drink could be a smidgen colder. Maybe you should set the bottles outside to chill."

"And risk getting them lifted?" Bert shook his head. "Nothing doing."

"Don't try to dodge the question, Bearcat."

Lizzie took a deep breath, then let it out slowly. "Jacob thinks I'm an undercover cop or a snitch of some kind. Doesn't believe I'm really his cousin. I told him I worked for Gardner and let him think I was a housemaid. The barmaid doesn't trust me, either. Maybe she thinks he's sweet on me. So my guess is she crashed the sing-along to try to figure out what's what, either on her own or at Jacob's suggestion."

"Hard to envision you as a housemaid, but I know what a good actress you are," Sidney said, tapping ash from his cigarette into a glass dish shaped like a leaf. "What else? Spill."

"Some guy might be tailing me. A few times when I was out walking, I noticed a fella following me. He never got close enough for me to see his face clearly, but he wears a green plaid cap and walks with a limp."

"You think your cousin's got him dogging you?" Bert asked.

"It crossed my mind." Lizzie held up her glass. "While you're meandering about, Bert, be a peach and get me a refill, will you?"

"How 'bout you, Sid? Want another?"

"Make mine a double." He let out a long sigh and crushed his cigarette butt in the ashtray. "Bearcat, we can't afford to wreck this engagement—we've got too much at stake. First, there was the business with Peabody and Sarah Gardner. Now this balled-up mess with your cousin and his wench—"

"I know, Sid, and I'm sorry. Truly, I never meant for any of this to happen."

"Must be tough being hot stuff like you," Bert joked as he handed over her drink. "You can't help starting fires wherever you go."

# Chapter Twenty-One

"Beware the man whose handwriting sways like a reed in the wind."

— *Confucius*

After donning the drab brown coat and headscarf Cora loaned her, Lizzie walked into the center of town. First she stopped at the Hawthorne Hotel and sent a telegram to Alan, inquiring about his mother's health. Then she continued on toward the harbor and Misery Tavern. She didn't know if it would be open, considering the police had raided the establishment the night before last and hauled off an undisclosed number of patrons for crimes yet to be revealed. But Lizzie didn't intend to give the pub's brazen barmaid the satisfaction of thinking she'd intimidated her.

On her way to the tavern, she passed the Custom House and noticed the famous landmark was open. The handsome brick building with its cupola and white balustrades made her think of the jigsaw puzzle of William Gardner's ships moored in Salem Harbor. She only had a few more days to finish it before The Troubadours returned to New York.

She climbed the steps and entered the building. A group of eight people had just started a guided tour led by a bookish young man in a too-big suit that looked as if it belonged to an older brother. She hurried to join them.

The guide showed them through the impressive, Federal-style structure, "the last of thirteen customhouses built in Salem since 1649," he told them. He described the handsome appointments, explaining that they "imparted a sense of the city's prosperity and stability." Nathaniel Hawthorne worked there as an inspector in the mid-1800s, a position that inspired his novel *The Scarlet Letter*. At the end of the tour, the young man directed them to an adjoining warehouse known as the Public Stores, where inspectors housed impounded cargo. Lizzie noticed he didn't mention the secret smugglers' tunnels that led from the harbor to Salem Common.

After leaving the Custom House, she walked a few blocks farther on to the dark and eerie-looking mansion known as the House of the Seven Gables. Built on the edge of the harbor in 1668 by a ship's captain, it once belonged to relatives of Hawthorne. A "Closed" sign hung on the door, but Lizzie spotted a stoop-shouldered woman wearing a heavy woolen coat sweeping the sidewalk in front of the sprawling structure.

"Good morning," she greeted the woman. "I keep hoping to see the legendary house from Mr. Hawthorne's famous novel, but it seems I always come by when it's closed."

"Well it's the holiday weekend, isn't it? Come back on Monday if you want a tour," the woman said brusquely. "It's recently been restored—not to its original state, mind you, but to make it fit the way Mr. Hawthorne described it in his story."

Lizzie sensed from the woman's tone that she didn't approve of the remodeling. "Thanks, I'll try again next week. Happy New Year."

Despite the bright sunshine, the morning temperature remained below freezing, and an icy breeze blew in off the water. Lizzie clutched the shabby coat tightly around her, longing for her good cashmere one with its warm, curly lamb collar. After several blocks, she reached Misery Tavern, half-expecting to see it shuttered too. The pub, however, was open and doing a brisk business. *Scandal and crime always draw gawkers*; she thought as she entered the crowded, low-ceilinged room where cigarette smoke hung thick as fog.

Avoiding eye contact with the patrons who studied her from head to toe, she crossed to the bar. Jacob Watkins stood behind the counter, the sleeves of his flannel shirt rolled up to his elbows, exposing forearms furred with thick, dark hair. He glanced up at her and narrowed his eyes as she slid onto a stool.

"Happy New Year, Cousin," she said, effecting a cheery tone.

"And to you," he replied. "What'll you be having?"

"Lunch. What's on the menu?"

He pulled a sheet of grease-spotted paper from under the counter and handed it to Lizzie. As her eyes scanned the handwritten menu, a niggling memory began to emerge. The crudely drawn letters and uneven lines of script on the paper reminded her of the note she'd seen tucked into Matthew Gardner's backgammon set.

"Heard you had some excitement here New Year's Eve," Lizzie said, removing her headscarf and unbuttoning her coat.

"That kind of excitement I can do without."

"Were the cops looking for hooch?"

"Nobody bought any drink in here," he insisted.

"I guess if you operate a tavern, you're always under suspicion."

"I've got no beef with the cops." Watkins wiped his forehead with a handkerchief, then shoved the dirty cloth back in his pants pocket. "You ask me, it was a set-up."

"Oh? What makes you think that? Is someone trying to cause you trouble?"

Lizzie wondered how much the barmaid had told him about yesterday's encounter at the Gardners' sing-along. Did he, too, suspect Lizzie had a hand in the raid? Again, she wondered if Matthew Gardner might have been involved in some way, and if he and Jacob were competing for the same woman's favors. Then her thoughts turned to the thief who died nearby on the night The Troubadours arrived in Salem before he could deliver his message to Gardner. Witnesses claimed to have seen the man in Misery Tavern that evening. *And look what happened to him.*

Watkins grabbed a wet rag and began wiping down the bar. "What's it to you?"

"Just curious, I guess."

"You know the saying 'curiosity killed the cat,' don't you?"

Two seats down, a man with a stubble of beard and an ear that looked as though someone had chewed off the lobe had been staring unabashedly at Lizzie since she sat down. Watkins banged his big fist on the counter in front of the man, a move so sudden and loud it startled her.

"You got an eyeful, pal, now pay your tab and hit the road," he ordered, jerking his thumb at the door.

Watkins' unexpected protectiveness surprised her, though most likely, he just wanted to avoid any more trouble. The man tossed a handful of coins on the counter and ambled toward the door.

"Thanks," Lizzie said.

She scanned the handwritten menu, which listed three offerings: chicken potpie, meatloaf, and fried cod. "I'll have the cod and a Coca-Cola, please."

Jacob withdrew a pale green bottle from an ice chest, uncapped it, and set it on the bar, along with a glass.

"Do you have any children?" Lizzie asked, trying to get him to warm up. She felt like she was pulling each response out of him with forceps.

"More questions, eh? Sure you're not a cop?"

"I just want to know more about my relatives—any harm in that?"

"Three. Howard, Charles, and Peg."

"How old are they?"

"Eighteen, fourteen, and eleven. Howard crews on the *Eventide*."

The boat's name meant nothing to Lizzie, but the boy's did. "Howard. He's named after your grandfather, right? The one who survived when *Peregrine* sank."

"Right."

Although she kept trying to engage him in conversation, Watkins held his cloak of reserve wrapped tight around him. He stayed as far away from her as he could, given the narrow confines of the bar, tending to other customers as if he not only wanted to service them but to shut her out as well. When he set her lunch down on the counter in front of her—a good-sized piece of golden-brown cod, fried potatoes, and baked beans—she gave up. She ate a few bites, then swiveled on the stool and scanned the pub for the barmaid who'd accosted her yesterday at the Gardners' party.

In the rear of the noisy tavern, a buxom, broad-hipped woman wearing a kerchief over her brown curls served a table of four seamen with weather-hardened faces. The waitress exuded a coarse sensuality that some men found attractive. Matthew Gardner, perhaps, whose refined, delicate wife was the exact opposite. Was the waitress the one Watkins claimed he'd been taking care of?

The pub door swung open. An adolescent girl with waist-length braids and a face full of freckles burst into the tavern. She skipped across the room, leapt up on the barstool beside Lizzie, and banged her scuffed shoes on the footrest.

Watkins leaned over the bar and tugged one of the girl's pigtails playfully. "Ah, Peg o' my heart."

He pulled a bottle of root beer from the ice chest, uncapped it, and handed it to her. For a moment, Lizzie thought he might introduce the girl, whom she assumed was his daughter. When he didn't, Lizzie introduced herself.

"Hi, Peg. I'm Lizzie Crane. If you're this fella's daughter then you and I are cousins."

The girl frowned and stopped kicking the barstool. "Is she really my cousin?" Peg asked her father.

"I don't know who she is," Watkins replied. "Go back in the kitchen and eat your lunch."

Lizzie finished her meal, giving up hope of finding out anything more about her family, the New Year's Eve raid, or the belligerent barmaid. She folded the handwritten menu and tucked it in her coat pocket.

Before going back out into the cold, she turned down a dimly lit hallway and pushed through a door marked "Ladies." An acrid odor assaulted her nostrils. Rust stained the sink. Dried mud and who-knew-what-else streaked the scarred wooden floor.

*Drat, no toilet paper,* she noticed upon entering the single stall. Glancing around the dingy restroom, she spotted a doorway and opened it. Inside, a bucket, mop, and an array of cleaning supplies stood waiting for some enterprising soul to put them to use. A stack of toilet paper rolls leaned against the back of the shallow closet. Lizzie reached for one, but her coat sleeve caught on a rack of threadbare towels. The rack and the stack of toilet paper spilled onto the floor, revealing another door about three feet high. Curious, Lizzie opened it.

A dank, musty smell like that of a cellar rose from the opening. Leaning through the tiny door, Lizzie saw a flight of wooden steps descending into the moldy darkness. But without some sort of light she couldn't tell where they led. *Access to the pub's plumbing,* she decided. As she backed out of the utility closet and began gathering up the supplies she'd scattered all over the floor, the barmaid entered the ladies' room.

"What are you doing?" she demanded.

"I've accidentally made a bit of a mess here," Lizzie answered as she collected several errant rolls of toilet paper.

"Can't bear to stay away from here and leave us alone, can you?"

Lizzie stood and stared down at the woman who was several inches shorter than her but stockier, with well-muscled arms from carrying heavy-laden trays. Her forehead glistened with sweat. The woman stood with her hands on her hips, daring Lizzie to try to get past her.

"Why did you come to Matthew Gardner's home yesterday and threaten me?" Lizzie shot back.

"You been nosin' around here this past week, sizin' us up. Turn about's fair play."

"This is a public establishment. And I really am Joseph's cousin—that's my only reason for coming here," Lizzie said. "Okay, so I'm not a housemaid. I'm an entertainer from New York, hired by Gardner. I dressed this way because I didn't want to attract attention, maybe get my pocket picked. But I'm not your enemy, and I don't want any trouble with you."

The woman glanced at the closet where the door that led to the pub's basement still hung open. "Just leave everything. I'll see to it," she said, exasperation lacing her voice.

Lizzie pushed past the barmaid and out into the pub. As she made her way toward the front door of the tavern, a splash of green hanging on a pegboard caught her eye. A green plaid cap.

\* \* \*

Why hadn't her parents mentioned her relatives before? What kept Lizzie's mother apart from her kin? Jacob Watkins could hardly be considered congenial, but was there a reason beyond New England reserve that contributed to his off-putting behavior? Despite his brusque manner, he'd shown affection for his young daughter Peg. That alone gave Lizzie reason to think more favorably toward him.

*I'll ask about him when I get back to New York,* she decided.

She pulled the grease-stained menu from the pocket of Cora's old coat. Running her fingertips over the words on the menu, she wished she could compare it to the note she'd seen in the Gardners' backgammon set. She'd read that each individual's handwriting was as unique as his fingerprints. But why would Jacob Watkins have penned that note? Again, images of Gardner and Jacob in the cemetery flashed in her memory. And if he had, what did it mean, and how could Jacob have managed to slip it into Gardner's backgammon box? Who was the "new player" the author mentioned?

*It's all too confusing.* Lizzie shook her head, trying to dismiss the questions that buzzed like hornets in her brain. She folded the menu again and slid it back into the coat pocket. As she hung the coat in the wardrobe, she contemplated the note the police had found on the body of the thief who died near Misery Tavern. *If I could compare them,* she wondered, *would the handwriting match?*

# Chapter Twenty-Two

"Three may keep a secret if two of them are dead."

— *Benjamin Franklin, Poor Richard's Almanac*

From the bottom shelf of the mahogany wardrobe, Lizzie pulled the bottle of scotch Cora had given her and uncapped it. The only glass she had was a tumbler from the bathroom. *It will have to do.* Making a mental note to pinch a pretty glass from the kitchen, she poured herself two fingers worth of Scottish Highlands' whisky and curled up in one of the bedroom's velvet armchairs, tucking her feet beneath her.

*How have I managed to make so many enemies in such a short period of time?* she lamented, waiting for the golden liquor to calm the anxious twinge in her stomach. She had to finish this engagement with the Gardners, which meant she couldn't avoid Abigail and Sarah. But she didn't need to go back to Misery Tavern again and subject herself to the jealous barmaid's animosity or her cousin's indifference.

Then there was the business of the man with the green plaid cap. *He was there today.* The thought made her skin crawl. Lizzie tried to remember the faces of the people in the crowded tavern this afternoon. Was he one of the rough-looking seamen sitting at the back of the pub? She realized she couldn't have recognized the man whom she now felt certain was following her—she'd never gotten a good look at his face. Only his cap and his limp gave him away. But why was he tailing her? And at whose behest? Jacob's most likely, if he believed Lizzie was spying on him—and if he really was selling booze illegally. He might even have sent the pub's waitress to the Gardners' sing-along to get info about his cousin.

As she sipped the peaty scotch, she contemplated the possibility that Matthew Gardner could have hired the mystery man to keep an eye on her. Her host had invested a good deal of money in The Troubadours and this series of holiday events, after all, and he might be looking after his investment. She had to admit that the man hadn't attempted to harm her in any way, nor had he tried very hard to avoid detection. Maybe Cora told Gardner about the catastrophes that had taken place at the musicians' previous two stints. If so, had her employer engaged a watchdog to make sure Lizzie stayed out of trouble during their tenure in Salem?

The bedchamber door opened, and Melody entered, carrying several shopping bags. Bubbling with excitement, she set them down on her bed and peeled off her coat, hat, and mittens.

"What do you have there?" Lizzie asked.

"Presents." She unwrapped a tissue-covered block and passed it to Lizzie. "A jewelry box for Mom. It's made of sandalwood from India—and look at the pretty mother-of-pearl inlay."

Lizzie ran her fingertips over the carvings and commented on its finery. "It smells nice, too," she said.

Next, Melody handed her an intricately carved ivory pagoda in a glass case that she'd purchased for her architect father. "Can you believe someone had the patience and skill to make this? It's so fragile; I'll have to carry it on my lap the whole way home."

From another bag, she pulled a whitish oval the size of her palm. "This is for Douglas. It's a paperweight made of whalebone. Sailors on whaling ships began engraving pictures like this on bones and walrus tusks in the mid-1800s—it's called scrimshaw."

"How handsome," Lizzie said as she studied the meticulously etched image of a clipper ship, its sails billowing in the wind. "You've had quite a shopping spree."

"It was fun. I learned a lot too." Melody dug into another bag and withdrew a small red velvet pouch. "Here, this is for you."

"For me? Why?"

"Open it, you'll see."

Lizzie untied the pouch and shook out a green disc with a Chinese character carved on it. She turned it over, as if expecting an interpretation on the backside. "I give up. What is it?"

"A lucky charm. The Chinese believe jade brings good fortune. The symbol means 'love.' It's supposed to make Alan Peabody fall in love with you."

Lizzie laughed and hugged her friend. "Thank you, Melody. I need all the good luck I can get."

\* \* \*

Lizzie barely had time for a bath before the Gardners' five o'clock cocktail party. As she applied her makeup, she wondered if her hosts would serve alcohol this evening. How could you have a cocktail party without booze? Even though it wasn't a crime to consume spirits in your home, some people chose not to chance it—unlike Isaac Roman, whose mansion on Salem Common had literally flowed with champagne on the eve before New Year's Eve. Others who could afford it, like Cora, had stashed away what they hoped would see them through until Prohibition ended and doled it out sparingly. Matthew and Abigail Gardner, she decided, might fall into the latter category.

While Melody carefully arranged her golden curls, Lizzie slipped on a sapphire blue dress with a petal skirt and low-cut back that complemented the flutist's more modest silvery-blue frock with its ruffled chiffon hem. She rolled up her silk stockings and buckled on her *peau de soie* pumps. With a swipe of lipstick, she said, "Ready to ankle, Mel?"

Melody tucked a rhinestone comb in her hair. "Ready."

Tonight would be low-key, two hours of cool jazz, show tunes, and popular songs so the Gardners' friends could socialize in a congenial atmosphere. Dancing would be allowed, but not encouraged; therefore, The Troubadours planned to modulate the volume of their music to permit easy conversation.

Although hors d'oeuvres would be served, guests were expected to depart before supper.

As they started down the mahogany stairway into the center of the mansion, Lizzie's right foot twisted. Before she could grab the banister, she tumbled down the stairs. Her knee, then her shoulder, banged on the steps. Melody's cry of alarm rang out above her as she rolled down the entire flight, finally slamming into the newel post at the bottom.

Melody rushed down the stairs as several housemaids, alerted by her yelp, hurried to the scene. "Are you all right?" she asked, her pretty face contorted with worry.

Shaken, Lizzie eased herself up on one elbow and stretched out her legs. They seemed to work normally, but her ankle screamed in pain when she tried to rotate it. Her right hip smarted, too.

Housemaids hovered around them, uncertain what they could or should do. The housekeeper, Violet Platt, pushed through them. A few girls scurried away, back to their chores. The others huddled together in the foyer, eager to see what would transpire.

Bending over Lizzie, Mrs. Platt asked, "Are you injured? Should we send for a doctor?"

Still stunned, Lizzie pushed herself into a sitting position and gingerly tested her appendages. She turned her head slowly from side to side. Thankfully, her neck and back felt fine. *At least it seems I'm not crippled,* she thought with relief. Holding on to the railing for support, she slowly stood. Her ankle felt as if a sharp-toothed animal were biting it. Her shoulder throbbed. But despite pangs and twinges radiating from numerous parts of her body, nothing seemed grievously damaged.

"I think I'm copacetic," she told Mrs. Platt. "Could I have some ice for my ankle, please?"

Melody slid an arm around Lizzie's waist. "Can you walk back to our room?"

"I think so."

When a housemaid returned with ice wrapped in a dishtowel, Mrs. Platt instructed the girl to assist Melody. Together they guided Lizzie up the stairs into her bedroom.

"Drat, I've ruined my stockings," Lizzie said as they positioned her on her bed.

"That's the least of your problems," Melody said, taking the ice from the maid. "Would you please tell the Gardners and our colleagues that Miss Crane won't be performing tonight?"

Lizzie balked. "Wait a minute. I can sing. There's nothing wrong with my voice." She looked at her right ankle, which was already beginning to swell. "I just need a new pair of stockings—these are shredded."

"I think you should take it easy tonight. We can manage without you."

"That's what I'm afraid of," Lizzie said.

Melody removed her friend's shoes and unrolled her torn stockings. "Oh, the heel's missing from the right shoe," she said. "Strange that it would just snap off like that."

"Hand it to me, will you, Mel?" As Lizzie inspected it, a frown lined her forehead. "Look here. It's not a jagged break, as might be expected as the result of a fall. It's neat and clean, as if someone sawed through the heel. Or pried it loose—see these little scrape marks?"

"So it seems," Melody said, examining the damaged shoe. "But who would do such a thing?"

"I don't know," Lizzie answered, holding the ice to her ankle. The first person who came to mind was Sarah Gardner. The girl's New Year's Eve threat, "I'll get even with you!" echoed in her ears.

Emma had said, perhaps jokingly, that her jealous sister would like to see Lizzie drawn and quartered. Was Sarah capable of actually instigating an injury? Whoever sliced the shoe had to be a member of the Gardners' household—no one else had access to the singer's clothing. Before Lizzie walked into town earlier, she'd laid out what she planned to wear this evening. That meant the guilty person must have done the deed this afternoon while both she and Melody were away. A chill ran up her spine.

"I'm going to sing tonight," Lizzie insisted.

She had no intention of caving in to intimidation. Pushing herself up from the bed, she painfully made her way to the wardrobe. She stripped off her short flapper dress and chose a long gown instead that would cover the injured ankle. After pulling on new stockings she checked the rest of her shoes to make sure they hadn't been tampered with too.

"Drat, those were my favorite shoes," she said, slipping her feet into her second-best pumps.

"Are you sure you're okay?" Melody asked dubiously, concern lacing her voice.

"Ab-so-lute-ly," she said, trying to sound more confident than she felt. "Whoever's got it in for me can't get rid of me that easily. On with the show."

\* \* \*

While the guests said their thank-yous and goodbyes and stepped outside to their waiting autos, Emma Gardner approached the Steinway and leaned against its black lacquered body as if the piano were a lover. *Well,* Lizzie thought, *in a way, it is.*

"If your parents will allow it, would you like to play a song or two with us tomorrow?" Sidney asked the girl.

"Do you think I could? I mean, do you think I'm good enough?"

"I wouldn't have suggested it if I didn't think so. But only if you want to."

Emma jumped up and down, like an excited child. "Oh, I do! I do!"

Lizzie sidled up to the piano and waited for her to settle down before saying, "Emma, may I have a word with you?"

The girl's jovial behavior ceased instantly, and she regarded Lizzie warily. "Did I do something wrong?"

"No, of course not. I just wanted to ask you a question, woman to woman."

She motioned for Emma to follow her to the front parlor, out of earshot of the other musicians. Lizzie's right ankle screamed in pain with every step she took. She eased herself down onto one of the damask-covered settees and stretched out her legs.

"Yesterday, you said your sister was angry with me." Lizzie raised her skirt to reveal the bruise that had spread up her right calf. "On my way to perform here this afternoon, I fell down the stairs. The heel of my shoe had been cut, which resulted in this injury."

"Do you think you should see a doctor?" Emma said.

Lizzie waved the suggestion away. "Somebody did this intentionally. Somebody wanted me to get hurt, or worse. What I want to know is, do you think your sister was responsible?"

# Chapter Twenty-Three

"Here's to alcohol, the rose-colored glasses of life."

— *F. Scott Fitzgerald, The Beautiful and Damned*

A young man wearing a white dinner jacket stood behind a table draped in festive red damask, pouring drinks. *So the Gardners have finally decided to bring out what Fitzgerald called "the rose-colored glasses of life,"* Lizzie thought with a satisfied smile. As soon as The Troubadours took a break, she planned to sample the proffered spirits. Gardner could afford to serve top-shelf booze, unlike what she was accustomed to getting at the speakeasies back home in the Village.

Searching for Alan Peabody, she scanned the faces of the guests who mingled in the double parlor, but she really didn't expect to see him. After offending the Gardners on New Year's Eve, he might never be invited here again. Surely Abigail Gardner wouldn't risk bringing him and Lizzie together.

Lizzie wondered if Alan's attention to her—and the snub to Sarah—could damage his business relationship with Matthew Gardner. But that was giving herself too much importance. Money always came first, and if Alan's firm made money for Gardner, a mere romantic dalliance wouldn't interfere with a profitable arrangement.

Abigail Gardner, however, would take the affront more seriously, Lizzie suspected. She'd view Alan's breach of etiquette and his lack of interest in her daughter as a personal insult. What was it Cora had said about Abigail? "She can be a real vixen if you cross her." Watching her diminutive hostess, dressed in an understated but perfectly cut taffeta cocktail dress, Lizzie wondered if Abigail might have damaged her shoe in hopes of eliminating Sarah's competition. Most of the Gardners' holiday entertainments had been fulfilled. An injury to one of the performers would provide a valid excuse for cancelling the remaining events without losing face.

*I could've broken my neck falling down those stairs,* Lizzie realized. Her right ankle ached, and she shifted most of her weight to her left leg, determined not to show her discomfort. If either Abigail or Sarah was responsible, she refused to give them the satisfaction of knowing they'd drawn blood. But would the failed attempt to sideline Lizzie cause her adversary to strike again?

She and Sidney finished singing "Tea for Two" from the Broadway play *No, No, Nanette*. This time she begged off from doing their usual dance routine. "Let's take a break," she told her friend. "I'm dying for a drink."

"You're limping," he said.

"I thought I'd hidden it better, but yes, I took a bit of a tumble. Now that you're aware of my physical limitations, why don't you be a peach and fetch me a highball to ease my discomfort?"

While he went to get their drinks, Lizzie made her way to the front parlor, gritting her teeth with each step, and lowered herself onto one of the settees. She didn't want to worry him. Sid was overly protective even in the best of circumstances, and if he thought one of the Gardners had it in for her, well...

"Here you go." He handed her a squat glass with a generous splash of Kentucky bourbon in it and sat down beside her. "Now, what's the story with this 'tumble'?"

"Thanks. Just what the doctor ordered." Lizzie sipped her drink, trying to decide how much to tell him. "The heel of my shoe snapped off while I was coming downstairs for this evening's performance. I twisted my ankle. Nothing's broken. I'm okay-ski."

"So you say-ski."

"Really. And this lovely drink will help tremendously."

*  *  *

Sid had invited Emma to join the group for a song during the second hour. Although the girl displayed a few jitters, she played well—well enough that Matthew Gardner, surprised to see her in the spotlight, stood and loudly applauded his younger daughter. Lizzie then asked him to sing with them while Emma played piano. The father-daughter combination received an enthusiastic response from the audience—all except Abigail and Sarah, who remained as stiff and silent as a pair of andirons.

When the cocktail party wound down, guests closed in around The Troubadours to offer compliments. Sidney, as usual, beamed under the attention while Melody hung back as if trying to blend into the furnishings. Bert awkwardly shifted his weight from one foot to the other, bobbing his head and blushing endearingly whenever someone praised him. He hugged his saxophone to his chest like a child clutching his favorite toy. Three men older than Lizzie's father gave her their calling cards, but she politely dodged their come-ons and referred them to Sidney, explaining, "Mr. Somerset handles all our business arrangements."

As soon as she could, Lizzie excused herself and headed for the kitchen, where Pearl and her staff wrapped leftovers and washed up. Maids carried platters littered with half-eaten canapés and empty glasses into the bustling kitchen, unloaded them, and went back to collect more. Amid the cacophony, Lizzie sat at the corner worktable out of the way and waited to catch the cook's eye.

It didn't take long for Pearl to spot her. The turbaned woman wiped her hands on her apron and maneuvered through the crowded kitchen like a boat rolling with the tide.

"What you be needin', Miz Liz?"

"Some ice. I twisted my ankle, and it's starting to swell."

"Put your foot up on that there stool. Be right back."

Lizzie did as she was told, hiking the skirt of her gown up to her knee to examine the damage. The graceful curve of her ankle had practically disappeared with the swelling. A patchwork of purple, blue, and crimson bruises crept up her calf. *Looks like I'll be wearing long dresses for the rest of this stint,* she rued.

Pearl returned carrying a chunk of ice wrapped in a linen dishtowel. "Here you go. Take off them stockings and hold this on your leg."

Lizzie obeyed. When the ice had melted, Pearl handed her a muslin bag the size of her fist. "Before you go to bed, soak this here bundle in water, squeeze it out, and put it on your ankle for half an hour or so. Again in the mornin' too. Should do the trick."

"What is it?"

"Just a few plants, mullein, parsley, an' such. Some good juju."

"Thanks, Pearl. You're a peach."

Without actually touching Lizzie's leg, the cook ran her hand slowly from the ankle up to the knee and back a few times. "Now get on up to your room an' rest. I got work to do an' you in the way. 'Member, keep that leg up. You be dancin' again in a day or two."

\* \* \*

By the time Lizzie dragged herself upstairs to their bedchamber, Melody had already changed into her nightgown and settled into bed with a book. Lizzie stripped off her evening gown and hung it up. She pulled the bottle of scotch from the bottom of the wardrobe and poured two fingers' worth in the bathroom tumbler. *Drat, I should've asked Pearl for a better glass,* she thought as she sank into one of the room's armchairs and propped her injured leg on the other.

Melody laid her book aside. "How are you feeling?"

"By the time I finish this drink, I should be copacetic."

"Sid's worried about you."

"Sid's *always* worried about me."

"That's because he cares about you."

"I know, but seriously, I'm okay. Still in one piece. Pearl, the cook, gave me some herbs to bring down the swelling. If only I didn't have this ugly bruise—it doesn't match any of my outfits."

Melody laughed, but then asked, "Are you afraid?"

Playing down her anxiety to avoid upsetting her friend, Lizzie said, "Not enough to skedaddle out of here, if that's what you mean. The Gardner women may be trying to intimidate me, but they won't run me off that easily. I'm thinking about adding the price of those shoes to our bill."

"You'll be careful, won't you?"

"Of course." Lizzie sipped her scotch, enjoying the way its golden warmth was beginning to soothe her aches. "Say, maybe I can find someone to make a magic protection charm for me. This is Salem, after all. There still must be some witches around here plying their trade."

# Chapter Twenty-Four

"Revenge may be wicked, but it's natural."

— *William Makepeace Thackeray*

Sidney pushed away from the piano and stood to greet Lizzie when she entered the double parlor, limping slightly. He crooked his arm for her to grasp, as if offering support to an elderly lady. "How's your leg?"

"Much better, thank you. And it's just my ankle."

"Melody told me Sarah Gardner sawed the heel off your shoe. Why didn't you say so last night?"

"That's still speculation. Besides, I didn't want to worry you. You know what a fussbudget you can be sometimes."

Guiding her to one of the Chippendale armchairs, he held onto her hand until she was comfortably seated.

"I like attention as much as the next girl, but honestly, Sid, I'm okay."

He fitted a cigarette into his silver holder and lit it. "I seem to recall the elder Gardner girl threatening revenge because Peabody showed an interest in you." He puffed out a few perfect smoke rings and watched them float up toward the ceiling. "I warned you, Bearcat, that man would bring trouble."

"Men usually do."

As she contemplated the incident, however, another possibility surfaced in her mind. Did Matthew Gardner—not his daughter or wife—wish her

156

harm? She still didn't know if he'd seen her in the cemetery a week ago, when she heard him admit interest in a woman other than his wife. If he feared Lizzie would expose him, might he have paid a servant to damage her shoe? And if so, would he try again to silence her?

In the dining room across the hall, housemaids were busy setting up for Sunday's brunch. Lizzie heard dishes breaking, followed by a cry of alarm. She recalled the Chinese vase that had gotten smashed on the second day of The Troubadours' stay when Lizzie insisted on moving the Gardners' dining table. *How long ago that mishap seems,* she thought. *I hope today's breakage won't be deducted from that poor girl's pay.*

"Do you feel well enough to perform this morning?" Sidney asked.

"Ab-so-lute-ly. I sang last night, and it hurt more then." Lizzie squeezed his hand reassuringly. "Don't worry, Sid. It'll take more than a sprained ankle to put me off my game. This engagement means as much to me as it does to you, and I intend to complete it."

The maid with blond braids, wearing a starched white apron over her gray woolen dress, interrupted them, bearing a tray with coffee and blueberry muffins.

"Thank you," Lizzie said as the girl set the tray on an eighteenth-century mahogany tea table.

"Would you like anything else, ma'am? Sir?"

"No, thanks," Sid said, and the maid retreated as gracefully and quietly as a cat.

For the next half-hour, they drank coffee and finalized the songs they planned to play during brunch. But Lizzie had a hard time keeping her mind on work. Her thoughts kept circling back to her fall and the fact that someone in this very household wished her harm. Was this just a warning shot over her bow, or did her assailant have more sinister intentions? And how could she defend herself against an enemy whose identity and purpose remained unknown?

\* \* \*

Lizzie hadn't planned to wear a long gown to the Sunday morning brunch—it was entirely too formal for such an occasion—but she didn't want to show the purple bruises on her ankle and calf. Not only might the Gardners' guests think it unsightly, it would also reveal the injury to her attacker. Surely her hosts must have heard about her fall by now, but none of them had expressed concern or sympathy or even acknowledged the incident. Their silence increased her suspicion that one of them meant her harm.

She pulled one frock after another from the wardrobe, considered them, and then put them back. Finally, she held up a floor-length, celadon silk gown with a boat neckline and long, tight sleeves.

"What do you think?" she asked Melody.

"I know you'd rather wear something short and fun, but that one's lovely."

"Will you wear your long violet number so we'll both seem a bit over-dressed for the occasion?" Lizzie laid the gown on her bed, then sat at the vanity and propped her leg up, examining it with annoyance. She pressed her ankle with her fingertip to test the pain level. It felt much better than it had last night. "This blasted bruise is really a nuisance."

"At least it's nothing more serious. You should be thankful. You could've been crippled for life falling down stairs like that, you know."

"True."

Melody sat cross-legged on her bed, fingering the amethyst necklace she wore for good luck. "What if the person who wanted to hurt you tries again? Are you scared?"

Lizzie slid her leg off the vanity and leaned toward the mirror to check her face. She picked up a brush with a Bakelite handle and ran it through her short, dark hair. More to herself than to Melody, she said, "I've been afraid of so many things in my life. When I was a little girl, I feared my parents wouldn't have enough money to feed my siblings and me or heat our apartment in the winter. I was afraid during the War and the influenza, and I'm still scared of polio and tuberculosis and a million other plagues and pestilences. In school, I was afraid I was too tall and boys wouldn't like me. And when I struck out on my own, I worried I wasn't good enough to make it as a singer. I still get jitters every time I step onstage and look out at my audience. Will they like me? Will I choke up or forget the words? Will I fall flat on my face?"

"I'm not nervous about performing," Melody said. "But I get all tongue-tied when I have to talk to strangers. I never know what to say. Everybody seems smarter and more sophisticated than me."

Lizzie flashed back to the man with the green plaid cap, whom she suspected was trailing her. "I'm afraid all sorts of people might do me harm. People I don't know—and even some I do."

"No one would ever think you're afraid," Melody said. "You always seem so sure of yourself."

"It's an act, partly," Lizzie said as she smoothed rouge on her cheeks and swiped jade-green eye shadow on her lids.

Melody got up and pulled her violet silk gown from the wardrobe. She held it against her delicate figure, examining her reflection in the mirror. The gown's rich hue brought out a cheery color in her fair cheeks. "Do you think men are afraid too?"

"I'm sure they are. They just hide it better."

Lizzie stepped into the celadon gown. She eased the shimmering silk up over her full hips and breasts and slid her arms into the fitted sleeves. "Button me up, will you, Mel?"

While her friend fastened a line of tiny rhinestone buttons that ran from her neckline to the base of her spine, Lizzie clipped on a pair of emerald earrings. "We can't let fear get the upper hand," she said as she searched her jewelry box for the right necklace to wear. "If we do, we'll never enjoy life, and we'll never know what we might have accomplished if we hadn't let our worries get in the way."

\* \* \*

With Melody at her side, Lizzie carefully descended the stairway that led to the mansion's central hall. Each step brought anxious memories of toppling painfully down that sweeping expanse, unable to stop her fall. In light of yesterday's injury, she now moved more cautiously and studied everything—people, as well as her environment—trying to anticipate what might hold danger. She chastised herself for succumbing to intimidation. Yet turning a blind eye to the peculiarities going on around her was naive or foolish at best.

If someone in the Gardners' household had orchestrated Lizzie's accident, he or she didn't reveal it. No one except Pearl even inquired about her fall. Either they didn't know, didn't want to admit they knew, or didn't want anyone else to know.

Two dozen guests, dressed in their Sunday best, having come straight from church, gathered in the dining room to partake of the Gardners' brunch. Across the hall, The Troubadours played light jazz. At one point, Emma Gardner slipped into the parlor and scooted onto the piano bench beside Sidney. He nodded to her, and she joined in.

"I'm not invited to the brunch, and neither is Sarah," Emma said after they finished the song. She seemed pleased that her sister had been demoted from her former status among the adult guests.

"Why not?" Lizzie asked.

"She and Mother had words this morning. Mother thinks Sarah isn't trying hard enough to attract a husband. Sarah says it's your fault Mr. Peabody doesn't like her. She's still sulking."

"Hmm. Do you think she's mad enough to retaliate?"

"What does retaliate mean?"

"Do something to get back at me."

Emma nodded. "Once, when she was mad at me, she cut up my favorite doll into pieces. And she pushed our cousin out of a window when he called her a bad name."

*So Sarah's a vixen when crossed, like her mother,* Lizzie surmised, remembering Cora's warning.

"Emma, I think you should go back up to your room now and let us do our job," Sidney told her.

The girl's face fell, but she obediently left the parlor as Bert and Sid struck the first notes of "Rhapsody in Blue."

* * *

After the Gardners' guests had departed, the housemaids set about putting the double parlor to rights again. Lizzie moseyed about the balsam-scented space, uncertain what to do next. The Troubadours had finished their commitment for the day, and she had no obligations until tomorrow. She longed to flee from whatever covert threats might be lurking in the Gardners' household, but even though the weather had warmed up to a respectable 40 degrees, she was in no condition to go walking around town.

To her surprise, the wooden jigsaw puzzle of William Gardner's ships moored in Salem Harbor remained as she'd left it the morning after Isaac Roman's bash, still unfinished on a mahogany game table in a corner of the back parlor. She pulled up a chair and sat down to study the pretty composition. Only a few areas of the dockside activity, a section of the Custom House, and part of a ship's hull were still incomplete.

The gap in the hull made her think of the hole ripped in *Peregrine* when the clipper crashed on the rocks at Misery Island. How quickly had the ship sunk? The islands weren't far from the mainland, yet only Jacob Watkins' father had managed to make it to shore on that stormy night. And what happened to *Peregrine*'s cargo? According to Matthew Gardner, only part of it had been recovered.

She fit a few pieces into the puzzle, filling in the Custom House's roof on which a golden eagle perched, staring out to sea. Below him, horse-drawn carriages rolled along Derby Street, giving spectators a glimpse of the excitement taking place on the wharf. Longshoremen ferried cargo from ship to shore. Merchants bartered for exotic goods and huge sums of money traded hands. *How much of the booty disappeared down Salem's smuggling tunnels, before the revenuers had a chance to tax it?* Lizzie wondered.

However, the hefty profits from these Oriental sojourns didn't filter down to the common seamen who manned the clippers. And sailors weren't known for their financial savvy or inclination to save money for the future. She recalled her cousin's bitter statement when she'd inquired about *Peregrine*'s sinking: "When a ship goes down, rich men lose their investment. Poor men lose their lives." Jacob Watkins' father was lucky. The only survivor of that disaster, he'd managed to leave a viable business for his son. Because of Howard's legacy, Jacob never had to go to sea.

Wishing she could put the pieces of her own life together to form a pretty picture, Lizzie slid the last few bits of the puzzle into the shipside scene, where a man weighed unknown substances on a brass scale. Had Watkins escaped after the wreck with a secret cache of precious spices or opium that William Gardner believed lost at sea? Had stolen goods allowed the sailor to make a better life for himself and his family in Salem?

Admiring the completed jigsaw puzzle, she pushed herself up from the game table. *Too bad it will soon be knocked apart,* she sighed. *But that gives someone else the pleasure of solving it.*

Pain shot up her leg, and she shifted her weight, taking pressure off her injured ankle. Although she didn't like admitting weakness, she wished she had a cane—or better yet, a handsome man—to support her to her bedchamber. *I must ask Pearl for more of those healing herbs.*

As she pulled herself up the staircase to the mansion's third floor, she contemplated the possibility that Howard Watkins might have made off with valuable loot from the doomed clipper. If he had, did his son Jacob know about it? Did Matthew Gardner?

# Chapter Twenty-Five

"If you want to know what God thinks of money, just look at the people he gave it to."

— *Dorothy Parker, The Natural History of the Rich*

When she climbed out of bed Monday morning, Lizzie was surprised to discover that the pain in her ankle had diminished significantly—it barely hurt to stand. She lifted her nightgown to inspect the injury and saw that the swelling had gone down. The purple bruise had faded to an ugly green.

Melody's bed was already made, and she'd gone about her day. Lizzie pulled on a woolen crepe skirt that fell almost to her ankles, brushed her bobbed hair, and applied a hint of rouge to her cheeks. Then she measured her steps carefully as she made her way down to the kitchen, pleased that she could navigate the stairs without much difficulty.

As usual, the sunny kitchen bustled with activity. Tonight the Gardners had invited some of Salem's politicians and business leaders for dinner. The Troubadours planned to play a mix of classical pieces and cool jazz that required no practice or preparation beforehand. That gave Lizzie the day off to do whatever she pleased.

She spotted Pearl, wearing a purple turban. The cook bent over her eldest daughter, Ruby, supervising the girl in making a cake. Lizzie suspected Pearl's secret recipe contained not only flour, sugar, cocoa, and eggs, but also a dash of good juju. After a few moments, Pearl noticed Lizzie and raised a hand with rings on every finger. A wave of that bejeweled hand brought a kitchen maid carrying a coffeepot to the corner work table where Lizzie sat, her foot propped on a stool.

The girl poured the singer a cup of the fragrant, dark brew. "Will there be anything else, ma'am?"

"Eggs, bacon, muffins, whatever you've got," Lizzie said. "And if Pearl has a free moment, a word with her, please."

She'd nearly finished a plateful of fried eggs, sausage, and toast slathered with raspberry jam by the time Pearl freed herself from the cacophony of the kitchen. The cook dabbed her forehead with her apron and eased herself onto a stool at the work table.

"How you doin', Miz Liz?"

"Much better than I could've imagined, thanks to you."

Pearl nodded. "Lemme see how it is."

Lizzie pulled up her skirt to reveal the olive-green bruise that circled her ankle and stretched up her calf. "Look, it's almost healed. Those herbs you gave me really worked."

"Uh-huh." For a few moments, Pearl studied the wounded ankle, gently prodding and manipulating it. "You okay on this one. But what brought it on…." She shook her head. "I can't keep that at bay."

"What do you mean?"

"All I'm sayin' is watch yourself, girl."

\* \* \*

The Tibetan temple bells hanging on the antiquarian shop's door jingled, and Lizzie turned toward the man who entered. Dressed in a double-breasted maroon suit with chalk-white stripes and pointed lapels, Isaac Roman looked every bit the gangster. But the gray cape thrown over his shoulders gave him a theatrical flair that made his mob boss outfit seem all for show.

"Miss Crane, what a pleasant coincidence," he said, removing his fedora from his shoulder-length, snow-white hair.

Lizzie held out her gloved hand. "Good afternoon, Mr. Roman."

"What brings you to my friend Theodore's shop, if I may ask?"

"I'm visiting a goddess your friend has been kind enough to take care of for me until I can bring her back to New York."

"Ah, and which goddess might that be?"

"Quan Yin, the Chinese goddess of mercy."

Roman nodded. "Yes, I'm familiar with her. She's the patron goddess of seafarers, too, as I recall."

The elderly storekeeper indicated a locked display cabinet. "The lady is over here, awaiting you. Have you come to take her to her new home, miss?"

"Not until Thursday," Lizzie answered. "I just wanted to stop by to say hello and make sure you knew I haven't forgotten her."

"I never thought you would." The old man smiled, and his watery blue eyes twinkled behind his spectacles. "Of course, if you did by chance forget, I'd be the beneficiary of your absentmindedness, for I'd get to keep the lady *and* your deposit."

"Let's pay our respects to the goddess, shall we?" Roman said.

He followed Lizzie to the oak-and-glass display case, where an incandescent light illuminated the precious pieces inside. The shelves held ornate silver saltcellars, figurines carved of ivory, and porcelain vases so thin the light shown through them. She noticed a Fabergé egg—or more likely, a convincing replica—had been added to the locked vitrine since the last time she was here.

Lizzie pointed to the delicate jade statue. "That's my goddess. Isn't she exquisite?"

"She is indeed," Roman answered and snapped his fingers. "Too bad you saw her before I did. Otherwise, I'd have snatched her up myself."

"I've heard you're an art collector."

"Then you've probably also heard I traffic in stolen artwork."

His cavalier admission surprised Lizzie. But by acknowledging the rumor so casually, he managed to diminish its legitimacy and make the whole idea seem silly.

"Well, yes, I did hear mention of something like that. But then one hears all sorts of things that may have no substance and can't be proved."

Roman grinned. "Good God, let's hope not!"

With a last look at the Quan Yin statue, Lizzie turned to the shopkeeper, who'd gone back to reading his newspaper. "Excuse me, sir. Thank you for protecting my goddess from Mr. Roman. I trust you won't sell her out from under me, even if he offers you a higher price."

"Certainly not, miss," he assured her. "She'll be right here when you return on Thursday."

Roman seemed more amused than offended by her insinuation. "Miss Crane, would you care to see some of the artwork I've been fortunate to acquire over the years? I can't compete with Isabella Stewart Gardner when it comes to treasure hunting, but I dare say you won't be disappointed."

"Yes indeed, I'd like that very much. If my musician friends and I are going to be performing for you in the spring, I suppose I should get to know you better."

Roman crooked his arm for her to grasp. "Shall we stroll across the Common to my house? The weather's finally warmed up enough that we're no longer in danger of getting frostbite on the way."

Lizzie flexed her ankle, questioning whether it would carry her that far. "I must admit, I may not be up for a walk. I injured my ankle in a fall recently, and it's only now beginning to heal."

"Perhaps I should carry you then?" His eyes swept her figure, unabashedly studying her from head to toe as if he were trying to gauge her weight.

"Maybe we could fly?" she suggested, pointing to his cape.

Roman threw his head back and laughed. "I'm afraid this garment lacks magical properties, and I don't own a witch's broom."

Feigning surprise, she asked, "What? You're not a witch?"

"I'm whatever I want to be—or need to be."

They said *adieu* to the old shopkeeper and headed out into the sunny afternoon that seemed almost balmy after the ten-day cold streak. Lizzie held on to Roman's arm just in case her ankle gave out, and she needed support. *Besides, it never hurts to let people believe you're weaker than you really are,* she thought as they crossed Salem Common.

When they reached his Federal Period brick mansion, Roman opened the front door and guided her inside. Unlike his garish ballroom, the spacious entryway was tastefully furnished with Sheraton pieces, the walls covered with hand-painted French wallpaper. Instantly, a housemaid appeared to take their wraps.

"You haven't said yet, Miss Crane, whether you enjoyed my party."

"Oh, ab-so-lute-ly, it was the cat's meow," she answered. "Except the fire, of course. That was unfortunate."

"Maybe, maybe not. My guests seemed to like it—some of them thought it was planned as part of the evening's entertainment."

A staircase with a polished balustrade and ornate spindles led to the second floor. Roman signaled her to climb ahead of him, ostensibly to catch her if she fell again. But she suspected he wasn't just being polite; he wanted to appraise her backside. She took a few steps, testing her ankle. Only a slight ache remained.

At the top of the stairs, he steered her down a hallway until they came to a paneled wooden door with two locks. One, a cunning brass creation known as a detector lock, counted the times it was opened so that Roman could tell if anyone other than him had accessed the gallery. He withdrew a key from his pocket and opened the door, revealing a metal grate behind it, also locked.

"Jeepers creepers, I feel like I'm entering a vault," Lizzie said as he slid the grate aside.

"Can't be too careful. The artwork in here is priceless. These pieces can never be replaced."

The room was larger than the Gardners' double parlor, with soft gray walls, Persian rugs laid over waxed wooden floors, and iron bars on the windows. Heavy velvet drapes prevented sunlight from damaging the artwork. Roman switched on electric lights, and Lizzie took a moment to rein in her initial surprise, before stepping closer to a wall of paintings. She'd spent enough time at New York's Metropolitan Museum of Art to recognize a Renoir and a Matisse. Bronze and marble sculptures that might date back to the Renaissance—perhaps even to ancient Greece or Rome—perched on pedestals. That such a collection belonged to one man was hard for her to fathom.

Slowly, almost reverently, she made her way around the room while Roman stood in the center, watching her. It occurred to Lizzie that these pieces might be fakes, clever copies made to trick unsuspecting buyers. Or, they might be stolen. Karl Blume had said an opening into Salem's infamous smuggling tunnels lay beneath this house. She let her eyes roam about the gallery, searching for signs of a secret staircase or elevator that led down into those clandestine depths.

"What's to prevent someone from cutting through from above or below and stealing your treasures?" she asked.

"Metal plates installed between the floors."

"Ah, so I really am in a vault."

He chuckled. "Yes, I suppose you could say that."

One corner of Roman's private museum was dedicated to Oriental art brought to Salem during the China trade. Jade dragons coiled on teak shelves beside Ming vases and ivory pagodas. *My goddess would feel right at home here,* Lizzie thought. As she admired a life-size bronze figure of the Buddha sitting cross-legged on a carved teak dais, a question rose in her mind.

"What if a clipper sailing home from a trip to the Orient was shipwrecked before it reached harbor, and what if some of the cargo was rescued?" she asked. "Who'd own the salvaged goods?"

"That depends," Roman answered. "If the cargo was rescued at the time of the wreck, it would likely belong to the owner of the ship unless someone else had purchased the goods in advance or helped to underwrite the voyage. If the ship was insured, which was usually the case, and the ship owner collected on his loss, anything recovered later might belong to the insurance company. Typically, insurance companies only paid three-quarters of the value of the cargo, though."

"What about the rest?"

"Some ship owners in the last century banded together to form what were known as protection and indemnity clubs that distributed the liability among themselves to cover what the insurance agencies didn't. If a ship owner belonged to such a club and the club reimbursed him for his loss, a portion of the cargo—if it were salvaged later—could go to the club members." Roman crossed the room to the display of Oriental *objets d'art* where Lizzie stood studying the amassed riches from a faraway land.

"What about finder's keepers?" she asked. "Would the person who saved the goods have any claim to them?"

Roman toyed with his silk tie, adjusting it so the knot rested perfectly in the hollow at the base of his throat. "Why do you ask?"

"You may know that Matthew Gardner's grandfather's ship *Peregrine* wrecked on Misery Islands in 1868."

"Yes, and if my memory serves me, only one man survived."

"Right. Howard Watkins, who established a pub he named Misery Tavern after the islands. I've wondered how he could afford to do that on a sailor's wages."

Roman pointed to a porcelain vase about two feet high, decorated with phoenixes and peony flowers. "What do you think this is worth?" he asked.

"Haven't the foggiest."

"About $3,000."

"Holy moly, that's two years' salary for a skilled tradesman."

"And this one," Roman indicated a larger jar shaped like a bell and rimmed in gold, "might fetch twice that much. I don't know what their values were in 1868, but if Watkins escaped in a lifeboat with one of these sweethearts my guess is he could've sold it for enough to set up shop."

As Lizzie's eyes fell on one after another of the antiques, she mentally tallied up what they might be worth. *No surprise so many people wanted to get in on the China trade, despite the risks.*

"Other than idle curiosity, what's your interest in this?" Roman asked.

"Well, as you know, Matthew Gardner has hired my friends and me to perform for his guests during the holidays. Jacob Watkins, Howard's son, is my cousin." She considered the message addressed to Gardner that police found in the pocket of the dead man near Misery Tavern and the meeting she'd observed between Gardner and Watkins in the graveyard. "I get the feeling there's a peculiar connection between them, something more than

169

the elder Watkins crewing on the elder Gardner's ill-fated ship."

Roman let out a low whistle. "I'd say you've got yourself in a bit of a pickle. A whole barrel full of pickles."

"Why do you say that?"

"Do they know you're a link between them?"

"Jacob knows I'm working for Gardner. I'm not sure about Gardner, but I don't think he realizes I'm related to Jacob."

"My advice is don't tell either of them what you've just told me."

# Chapter Twenty-Six

"I want to be with those who know secret things."

— *Rainer Maria Rilke*

Themselves the highballs she'd drunk in Sidney's apartment after they finished entertaining Gardner's business and political associates had numbed Lizzie's ankle. It no longer registered even a twinge of pain as she walked across the frozen backyard to the mansion. She'd tipped the maid Fanny to leave the back door open, and she slipped in through the kitchen. At this time of night, the cavernous space—usually so bright and boisterous—was strangely dark and still. She aimed the flashlight Sidney had loaned her at the floor and followed its beam down the hallway.

The double parlor, too, rested quietly in the aftermath of the evening. Strings of multicolored lights, hanging along the mantel and on the Christmas tree at the front window, glowed like captured rainbows. In the fireplace, orange coals gave off a last vestige of warmth. She turned off the flashlight and flipped on the overhead electric lights.

*I'll just grab a book to help me fall asleep,* she thought as she made her way to the back of the room where floor-to-ceiling shelves lined the walls. She was glad Matthew Gardner had given her permission to access this library, which contained a wealth of information about Salem and its history. She'd read several of her host's volumes about the city's architecture, its shipping trade, and the witchcraft hysteria, but wished she had time to delve deeper.

Holding on to its railing, Lizzie mounted the library ladder. She tilted her head toward her right shoulder and read the spines of the neatly aligned texts. Bypassing leather-bound tomes of philosophy, pharmacopeia, and engineering, she searched for a novel by Jane Austen or perhaps Edith Wharton. She was about to climb down and slide the ladder to a section that promised more entertaining fare when she spotted a series of ledgers.

She pulled a ledger from the shelf and rested it on one of the ladder's rungs. Opening it, she flipped through pages of records written by her host's grandfather, William Gardner, related to his shipping business. Here, in a precise script, he'd kept accounts of his ships' voyages between 1853 and 1856. His notations described where they traveled, what goods the ships carried, the names of passengers and crew, and so on. Lizzie slid the ledger back into place and took down another.

This one covered the years 1857 through 1860. In addition to the mercantile records, Gardner occasionally included asides that Lizzie found amusing. One said, "It has been reported to me that three sailors professed to witness mermaids riding the waves whilst singing with the most beauteous voices, such that the men fell under the sirens' spell and would have dived into the waters had not other stalwart members of the crew used force to restrain them. I suspect them overwrought by fantasies not uncommon to young lads long at sea without the company of women." In another, William Gardner noted, "The captain of *Merryweather* has explained to me, whilst apologizing profusely, that a seaman did not return to the ship after docking in Shanghai. It is believed he absconded in pursuit of a local girl; however, this cannot be proved, and the ship was obliged to depart without him. I am now confounded as to what I shall tell his wife and whether I shall be required to pay her a sum for the loss of her husband."

She replaced the ledger and withdrew one that began in 1866 and ended in 1869. Curious, she turned the pages until she came to February 1868, the date *Peregrine* sank. Among the names of the crew aboard the ship, she saw Howard Watkins listed. At the bottom of the page, Gardner had written, "Captain Stevenson and all hands, save Howard Watkins, went down with the ship. God rest their souls."

A sheet of paper in another person's handwriting followed. The yellowed document bearing fold marks had been glued to a page in the ledger. It described *Peregrine*'s cargo in detail and was signed Hu Chen, with Chinese characters inked beneath the signature. The ship's manifest. During her visit to Salem's Custom House, Lizzie had learned that, for tax purposes, inspectors required cargo manifests when a ship docked.

Presumably, any paperwork onboard *Peregrine* would have been destroyed when she sank. Was this a copy drawn up by Gardner's agent in China and mailed after the wreck? As Lizzie scanned the list—crates of tea and spices, bolts of silk cloth, porcelain, carpets, teak, and rosewood furniture—something unusual caught her eye: "A statue of Quan Yin, fashioned from jade, ivory, and gold, measuring some thirty inches in height."

*Quan Yin.* The goddess who protected seafarers and rescued shipwrecked sailors. The same goddess whose likeness had captivated Lizzie. What had become of that statue? Was she lying at the bottom of the sea off Misery Islands, having failed to save the drowning sailors aboard *Peregrine*? The thought made Lizzie want to cry. She repositioned the ledger on the shelf and backed down the ladder. *I must talk to the old man at the antiquities shop.*

\* \* \*

When she awoke, Lizzie saw an envelope lying on the floor of her bedchamber near the door. She scooped it up and read her name penned in Alan Peabody's graceful hand on the thick, creamy paper. For a moment, she hesitated opening it. What if he'd written to end a relationship that had barely begun? She hadn't seen him since New Year's Eve, and he hadn't replied to her telegram inquiring about his mother's health. Were all his pretty words and attentions intended solely to get her into bed, and now he'd given up on her?

Lizzie carried the letter to the marble-topped vanity. The good luck charm Melody had given her lay between her hairbrush and a bottle of perfume. She touched the jade charm, closed her eyes, and made a wish. Then she tore open the envelope and withdrew the sheet of paper tucked inside.

Dear Lizzie,

I hope you can forgive my silence since our last meeting. Please know that I have thought of you countless times and longed to be with you. My mother's ill health has occupied a great deal of my time and energy of late, but fortunately, she appears to have turned a corner and, although not yet out of danger, she is much improved. Thank you for your telegram asking about her well-being.

My calendar reminds me that you plan to return to New York on Thursday. Can it possibly be so soon? Is there a chance you could find time to see me before you leave? If not, I wish you a safe trip home and a happy New Year.

Fondly,

Alan

She read the letter again before folding it and slipping it back into its envelope. The final commitment on The Troubadours' schedule was performing at a tea tomorrow afternoon. *Perhaps he'd be willing to meet me tomorrow evening? Sid will have kittens, but ish kabibble.* After breakfast, she'd send Alan a telegram and hope for the best.

Lizzie picked up the jade charm and kissed it. Maybe this magic stuff really did work.

\* \* \*

On her way out, Lizzie heard music coming from the double parlor. She peeked inside and saw Melody playing Bert's clarinet, Bert playing Melody's flute, and Emma Gardner seated at the Steinway Grand. Chopin's "Nocturne in C# Minor" filled the space, but her friends had adapted the piece to include the clarinet, which gave it a slightly heavier feeling than the original. She wondered if the sensitive composer would have approved.

When they finished, Lizzie applauded. *"Magnifique."*

Emma beamed. Bert blushed.

Melody rested the clarinet, which Lizzie thought seemed disproportionately large for her petite frame, on her shoulder like a hobo's pole. "Where are you off to this morning?" she asked Lizzie.

"To send a telegram."

"Would you send one to my parents for me?"

"Sure. Write down what you want it to say," Lizzie told her. "Where's Sid?"

"One of the breezer's tires had a leak. He went to get it fixed," Bert said. "Don't want to have a flat on our way home."

*Home.* The word triggered mixed feelings. Lizzie would be glad to get back to her life in the City, but she worried about putting two hundred miles between her and Alan. *That can't possibly be good, never mind what they say about absence making the heart grow fonder.* Boston had too many other beautiful women to entertain him in her absence.

Melody scribbled a note and handed it to Lizzie, who tucked it in her coat pocket. "Anybody else need anything while I'm in town?"

Bert motioned her toward the front of the parlor, away from the others. "I want to buy the girl I've been seeing a gift, but I don't know what she'd like. Would you pick something out for me?"

"Is this a goodbye present or a token of continued affection?"

He shifted his weight from one foot to the other and stared up at the angel atop the Christmas tree, as if hoping it might provide an answer. After a bit, he said, "I'd like to think the latter, but it's probably the former."

Lizzie patted his arm. "Okay, I understand."

\* \* \*

After sending telegrams to Alan and to Melody's parents, Lizzie entered the antiquarian shop and found its white-bearded owner seated in an oak swivel chair behind the counter. He looked up from the morning edition of *The Boston Globe* and frowned at her.

"Good heavens, is it Thursday already?"

Lizzie laughed and shook her head. "No, it's Tuesday. But I have a question and thought maybe you could answer it."

"I'll try," he said, folding his paper and setting it aside.

"Have you ever heard about a valuable statue of Quan Yin that went missing when the ship *Peregrine* wrecked on Misery Islands in 1868? Supposedly, the statue was among the ship's cargo."

The elderly man removed his spectacles and rubbed the bridge of his nose. "Hmm, yes, now that you mention it, I seem to remember hearing something about that. It's been a long time, though. Why do you ask?"

She told him about the ship's manifest she'd found in William Gardner's ledger. "Do you know if the statue was ever recovered?"

"No, I don't. But if you could get your hands on some old editions of *The Salem News*, they might provide some information." He drained a cup of coffee he'd been nursing, then asked, "I'm going to get myself a refill. Would you care for some?"

"Yes, thanks, that would be swell."

The old man pushed himself up from his chair and straightened his bent arthritic frame inch by inch. Slowly he crossed to an oak file cabinet on which an electric percolator sat, steam issuing from its spout. He poured coffee into a cup for Lizzie, then filled his own and set them both on a Queen Anne table. He pulled out a chair and motioned for her to sit.

"If a statue such as you've described were rescued from the drink, it would've made the news. Especially under the circumstances," the shopkeeper said.

"Unless whoever rescued it kept it for himself or sold it secretly."

"In that case, Miss Crane, its whereabouts may never be discovered."

"How much might a treasure like that be worth?"

"It's hard to tell without seeing it. The value would depend on its age, the quality of the workmanship, the composition of the materials involved, the artist who fashioned it, and many other things."

Lizzie repeated the description she'd read in Gardner's manifest.

The old man tapped his right temple, just above the arm of his eyeglasses. "A wild guess? A few thousand, anyway. Perhaps a good deal more."

"Holy moly." She sipped the weak black coffee while curious thoughts tumbled about in her mind.

"The lady is not so easily won," said the note found in the dead thief's pocket on the night The Troubadours arrived in Salem.

"She's mine, and I want her back," Matthew Gardner had demanded of Jacob Watkins in the cemetery.

"I'm the one who's taken care of her all this time," Watkins had countered.

What if the "lady" wasn't a flesh-and-blood woman after all? What if she was a Chinese goddess made of jade, ivory, and gold?

# Chapter Twenty-Seven

"He had two lives: one, open, seen and known by all who cared to know, full of relative truth and of relative falsehood, exactly like the lives of his friends and acquaintances; and another life running its course in secret."

— *Anton Chekhov*

When Lizzie learned that the Gardners would host a dinner in honor of the up-and-coming painter Edward Hopper, she could barely wait to make his acquaintance. She immediately recognized Hopper, standing in the front of the double parlor near the Christmas tree, from a self-portrait displayed at the Whitney Studio Club, but she hadn't expected him to be so very tall. He towered over the rest of the guests—Matthew and Abigail Gardner looked like children beside the artist. In the pictures she'd seen of Hopper, he appeared to be an ordinary, middle-aged man with a serious, contemplative demeanor. Up close in real life, however, he exuded a barely restrained intensity that matched his paintings.

"I'm going to say hello," she told Sidney as she broke away from her friends.

Three couples, whom she guessed must be art enthusiasts, had gathered around the painter and his gregarious wife, Josephine, an artist in her own right. Serving girls slid seamlessly between the guests, carrying trays of hors d'oeuvres. As soon as Lizzie spotted an opening, she edged her way into the group of fashionably dressed ladies and gentlemen and introduced herself.

"Mr. Hopper, I'm Elizabeth Crane." She held out her hand, and he tentatively grasped her fingers the way big men often did, as if he feared he might inadvertently hurt her. "I'm so pleased to have this opportunity to meet you. I very much enjoyed your exhibit of Gloucester scenes at the Brooklyn Museum. Like you, I'm from New York, but I've had the opportunity to visit Gloucester a couple times. Your paintings wonderfully capture the vibrancy of that seaport."

"Thank you, Miss Crane. You've seen Gloucester, then? Such an interesting town. Did you know it's the oldest fishing community in America?"

Jo Hopper sidled up to her husband and grasped his arm as if laying claim to her property. "Eddie and I met in Gloucester," she said.

"What about my pictures appealed to you?" he asked Lizzie.

"The way you made the buildings seem alive as if they're bursting with stories to tell. And the way the light transforms ordinary houses into places full of magic and mystery."

Hopper nodded and stroked his chin. "My favorite thing is painting sunlight on the side of a house."

Matthew Gardner interrupted their discussion of Gloucester's architecture. "I see you've met our chanteuse, Miss Crane."

Lizzie got the impression Gardner felt she'd been too forward in taking it upon herself to engage the guest of honor in conversation. She was paid to sing, not socialize.

"She recognizes the underlying force that animates the surface," Hopper told Gardner.

"I must get back to my colleagues," Lizzie excused herself, wishing she could spend the entire evening talking with this intriguing artist. "I look forward to seeing more paintings of yours in the future, Mr. Hopper."

"You will, Miss Crane. You will."

⅄ ⅄ ⅄

After the guests had departed, Matthew Gardner approached The Troubadours.

"Miss Crane, may I have a word?"

"Of course, Mr. Gardner."

"In private."

*Uh-oh, this doesn't sound good,* she thought as she followed him upstairs to the second floor of the mansion—a level she'd never visited before—where the family had their private quarters. He led her down a hallway to a room furnished with a walnut desk, several chairs upholstered in tapestry fabric, and a number of cabinets of varying sizes and pedigrees. An Oriental carpet in blue and orange tones lay on the floor. Delft lamps at either end of a tufted Chippendale sofa cast a soft, golden glow in the handsome room. Gardner motioned her toward an armchair and closed the door before taking his place on the sofa.

"Was there a problem with our performance tonight?" she asked.

All in all, she'd considered it a bit lackluster, coming as it did at the end of their lengthy engagement and the inevitable letdown that followed the busy holiday season, but she hadn't realized her host might have sensed that too. Although Lizzie was painfully aware of every misstep and errant note the troupe played, clients never noticed. Gardner, however, had a keen interest in music and was more particular than most. Or, maybe he objected to the way she'd approached Edward Hopper uninvited.

"Your performance? Oh, no, nothing of the sort. The entertainment you've provided has been exemplary." Gardner ran a hand through his wavy, graying hair. He took a deep breath, then let it out slowly. "Miss Crane, it's come to my attention that you are acquainted with a man named Jacob Watkins."

His statement caught her by surprise. "Yes, sir, he's my second cousin. I only learned about him the day before coming here. Our families never had any contact while I was growing up."

"And now?"

"I was curious about him, so I visited his tavern and introduced myself." Wondering how much to reveal, Lizzie added, "He didn't seem interested in getting to know me."

Gardner considered her comment briefly, then stood up and crossed the carpet to the walnut desk. He opened a drawer and withdrew a meerschaum pipe, its bowl carved to resemble an old man's face. Gardner filled the bowl with loose tobacco, tamped it down, lit it, puffed on it a few times until it caught, then returned to his seat on the sofa.

"Miss Crane, may I speak to you in confidence? What I have to say must not leave this room."

"Certainly, Mr. Gardner."

"Your cousin has taken possession of something that belongs to me. I've asked him to return it, but he refuses."

"If he's stolen your property, shouldn't you notify the police?"

"It's a bit complicated. I'd rather not involve the police unnecessarily."

Lizzie shifted uncomfortably in her seat. "I don't understand why you're telling me this or how you think I might be of help."

Gardner exhaled a mouthful of smoke that swirled around his face like a cloud. "You're Watkins' cousin—perhaps you could talk sense to him. Make him see the validity of my request."

"Just what, exactly, is your request?"

"That he give back what's rightfully mine."

"Which is?" she prompted.

He leaned toward her, his eyes bright with suppressed anger. "A statue his father took from my grandfather's ship when it sank."

*So she still exists!* Quan Yin. The jade, ivory, and gold goddess described in *Peregrine*'s manifest. Lizzie struggled to contain her excitement and keep her expression blank.

"What makes you believe Jacob has this statue?"

Gardner stood again and pulled a key from his pocket. He opened a drawer in one of the cabinets and extracted a photograph. For a moment, he stared at the black-and-white image as if seeing it for the first time, then handed the picture to Lizzie. The photo showed Jacob Watkins holding a statue the size of a young child in his hands. Despite the poor quality of the photograph, the statue's exquisite beauty was obvious. Her ivory face glowed like the full

181

moon.

"Holy moly."

"Watkins has demanded an astronomical sum for the statue's return. He insists he deserves such a steep amount because it would've been lost if his father hadn't saved it. I'm a reasonable man and I've tried to negotiate with him, but he remains adamant."

Lizzie looked at the photograph again, and an idea popped into her head. "Mr. Gardner, did you hire that thief, Nickolas Owens, the one who died near Misery Tavern, to steal the statue from Jacob?"

After a long pause, Gardner admitted, "Yes, but I didn't kill him. I was here with my family and guests all evening, as you know."

*Did Jacob?* she wondered. The possibility raised goosebumps on her arms.

"So that's why you don't want to go to the police."

"Yes."

"Sir, I can't get involved in this. It's none of my business." Lizzie handed the photograph back to him. "Plus, it's dangerous. One man has died already. Another man's been following me, a man who wears a green plaid cap and walks with a limp. Did you put him on to me?"

Gardner shook his head. "I don't know anything about that."

He could be lying, she realized. Or maybe Jacob hired the man to trail her. She'd seen him—or at least his green cap—at Misery Tavern only a few days ago. *I know almost nothing about my cousin, and he seems determined to keep it that way.*

"I insist you help me, Miss Crane. I fear your cousin will sell the statue to someone else if I don't give him what he asks."

"I'm sorry, Mr. Gardner, but I can't help you. I shouldn't even be talking to you about this." Lizzie stood up and started toward the door.

"If you don't, I won't pay you and your friends for your work here. I'll put that money toward buying the statue instead." He chuckled in a way that lacked even a hint of mirth.

"You can't do that. We have a contract."

"Oh, but I can. All I have to do is say I've already compensated you. You can deny it, but who do you think will be believed, you or me?"

Lizzie strode across the blue-and-orange carpet, her angry footsteps muffled by the thick wool, and yanked the office door open. "Maybe *I* should go to the police."

\* \* \*

Melody sat at the dropleaf table in their bedchamber, doing a crossword puzzle. "What's a nine-letter word beginning with tre and ending with ry?"

"Treachery?" Lizzie said as she buttoned her coat with shaking hands.

"That fits," Melody said and penciled in the letters. "Where are you going?"

"I don't know," Lizzie answered.

"What's the matter? You didn't have an argument with Sid, did you?"

"No, nothing like that."

Melody laid the puzzle aside. "With Alan?"

"No." Lizzie pulled a gray cloche hat over her bobbed hair.

"Did Sarah Gardner do something horrible again?"

"I can't tell you, Melody."

"Are you in some kind of trouble?"

"Will you please stop asking questions?" Lizzie let out an exasperated sigh. "I'm just going out for some fresh air, okay? I won't be gone long."

She hurried downstairs and out onto Chestnut Street, her heart pounding with a mixture of anger, confusion, and fear. Streetlights glowed in the purple night. She couldn't tell the other members of The Troubadours about Gardner's threat. Nor could she discuss the possible danger involved. Sidney would get in a lather. Melody would worry. Bert would try to protect her and end up making things worse. Slipping her hands into her pockets, she touched the cloisonné trinket box she'd purchased for Bert's girl. *Drat, I forgot to give to him.*

A car drove by, its headlights briefly illuminating the sidewalk on the other side of the street. There a man wearing a greatcoat leaned against a wrought-iron fence, smoking a cigarette. In the dark, she couldn't distinguish the color of his cap, but she felt certain it was green. *I can't even take a quiet walk,* she thought irritably. She started to turn around and go back to the

183

Gardners' mansion, but then picked up a cobblestone instead. *I'm tired of this cat-and-mouse game.*

Lizzie stormed across the street and stopped in front of the man. "Who are you?" she demanded.

The man lifted his cap. "Evening, miss."

"Why are you following me?"

"What makes you think I'm following you? I don't even know you."

"Hooey. You've been dogging me for days, and I'm sick of it."

The man dropped his cigarette on the sidewalk and crushed the butt beneath his shoe. "What do you plan to do with that rock?"

"Bash in your skull if you don't leave me alone."

He laughed. "Is that a fact?"

"Did Jacob Watkins hire you to tail me?"

"Don't know anyone named Jacob Watkins."

"He owns Misery Tavern. I saw you there on Saturday."

The man shrugged. "It's a public place."

"Just go away before I call the cops!" Lizzie shouted.

A light came on in a window of the house behind the wrought-iron fence.

The man tipped his cap again. "Good evening, miss," he said and limped away.

Lizzie threw the stone at him. It missed by several feet.

She thought about going to Cora Delaney's house, but it was after ten o'clock, and she didn't want to disturb her friend. Cora might already be asleep, or Lizzie's unannounced arrival might alarm her. *Tomorrow I'll contact her. Maybe her lawyer friend Karl Blume can give me some advice about how to handle this situation with Gardner.* She didn't want to walk about town and risk running into the man in the green plaid cap again. If she'd had the keys to Sidney's Buick, she would've driven around until she cooled off, but that wasn't an option either. In New York, she could always find a friendly speakeasy in which to unwind, but she didn't know of any clandestine nightspots in Salem, and wandering into the wrong one—a woman alone—could be disastrous.

Finally, Lizzie resigned herself to going back to the Gardners' home, where her host, his wife, and their elder daughter all had it in for her. *How did I get myself into this balled-up mess?*

As she pushed through the front gate, Matthew Gardner's words echoed in her mind: "I fear your cousin will sell the statue to someone else if I don't give him what he asks." She recalled the clumsily written note she'd discovered in the backgammon box that said "Another player has entered the game." Did the cryptic note refer to a prospective buyer? Was it intended to put pressure on Gardner? Had Jacob Watkins penned it and paid a housemaid to put it there?

Surely, Lizzie reasoned as she climbed the stairs to the mansion's third floor, art enthusiasts in Boston and New York would be eager to acquire a treasure like the Quan Yin statue, especially given its colorful past. Even well-established auction houses like Sotheby might be interested. But the most logical collector was right here in Salem: Isaac Roman.

# Chapter Twenty-Eight

"If I maintain my silence about my secret it is my prisoner…if I let it slip from my tongue, I am its prisoner."

— *Arthur Schopenhauer*

Too wound up to sleep, Lizzie filled the bathtub and eased into the hot water, hoping to quiet the many questions that vied for attention in her addled brain. But she couldn't silence them all. As she soaped her tired body, one question kept hammering at her like a persistent woodpecker drilling into a tree in search of its quarry. *Where would Jacob Watkins hide the statue?*

The tavern was too public a place to store something so valuable, and he probably wouldn't chance keeping it in his home where family members might stumble upon it. Maybe he'd buried it someplace, perhaps the cemetery where she'd overheard her cousin and Gardner talking about the mysterious lady.

Then it came to her: the smuggling tunnels.

According to Karl Blume, the century-old tunnels ran from Salem Harbor to various speakeasies and distilleries along Derby Street and were still used for ferrying contraband throughout the city. She recalled the small, secret door in the closet of the ladies' room at Misery Tavern. Did it provide ingress to the tunnels? If so, Jacob might have stashed the Quan Yin statue there in a safe spot out of sight, yet close enough that he could keep an eye on her. Maybe her cousin was also shuttling booze through those infamous underground burrows.

Lizzie slid down in the deep cast-iron tub and reclined against its sloping back, letting the hot water cover her up to her shoulders. She closed her eyes and imagined people sneaking about like moles day and night beneath the streets of Salem, engaged in all manner of illicit commerce, leading their surreptitious lives in the midst of willingly blind eyes.

\* \* \*

A woman's voice interrupted her sleep. "And so she abides apart from you, in isolation and secrecy, until you welcome her home again in all her glory. She is timeless, yet the time whence you must act draws nigh."

Lizzie opened her eyes to near-total darkness, searching for the person who'd awakened her. In the brass bed beside her, Melody's deep, rhythmic breathing assured her that her friend hadn't been the one to speak. *Who then?* A sense of urgency gripped her, along with a feeling of foreboding. She lay motionless for several moments, trying to get her bearings.

Finally, she remembered where she was. *It's only a dream,* she told herself and turned over, pulling the counterpane tight around her shoulders.

\* \* \*

A knock on the bedchamber door dragged Lizzie out of a fitful sleep. Despite her weariness, she'd awakened every hour or so throughout the night. She still felt unsettled by the strange voice she'd heard in the wee hours of the morning urging her toward some unspecified action involving an unknown woman, perhaps the goddess Quan Yin.

Forcing herself out of bed, she grabbed her silk robe and tied it around her nightgown. Melody had already risen, made her bed, and left while Lizzie still dozed. She crossed the room to the door and opened it.

"Your breakfast, ma'am," the housemaid with the port wine birthmark said as she proffered a tray with pancakes, slices of pineapple, and a pot of steaming coffee.

"Thanks, Fanny. Put it over there on the table, would you please?"

"There's a telegram for you too, ma'am," the maid added.

Trying to hide her eagerness, Lizzie accepted the telegram from the girl, but waited until after she'd left to read it.

> Dear Lizzie,
>
> Thank you for agreeing to meet with me before you return to New York. If your schedule allows, I'd be honored if you would have dinner with me at the Hawthorne Hotel this evening. Because I am not currently welcome at the Gardners' home, I regret I cannot pick you up there. I hope it's not too much of an inconvenience for you to meet me in the hotel lobby at 7:00. Unless I hear otherwise from you, I will wait for you there.
>
> Fondly,
>
> Alan

She traced the words on the telegram with her fingertip as pictures of the man who'd sent it flashed in her mind's eye. Her thoughts raced from one imagined scenario to another, from fairytale romantic interludes to shamelessly torrid couplings. Finally, she laid the telegram aside and dug into her breakfast.

This afternoon's tea marked the end of the twelve days of Christmas and The Troubadours' commitment to Matthew and Abigail Gardner. But if Gardner refused to pay them unless Lizzie helped him take back the Quan Yin statue from her cousin, the entire engagement would be for naught. Even though she wasn't responsible for any of the problems between Gardner and Watkins, the loss would still fall on her shoulders if the troupe went home emptyhanded.

Then there was the possibility that Gardner would not only cheat them out of their fee, but discredit them as well and tarnish the reputation they'd worked so hard to build. She wished she could talk to Sidney about the whole tangled mess, but he'd get apoplectic. He wouldn't be able to offer any answers either. She needed someone more knowledgeable about legal matters to guide her through this miasma.

Forking a chunk of pineapple into her mouth, she contemplated visiting Cora—maybe the card reader could offer some advice. Today's tea was scheduled to begin at four and end around six. That gave her plenty of time to talk with Cora and, hopefully, her attorney friend Karl Blume as well.

After a few bites of pancake, however, another idea emerged. She could sneak through the secret door in Misery Tavern's closet that she suspected led to the tunnels and poke around herself. If her cousin had possession of the statue and wanted to keep tabs on it, he probably would have hidden it nearby. When Lizzie thought of actually seeing the magnificent statue of the goddess, her heart skipped a beat. *She's so close. I can't let her disappear forever without seeing her at least once.*

* * *

Lizzie opened the door to Misery Tavern and peeked inside. At ten o'clock in the morning, only three patrons sat at tables, nursing cups of coffee and reading newspapers, while the pub's staff prepared for the lunch crowd. Her cousin Jacob stood near the bar talking to a customer, his back to her. She scurried down the shadowy hallway and entered the foul-smelling ladies' room. It didn't look like anyone had cleaned it since the last time she was here.

She pushed aside the rolls of toilet paper, washrags, and other supplies in the closet, revealing the Alice-in-Wonderland door hidden at the back. As she pulled it open, a damp, moldy odor like rotting leaves rose from below. Lizzie switched on Sid's flashlight that she'd brought with her and shone it into the tomb-dark space beneath the tavern. A crude wooden ladder, green with mildew, led into the nether regions.

Clutching Cora's mother's shabby coat close to her body, Lizzie eased through the doorway and stepped onto the ladder. Cautiously, she tested her weight on each rotting rung before descending to the next. At the bottom, she swept the flashlight's beam from side to side down the length of a narrow corridor. A rat scurried away from the light. Brick walls dripping moisture bordered the walkway. Brackish water slicked a floor littered with broken plaster fallen from the tunnel's low ceiling.

A wave of claustrophobia washed over her. For a moment, Lizzie wanted nothing more than to rush up the ladder again, into the light, away from whatever nefarious dealings Jacob Watkins and Matthew Gardner were engaged in. *What am I doing here?* she asked herself. *Even if I do find the statue—what then?*

She took a few deep breaths, trying to calm her anxiety. But inhaling the tunnel's mold- and mildew-laced air caused her to start coughing instead. Tucking the flashlight under her arm, she bent over, hands clutching her chest, and hacked violently, as if she might turn herself inside out.

When the coughing fit finally passed, she blinked a few times and counted to ten, then twenty, willing herself to stay calm. *Get a grip. It's just a tunnel, not a crypt—and a colorful piece of history to boot.* She waited a minute, then another, listening. Was anyone else in the tunnel near enough to hear her?

When she heard no other sound, she slowly straightened up again. The flashlight illuminated a patch of brick wall a few feet above the floor where a long crack split the old mortar. Not an ordinary, irregular crack due to natural settling, but one so clean and straight it might have been cut with a saw. Lizzie stepped toward it and traced the crack with the flashlight's beam. She ran her finger along the cut's three-foot length, then followed it when it took a 90-degree turn north and rose for another three feet or so.

Curious, she pushed on the slab of mortared brick. It moved a couple inches. She pressed harder. With a dull, scraping sound, a segment of the wall edged aside, mounted on a metal slide to reveal a gaping hole, into which Lizzie pointed the flashlight. Its beam illuminated a box.

Tucking the torch under her arm, she reached in and tugged at the box. Its weight surprised her. After several, determined, incremental attempts, she managed to drag it inch by inch to the front of the opening. She lifted the lid and peered inside. An oilcloth swaddled an object the size of a small child.

Excitement rose like a geyser in Lizzie's chest as she began carefully unwrapping the oilcloth. As she peeled away the fabric, a pair of creamy-white feet standing on a golden lotus flower appeared, then a long, flowing gown the color of sea foam. Ivory hands with perfectly wrought fingers held a gold vase and a willow branch. Finally, Lizzie pulled aside the last of the wrapping to expose a face so serene and compassionate it brought tears to her eyes. A golden mantle encrusted with pearls draped the goddess's head and shoulders.

Caressing the holy relic, Lizzie ran her fingertips lightly across the statue's ivory cheek, then down the goddess's arm to the vase she held. A vase from which sacred water flowed, purifying the earth and nourishing humanity. Lizzie had never seen anything so beautiful. In the squalid tunnel, the statue seemed to glow with an inner light as if it really did embody the goddess.

*I can't leave her here,* Lizzie thought, trying to figure out how she could rescue the statue from its hiding place without being discovered. She slid her fingers under the goddess, but could barely lift the jade, gold, and ivory figure. She hadn't the strength even to carry the statue up the rickety ladder, much less sneak it through Misery Tavern and smuggle it more than a mile back to the Gardners' mansion.

# Chapter Twenty-Nine

"Truth is so often disconcerting."

— *Rafael Sabatini, Scaramouche*

A groan from the wooden ladder pulled Lizzie's attention away from the goddess. She turned to see Jacob Watkins step down onto the damp brick floor, a coil of rope hanging from his belt.

"Guess I was wrong about you being a copper. More likely, you're a thief."

"Hello, Cousin. I heard about Salem's infamous smuggling tunnels and wanted to see them for myself." She struggled to keep her tone of voice casual so he wouldn't realize how anxious she was.

"You expect me to believe you're just down here taking a little tour of the city's colorful history?" He nodded toward the opening in the wall and the metal box that held the precious statue of Quan Yin. "What've you found there, *Cousin?*"

"The lady you've been taking care of all these years. The one Matthew Gardner insists is his."

A look of surprise crossed his face as he realized she knew about his conversation with Gardner in the graveyard. "If my father hadn't risked his life to save that statue, she'd be lying in pieces at the bottom of the ocean."

"Hey, I'm not disputing your claim to her." Lizzie raised her hands in a gesture of resignation. "I just hate to see her stuck away in a box where no one can enjoy her."

Watkins frowned, his thick eyebrows knitting above his nose. "Are you telling me you didn't come to steal the statue for Gardner?"

"Of course not. But he says he won't pay my colleagues and me for our work here unless I help him get her back."

"So you admit you're working for him."

"As a singer, yes. As a thief, no."

"You wouldn't be the first thief Gardner sent to steal the lady."

"Nickolas Owens, you mean? Did you kill him?"

Watkins dropped his eyes and stared at the floor. "When I figured out what he was up to, I followed him out of the pub and slugged him. He fell and hit his head on the pavement. I didn't know he'd died 'til I read about it in the paper."

*That might make him guilty of manslaughter,* she realized. "Listen, Jacob. I don't give a fig who the statue belongs to. Gardner doesn't know I'm here. I just want to get paid and go home. So if I can help negotiate some sort of deal between the two of you, we'll all benefit. Obviously, you haven't succeeded in working out a deal yourself, or the lady wouldn't still be stuck in that hole."

"Why should I believe you?"

"For starters, I couldn't steal the goddess even if I wanted to. She's too heavy for me to carry off."

For a moment, he seemed to contemplate what she'd said, perhaps considering the advantages of using Lizzie as an intermediary. His thick fingers toyed with the rope at his side.

"Before you get any foolish ideas about tying me up and leaving me here to rot, my colleagues, my lawyer, and Isaac Roman all know I'm here," Lizzie bluffed, dropping Roman's name so Watkins understood she believed the art collector had his sights set on the statue too. "If I don't show up for my 3:00 performance this afternoon, you'll have more cops than rats crawling around this place."

"You know too much," he said.

Watkins lunged at her, but before he could grab her, she kicked his right foot out from under him in mid-stride. He slipped on the wet floor and fell hard. Lizzie darted around her cousin, scrambled up the rotting ladder, and squeezed through the secret door in the ladies' room. She shut both closet doors behind her, praying no one in the pub would hear if he cried out for help. Brushing herself off, she walked through Misery Tavern as casually as she could, trying not to attract attention.

After being in the dark, dank tunnel, the morning sunshine seemed impossibly bright. She shaded her eyes with her hand and hurried down Derby Street along the harbor. Silvery light, like schools of minnows, glinted on the water's dark green waves as they rolled in to shore. The bitter cold stretch had finally broken, and dozens of people, tired of being housebound, strolled beside the ocean, enjoying the fine weather.

Finally, her heartbeat returned to normal as she walked back toward Salem's McIntire District. *What am I going to do now? Instead of resolving the situation, I've made things worse. Now both Gardner and Watkins know I'm on to them.*

\* \* \*

Lizzie turned onto Federal Street and made her way along the buckling brick sidewalk toward Cora Delaney's house. Maybe her friend could offer some advice. She wished she could talk to Sidney about all of it, but that wasn't an option. He was looking forward to going back to New York tomorrow with a fat check in his pocket. She didn't even want to imagine how he'd react if he knew the trouble she'd gotten into.

Lizzie knocked on the mustard-colored door of Cora's house and after a minute, the gray-haired housekeeper opened it.

"Good morning, is Miss Delaney in?" she asked, then added, in case the woman didn't remember her, "I'm Elizabeth Crane."

The older woman stepped aside to let her enter. "Please wait here while I see if Miss Delaney is receiving."

Several minutes passed before the housekeeper reappeared at the top of the staircase, followed by Cora and her friend Karl Blume.

"What a nice surprise," Cora called down to Lizzie.

# CHAPTER TWENTY-NINE

"I apologize for stopping by unannounced."

"Not at all. We were just about to have some tea. Will you join us?"

As usual, the card reader was fashionably dressed in a two-piece outfit of blue wool with a calf-length skirt. Blume, too, looked dapper in a tweed suit, but Lizzie noticed he lacked his signature lapel flower. His presence here at this time of the day—and in Cora's private quarters on the second floor of the mansion rather than in the first-floor parlor—made her wonder once again about the nature of their relationship. *Perhaps he spent the night?*

Cora instructed the housekeeper to bring tea and ushered Lizzie into the parlor, where a fire crackled in the fireplace. "What are you up to this morning?" she asked, glancing at the worn brown coat she'd loaned to the singer as a disguise. "Looks like you've been to see your cousin again."

"I'm afraid I've gotten myself into a huge muddle."

"Oh? How so?" Cora settled herself in one of the wing chairs near the fireplace. Blume claimed the matching chair, and Cora motioned for Lizzie to sit on the Queen Anne sofa.

"It's complicated...."

A wry smile played at the corners of Blume's mouth. His icy blue eyes sparkled behind wire-rimmed spectacles. "Let's hear it," he urged, and she thought the lawyer appeared to relish the idea of dealing with a complicated problem.

For the next fifteen minutes, Lizzie recounted the events of the past eleven days, pausing only when the housekeeper entered the room to set out a tray of tea and fruitcake. Occasionally, Blume interrupted to clarify details or ask questions. Cora twined her pearls around her fingers, her expression shifting from fascination to disbelief to worry as the story unraveled.

The attorney took a sip of his lapsang souchong, then replaced the delicate porcelain cup in its saucer. "First point, I doubt Gardner will go through with his threat to withhold payment to you and your friends. You have a valid contract, right?"

"Yes, but he insists he can simply say he paid us cash, and no one will believe otherwise."

"If he paid in cash, he'd require a receipt from you acknowledging payment," Blume pointed out. "Businessmen don't just hand over large sums of money without any paperwork to back it up. He's probably claiming you as a business expense and that won't fly without a contract and a receipt."

"What if he writes us a check, then stops payment before we can cash it?"

"Demand a bank check."

Lizzie shook her head. "I don't know...he holds all the high cards. We've done our part; we don't have anything left to barter."

"Don't be so sure," Cora said. "You know where the statue is. And you've seen her—Matthew's only seen a photograph. My advice is tell him where to find it, collect your fee, and go back to New York tomorrow as planned."

"Jacob will move the goddess now that I know her whereabouts."

"Which brings us to point two," Blume said. "Go public with the information."

"What?"

"Tell the newspapers. They'll go into a feeding frenzy over a story like this."

Lizzie groaned at the idea of being caught up in a scandal. "If word gets out, it will tarnish The Troubadours' reputation around these parts and ruin our chance of playing for Isaac Roman."

Cora laughed. "Trust me, it won't bother him a bit. He thrives on controversy."

"Even if he's a part of it?"

"All the better if he's a part of it."

Lizzie thought about the rope her cousin had tied to his belt and the man with the green plaid cap. She shivered as possibilities crawled out from the dark recesses of her mind like rats in the tunnels. "But won't Gardner or Jacob try to shut me up?"

"Once the story's out there, they can't hush it up," Blume said. "You're in more danger if you keep it to yourself, and no one else knows what's going on or who's involved."

"If she's in danger, shouldn't she go to the police?" Cora asked him.

Blume poured himself another cup of tea and stirred in a heaping teaspoon of sugar. "It appears a crime may have been committed. A man died, even if your cousin is telling the truth and it was an accident. Gardner's waist-deep in it too. Contacting the police would be a prudent measure. As an attorney sworn to uphold the law, I always recommend staying on the right side of it."

"But that would mean we could be stuck here in Salem for ages while the cops investigate this whole balled-up mess," Lizzie said.

"True," Blume agreed. "Which leads to point three. Talk to the head of the Peabody Museum."

*The Peabody Museum, financed by Alan's relative, the famous philanthropist George Peabody.* Lizzie's focus shifted abruptly to the red-haired man whom she planned to meet for dinner this very evening. He should've occupied the center of her attention, but the morning's turmoil had temporarily upstaged thoughts of him.

"How can the museum help?" Lizzie asked.

"They'll be gaga over the goddess," Cora answered.

Blume smiled and pointed a finger at Lizzie. "Bingo. They'll salivate at the idea of getting their hands on her, and they have a lot of leverage. Plus, the museum will be more discreet than the newspapers or the police."

The idea of getting the museum involved appealed to Lizzie. "They'll keep Quan Yin safe, won't they?" she asked Blume. "I couldn't bear it if something happened to her...if I was responsible."

"If she's everything you've said, they'll go to the ends of the earth to acquire her." He pulled a business card from his wallet, jotted a note on the back, and handed it to Lizzie. "Gardner, Watkins, and even Roman won't stand a chance."

# Chapter Thirty

"The fishermen know that the sea is dangerous and the storm terrible, but they have never found these dangers sufficient reason for remaining ashore."

— *Vincent Van Gogh*

Blume used Cora's telephone to arrange meetings with the men he knew at the Peabody Museum and *The Salem Evening News*.

"I can't thank you enough," Lizzie said. "Both of you."

Blume shrugged. "I like to see right prevail whenever possible. It's a rare enough phenomenon."

"I expect a full report of what happens," Cora said as she opened the front door for Lizzie. "If I don't hear from you before you leave town tomorrow, I'm calling the cops."

\* \* \*

After changing clothes and applying her makeup, Lizzie walked the half-dozen blocks to the Peabody Museum. Shoppers crowded Essex Street, taking advantage of the salubrious weather. Men stood on street corners, smoking and chatting. Women pushed baby carriages along the brick sidewalks. Lizzie hurried around them, mentally rehearsing what she'd say to the man who held the power to rescue and protect the Quan Yin statue. *Will he believe me?* she fretted.

She entered the Greek Revival granite building and, after showing Blume's business card to a man at the front desk, was directed to an office at the end of a hallway. There a woman in a prim brown suit and starched white blouse showed Lizzie into a room with tall, arched windows through which light streamed like liquid gold.

A man with a horseshoe of gray hair around his head and spectacles perched on the end of his long nose stood when she entered. He came around from behind a satinwood Hepplewhite desk and said, "Please, come in, Miss Crane. May I take your wrap?"

Lizzie slipped off her cashmere coat, and he hung it on a bentwood coat tree in one corner of the room. She sat in an uncomfortable black-lacquered Chinese armchair. Like the museum itself, the office's furnishings were a mix of periods and styles that had found their way to Salem via sailing ships over the years.

"Thank you for seeing me on such short notice, Mr. Cushing."

"Dr. Cushing," he corrected her. "I understand you have a matter of some importance to discuss with me."

"I believe so. You see, the proprietor of Misery Tavern, a man named Jacob Watkins, is in possession of a magnificent statue of the Asian goddess Quan Yin made of jade, ivory, and gold. His father rescued it from the ship *Peregrine,* which wrecked near Salem's harbor in 1868."

"And does this gentleman wish to donate the statue to the museum?"

"Hardly." Lizzie chuckled at the idea. "He's been trying to sell it to a local businessman named Matthew Gardner, whose grandfather owned *Peregrine.* But that hasn't worked out."

Cushing tapped his fingers on his desk and squinted at Lizzie over the tops of his glasses. "And why, exactly, is this a matter of your concern? Or the museum's?"

Lizzie crossed her legs, then uncrossed them again, trying to decide how best to explain the complicated situation. She took a deep breath to calm her nerves and straightened her shoulders.

"My own concern is of less importance than the museum's, although I'll be glad to answer any questions you may have. What matters is that this statue be preserved for posterity. She's rare, precious, and beautiful beyond belief—she may be centuries old. You do know that Quan Yin is the goddess who protects seafarers, don't you Dr. Cushing?"

"I'm aware of that attribute, yes."

"I'm afraid that if your museum or some other trusted organization doesn't step in, Mr. Watkins may sell her to an unscrupulous buyer—perhaps someone overseas. But she belongs here as part of Salem's maritime history."

"You've seen this statue, Miss Crane?"

"Yes, sir, I have."

"And where is it now?"

"This morning, it was hidden in a metal box in a tunnel beneath Misery Tavern. I can't say where it is now. Jacob Watkins may have moved it elsewhere, given that he knows I know about its existence. That's why it's urgent that your museum acts promptly to ensure the statue's safety."

Cushing fingered Karl Blume's business card, rubbing his thumb over the engraved letters. "What makes you think the museum might be interested in acquiring this statue? How do you know it's authentic? Are you an expert in Asian art?"

"No, sir, I'm not. But she's the most wondrous thing I've ever seen. Someone who *is* an expert really should take a look at her before it's too late." Lizzie gazed down at her hands folded in her lap. "I simply can't bear to think that such a treasure might be lost forever."

"Well, I appreciate you coming to us with this information, and I'll take it under consideration." Cushing handed Blume's calling card back to her. "Before the museum makes an acquisition, a process of verification must be undergone, as well as a determination of an object's historical significance and its value to our collection. As you may expect, this can take some time."

"But there may not be much time," Lizzie insisted. "Already a noted dealer in stolen art is haggling for the statue, and others may be bidding for her too."

"The Peabody Museum is not in the business of acquiring stolen art, Miss

Crane. If there's a question of ownership…." Cushing stood, signaling an end to their meeting. "Thank you for bringing this to our attention. I'll get in touch with Mr. Blume if I have any more questions. Good day."

Lizzie wanted to cry or scream or throw the crystal paperweight on his desk at him. Instead, she choked back her anger. She shook Cushing's hand, thanked him for his time, and retrieved her coat from the coat tree without waiting for him to hold it for her.

As she crossed the museum's lobby, she glanced at an antique grandfather clock and noticed she had less than twenty minutes until her meeting with the *Salem News* reporter. *Maybe he'll be more interested in this story.*

* * *

Stephen Abernathy was a thin, dark-haired, disheveled man in his mid-thirties who seemed to be in constant motion. He waved Lizzie into his cramped office, which was barely more than a closet, and shifted a pile of paperwork from an oak schoolroom chair to an overflowing table to make a place for her to sit. Newspapers stacked one on top of another leaned precariously against a wall, reaching toward the ceiling. A newsprint Tower of Pisa.

"So, who stole the statue?" he asked, lighting a Camel cigarette with ink-and-nicotine-stained fingers.

"I don't know that anyone actually *stole* it—that's still up for debate," Lizzie answered. "But two men claim to own it, and another man has already died trying to steal it. A guy named Nicholas Owens—he turned up dead near the harbor the night after Christmas, having just left Misery Tavern."

"Yeah, I remember that."

Lizzie ran through the details, bringing him up to date. "Now the current holder of the statue—Jacob Watkins, proprietor of Misery Tavern—and local businessman Matthew Gardner—who hired Owens to steal the statue from Watkins—are fighting over who really owns it."

Abernathy scribbled some notes on a pad of paper. "And why is this newsworthy?"

"Other than Owens's suspicious death, you mean?" Lizzie asked sarcastically.

"You think he was murdered?"

"I don't know, but here are some more reasons to break this story," Lizzie said, ticking them off on her fingers. "Both Watkins and Gardner have threatened me. The statue's worth more money than either you or I can imagine. She's got a checkered past that involves a wealthy Salem merchant's sunken ship and an escaped seaman who absconded with a rare treasure. And right now, some pretty important people around here are trying to get their hands on that statue."

Abernathy sucked on his cigarette while writing as fast as he could on his notepad. "Sounds like the stuff of crime novels."

"It does, doesn't it?" Lizzie agreed. "Except it's all real."

"You said Watkins and Gardner have threatened you. How?"

While she described the events of the past few days, Abernathy paced back and forth across the tiny office, dropping ashes on the floor in his wake. Suddenly he stopped, thrust his left arm straight up above him, and tipped his head back, staring at the ceiling. He reminded Lizzie of a holy-roller preacher beseeching God for guidance.

"Okay, I've got the headline. 'New York showgirl risks life tracking down stolen statue worth millions.'" He crushed his cigarette in an overflowing ashtray on his burn-scarred desk. "What do you think?"

Lizzie winced. "How about something a little less lurid? Like 'Important Chinese artifact reemerges after nearly sixty years'?"

Abernathy feigned a yawn. "You want more than a filler at the bottom of page 6, don't you? Look, Miss Crane, I still have to verify what you've told me. Right now, all I have is your word. I'm not saying I don't believe you, but before I cast suspicion on local businessmen and put the paper's reputation on the line, I need to check out this matter more fully. How 'bout you leave me to do my job, and if I have any more questions, I'll contact you?"

"I don't have a telephone, and you can't contact me because I'm staying at the home of one of the men involved in this scandal: Matthew Gardner."

"The same guy who hired the thief to snatch the statue?"

Lizzie nodded.

"Well, now, that adds another twist to the tale." Abernathy tugged at his left earlobe as if adjusting a radio antennae, trying to hear something beyond the normal frequency range. "Okay, Miss Crane. You're gonna have to trust me on this one. I'll start looking into it right away. We can develop the story as it unfolds."

Lizzie stood and held out her hand to the reporter. "I suppose you're right. Thank you for your time."

As she walked back to the Gardners' home, Lizzie admitted to herself that she'd been unrealistic. She'd expected both Cushing and Abernathy to jump on her story and rush in like knights on white chargers to rescue the Quan Yin statue. But it was probably better that neither Gardner nor Watkins knew she'd implicated them until after The Troubadours were safely back in New York. Still, she'd have to tell her colleagues before the news hit the stands to prepare them for what could be a blow to their careers. She dreaded dragging her friends through all this. Sid, especially, would be furious. He'd invested so much into making The Troubadours what they were today. If Melody's parents heard about it, they might force her to resign and go back to a safe, normal life.

Lizzie opened the wrought-iron gate in front of the Gardners' mansion and walked around to the back door. She'd missed lunch and hoped Pearl would have some leftovers she could eat before her three o'clock performance—she didn't sing well on an empty stomach. As she entered the kitchen, abuzz with preparations for this afternoon's tea, she wished she'd never embarked on this misbegotten quest. Never met her cousin. Never come to Salem at all.

# Chapter Thirty-One

"The instinct of ownership is fundamental in man's nature."

— *William James, Writings 1902–1910*

L izzie worked through the afternoon tea as if in a trance, barely noticing her audience or the lyrics she sang, or the presence of her colleagues as they performed in their hosts' double parlor on the twelfth day of Christmas. All she wanted was to collect their pay, pack up, and skedaddle back to the Big Apple before Gardner learned about her meetings with the museum head and the newspaperman.

She still hadn't revealed the events of the past few days to Sidney and the others, not wanting to distract them from this, the last day of their engagement. Sid, she knew, liked to settle up financial matters immediately after The Troubadours finished their stint while the "bloom was still on the rose," as he put it. Tonight, more than ever, she was glad for that practice. Closing her eyes, she envisioned Matthew Gardner handing over a hefty bank check, as if willing it to be true. In the morning, they could load their bags into Sid's breezer and drive back to the City.

After she finished singing the last song of the evening, George and Ira Gershwin's "Oh, Lady Be Good," she took a bow. The applause of the Gardners' guests swirled around her like confetti, and she breathed a sigh of relief. *We did it! We can go home now.*

In the midst of the day's complications and distractions, she'd barely had time to think about Alan Peabody, the man who'd starred in her fantasies for months and whom she planned to meet in just two hours. Now her focus shifted to him. Tonight was her last chance to win him over. After she returned to New York, her possibilities would diminish significantly. With more than two hundred miles separating them—plus the demands of their respective careers and his mother's illness—well, no gambler would bet on the likelihood of a romantic relationship growing between them. *Okay, then, I'll make the very best of tonight,* she promised herself.

\* \* \*

On her way through the kitchen to meet with her friends in the carriage house apartment, Lizzie spotted Pearl and called out to her. "Do you have a moment?"

The cook ambled across the room, her golden skin sheened with sweat. "I hear you be leavin' tomorrow mornin', Miz Liz. Gonna miss you around here, but I 'spect you be glad to get home."

"I will," Lizzie agreed. "I came to say goodbye and to thank you again for all you've done for me."

"How's your ankle?"

"Almost normal, due to your good juju." She reached in her pocket and pulled out a pair of ruby earrings—a gift from a long-ago suitor—wrapped in a lace handkerchief. Knowing Pearl wouldn't accept them for herself, Lizzie handed them to her and said, "Here, these have your daughter's name on them."

Pearl unwrapped the handkerchief and frowned. She picked up one of the earrings and held the blood-red stone to the light. "These be valuable. Why you givin' them to her?"

"Because they're *rubies*, and my name's Lizzie."

As Lizzie closed the cook's strong, calloused fingers around the earrings, Pearl's brown eyes glistened. "Thank you, Miz Liz. She'll be real proud of these. You have a safe trip back to New York. If you get back to these parts again some day, I hope you stop by if you got the time."

205

"As it turns out, we'll be back in March. I'll see you then, Pearl."

\* \* \*

Sidney rattled the silver shaker as if it were a percussion instrument, then poured icy-cold gin into three martini glasses. "Here's to a job well done," he toasted. "To us!"

Lizzie and Bert cheered, "Hear, hear." Melody raised her glass of ginger ale.

"I can't wait to get back to the City," Sid said. "Being cooped up like this, in this outback town with these provincial people, has nearly petrified my brain."

"It seems like we've been gone forever," Melody said. "I'll be glad to see Douglas and my parents tomorrow."

Lizzie glanced at Bert and read the loneliness already descending on his face. "I know you'll miss your girl, Bert. Maybe she could take the train to New York and visit you? I'd be glad to put her up in my apartment."

"Maybe," he said, brightening a little at the thought.

"Besides, we'll be back in Salem in two months to play for Isaac Roman. She'll wait for you, won't she?"

"I hope so."

The four friends chatted amiably for a while, unwinding after the pressure of eleven straight days of performances. *I'm glad they don't know the whole of it*, Lizzie thought as she sipped her second martini. *For the moment, we can just revel in knowing we did a good job and made people happy with our music.*

At six o'clock, Lizzie gathered her nerve and, trying to appear casual about it, asked her longtime friend, "Say, Sid, do you think you could drive me to the Hawthorne Hotel in an hour?"

"What's up, Bearcat?"

"I'm having dinner with Alan Peabody," she said. "It's too far to walk in high heels."

Sidney frowned. "Why can't he pick you up for a date? Is he ashamed of you?"

His words stung like a lash, but she braced herself against his criticism and answered, "He and the Gardners had a bit of a falling out."

"You mean after he snubbed their daughter, coming here to call on you would be rubbing salt in the wound."

"Something like that. Anyway, this might be my last chance to spend time with him. Be a peach. Once we're back in New York, I may never hear from him again."

"All right," he agreed. "Get a wiggle on. I'll meet you at the breezer in an hour."

\* \* \*

At precisely seven, Sidney eased his Buick up to the curb in front of the Hawthorne Hotel.

"Has Gardner paid up?" Lizzie asked.

"In full. Did you doubt he would?"

Relief washed over her. *He didn't go through with his threat after all. Karl Blume was right.* "Just making sure everything's copacetic before we head home tomorrow."

"Be careful, Bearcat," Sid said.

"Surely you don't think I'm in any danger from Alan."

"Not physically. I just don't want you to get your heart broken."

"That's always the chance a girl takes, isn't it? But if I'm going to get hurt, at least I want to have one last night of fun."

"Then go play-ski."

Lizzie gave him a quick hug. "Okay-ski."

\* \* \*

She caught only a glimpse of a green cap before the man grabbed her and pressed a knife to her throat.

"Do as I say, or I'll make sure you never sing again," he ordered.

Trapped between one set of heavy doors leading into the hotel's lobby and another pair that opened to the street, Lizzie couldn't alert anyone inside or out to her plight. If she screamed, it might be the last sound she uttered. Her heart raced. Her stomach knotted.

"Compose yourself, Miss Crane. Then we're gonna walk back outside together, like a happy couple enjoying a pleasant evening," he said.

"Where are we going?"

"Just a couple blocks down Hawthorne Street to visit a mutual friend."

With his left hand, he gripped her elbow tightly enough to assure her he meant business. His right hand, holding the knife, disappeared into his coat pocket. As they made their way toward the harbor, the man in the green plaid cap limping beside her, the scent of the sea grew stronger. Several automobiles motored by. *If I weren't wearing these fancy shoes, I might be able to outrun him,* Lizzie thought ruefully.

"Here," the man said, pulling her toward the entrance to a three-story brick building. Inside, he pushed her ahead of him and followed her down a dimly lit hallway. "Last door on your right. Open it."

The spacious room had beamed ceilings and a floor made of honey pine on which Chinese carpets lay. Wooden shutters covered the windows. Floor-to-ceiling bookcases lined one wall. Two mahogany desks—a Sheraton double-pedestal and a graceful table desk with a gilded leather top—plus a sitting area with four leather armchairs and reading lamps gave the office an appearance of refinement and prosperity.

Matthew Gardner sat at the larger desk. "Good evening, Miss Crane. How nice of you to join us."

"As if I had a choice."

"Please, have a seat." He indicated a pair of chairs in front of his desk. The man in the green plaid cap remained standing a few feet behind her. "I see you and Mr. Smith are already acquainted, so let me get right to the point. Yesterday, I asked for your help in reclaiming a valuable object your cousin's father stole from my family. You refused. Today, I learned that you discussed said object with Dr. Cushing at the Peabody Museum and encouraged him to acquire it."

*Did Cushing contact Gardner after I left to confirm the goddess's validity?* she wondered. *So much for discretion.*

"I only wanted to make sure the statue would be safe, and people would be able to see her," Lizzie explained.

Gardner narrowed his eyes and glared at Lizzie. "The statue belongs to me. I will make sure she's safe as soon as she's back in my possession, and I will determine who sees her."

"With all due respect, sir, for whatever reason, you and my cousin haven't managed to come to terms. I'm guessing you're not the only person who's interested in the statue. What if Jacob sells her to a buyer overseas? Or an investor who'll stick her in a vault somewhere? You'll never see her again."

"All the more reason why you must help me, Miss Crane. You know where she is."

"Yesterday, she was in a hole in the wall of a tunnel that runs beneath Misery Tavern. But Jacob's probably moved her by now."

"If that's the case, you'll have to get him to show you where he's hidden her and convince him to hand her over."

Lizzie let out an exasperated sigh. The fear she'd felt earlier, when "Mr. Smith" put a knife to her throat, had morphed into annoyance. *I should be enjoying a lovely dinner with a lovely man instead of sitting here bickering with this arrogant fella who's living in his family's illustrious past and thinks he should still command the world.*

"Look, Mr. Gardner. You're mistaken if you think I have any power or influence over Jacob Watkins. My cousin doesn't give a fig about me—we'd never even met until I came here to Salem. Frankly, he'd be glad to see me dead and out of the way, so if you're thinking of using me as bait, forget it. The only thing he cares about is money, and he'll sell the statue to the highest bidder. Which right now doesn't seem to be you."

"Let's just see about that," Gardner said and nodded to Mr. Smith.

# Chapter Thirty-Two

"Everything we see hides another thing."

— *Rene Magritte*

At quarter past seven, Alan Peabody checked his Patek Philippe watch and decided Lizzie must be running late due to packing, settling up accounts, and preparing for her trip back to New York tomorrow. At half past, he wondered if perhaps he'd been stood up. He unfolded the telegram she'd sent, agreeing to meet him tonight, and reread it carefully to see if he might have misinterpreted her response. But no, her wording contained no ambiguity.

When she still hadn't arrived at quarter to eight, he started to worry.

He pulled on his overcoat and approached the hotel's front desk. "Have you seen a tall, beautiful, well-dressed young woman with short dark hair in this lobby during the past hour?" he asked the concierge.

"I haven't noticed anyone who fits that description, sir."

"You definitely would have noticed her," Alan assured him. He laid a business card and a folded bill on the counter. "If you do happen to spot her, would you kindly tell her I asked after her and give her a key to my room?"

"Yes indeed, sir. I'll keep an eye out for her."

Alan slid behind the wheel of his silver Bentley and turned the key in the ignition. The three-litre tourer roared to life, like a racehorse prancing at the gate. He flipped on the headlights, illuminating the streets of the beautiful city, and drove to the most beautiful one of all: Chestnut Street.

For several moments he parked in front of the Gardners' home, debating how to proceed, until he noticed a light shining at the top of a flight of stairs that led up to the second story of the carriage house behind the mansion. Shifting gears, he drove two blocks farther and turned onto a side street where his flashy automobile wouldn't be visible from the house. Then he walked back through the shadows, eased open the front gate, and quietly made his way around to the carriage house. He climbed the stairs and knocked on the door.

Sidney Somerset opened it.

Confusion contorted the pianist's face, and Alan sensed Sid's anxiety even before he spoke. "Has something happened to Lizzie?"

"I don't know. She didn't show up for our dinner engagement. I'd hoped to find her here."

"I dropped her off at the hotel at seven sharp. I thought she was with you."

Alan shook his head. "No, and the hotel's concierge hasn't seen her either. May I come in?"

"Oh, sure, sorry." Sidney stepped back to allow Alan to enter the apartment. He observed the copper-haired man's emerald cufflinks, the perfect knot in his silk tie, his precisely creased trousers, and beautifully made leather shoes. Remembering his manners, Sid said, "I'm having a splash of scotch. Care for a drink?"

"Yes, thank you." Alan slipped off his coat, draped it over the back of one of the apartment's worn leather armchairs, and lowered himself into another. "How did she seem to you when you dropped her off tonight?"

Sidney poured two fingers of Lagavulin into a tumbler and handed it to Alan. "Keyed up, but in a happy sort of way. I attributed it to having successfully completed our stint here. The end of an engagement like this is always a combination of elation and letdown. Plus, anticipation of going home tomorrow." He clinked his glass against Alan's. "And, yes, she was eager to see you too."

Alan leaned forward in his chair, resting his elbows on his knees. He rubbed his thumbs up and down the sides of the glass, gazing into it as if it were an oracle that might answer the questions spinning in his mind. "Is there anyplace else she might have gone?"

"None. I think we should go to the police."

Alan had been thinking the same thing, but he tried to rein in unfounded fears. "I don't disagree, but Lizzie's only been unaccountable for an hour. That's not enough time for the cops to concern themselves with her absence." He sipped the scotch and studied Sidney, who fit a cigarette into his ornate silver holder and lit it.

"What do you propose?" Sid asked.

"Who else might be privy to information about Lizzie? Friends, perhaps?"

"Melody might. You've met her—she's the blonde in our group, plays flute and violin." Sidney took a long drag on his cigarette and slowly exhaled the smoke. "I've known Lizzie for seven years. We've worked together in all kinds of situations. She's like a sister to me. And yet, even after all we've been through, I wonder how well I really know her. She keeps things from me, Alan. Maybe she's afraid I'll disapprove or get mad at her, but I'm only trying to protect her. She's too curious, always poking her nose into places where she shouldn't, and it gets her into trouble. Well, you know about that firsthand." He stood up, stubbed out his cigarette, and grabbed a jacket from a wall-hung coat rack. "Stay here. I'll be right back. Help yourself to more scotch."

Sidney hurried along the driveway to the back door of the Gardners' mansion, through the hallway that led past the larder and the laundry, and into the bustling kitchen. Girls scrubbed pots and pans, washed antique china, and polished silver. He spotted the cook, Pearl, and waved to her.

"What you be needing, Mr. Sid? Didn't you get your dinner on time? Or you want an extra dessert?" She scanned his tall, slender form on which evening clothes draped so elegantly, and grinned. "If you come for some fattenin' up, you come to the right place."

He shook off her light-hearted banter. "I'm looking for Lizzie. Have you seen her lately? She seems to have gone missing."

"Now, how can a lady like that go missing?"

"I don't know either, but would you please send one of your girls up to her room and ask Melody to come down here right away? I need to talk to her."

"Sounds serious." Pearl tucked a loose curl of black hair beneath her purple turban. "I'll send my daughter Ruby up there right away."

"Thanks, Pearl."

"You want a cup of coffee? Got some lip-smacking apple cobbler, too, in case you're of a mind."

"Not right now," he said.

She directed him to a worktable at the back of the kitchen, out of the way of the busy staff. "She come by here 'bout an hour ago to say goodbye. Maybe she ran off with that red-headed man she's took a fancy to."

Sidney sat on a stool at the work table. "I wish that were the case. She was supposed to have dinner with him this evening, but she didn't show."

"You go to the police?"

"No, it's too soon to file a missing persons report. They won't take it seriously yet—and by the time they do, it may be too late."

"You got a bad feelin' about this, Mr. Sid?"

He nodded, trying to sort through the myriad thoughts racing in his mind. "It's not like Lizzie to skip an appointment, especially with the fella she's 'took a fancy to,' as you put it. He's up in the carriage house apartment right now, and he's worried about her too."

They both turned as Melody hurried into the kitchen, followed by Ruby.

"Where's Lizzie?" Melody asked, her blue eyes wide with alarm.

"We don't know yet," Sid said. He pulled off his jacket and draped it around her thin shoulders. "Come with me."

"I'm gonna put the word out on her, Mr. Sid," the cook said. "Never know what you might hear when you listen to the street."

"Thanks, Pearl. Let me know what you find out."

\* \* \*

Sidney told Melody what little he knew as they crossed the distance to the carriage house.

"Lizzie wouldn't miss this chance to have dinner with Alan. She's goofy for

213

him," Melody said as they climbed the steps to the second-floor apartment.

"Don't I know it."

"She told me not to wait up for her; she'd see me in the morning. I think she planned to spend the night with him."

Sidney had gotten the same impression. He opened the door and ushered Melody inside.

Alan stood, drink in hand, when they entered. "Good evening."

"Sid tells me you haven't seen Lizzie and don't know why she didn't show up for dinner," Melody said.

"I thought perhaps you might have some information that could help us find her," Alan said. "Has she seemed strange lately? Troubled?"

"No, not that I noticed."

Not wanting to frighten the young woman, he reluctantly asked, "Did she have any enemies?"

"I don't think so. Other than the Gardners, the only people she knows here are Cora Delaney and Jacob Watkins. Jacob's Lizzie's cousin. He owns a pub near the harbor."

"It's called Misery Tavern, off Derby Street," Sidney added. "A real dive."

Melody nodded. "Lizzie wanted to get to know her cousin. She went there a couple times to talk to him, but I don't think she trusted him. He sounded a little shady to me."

"What about Cora?" Alan asked.

"You know Cora, from our stint at Halcyon Castle," Sidney said, lighting a cigarette. He offered one to Alan, who shook his head.

"I've known Cora much longer than that."

"She and Lizzie have gotten quite chummy since we've been here," Melody said. "I think we should talk to her."

Remembering the eve before New Year's Eve party at Isaac Roman's mansion that Cora had invited them to, Sidney said, "I agree."

"Let's walk over now, her house is only a few blocks from here," Alan said. "We don't have time to waste."

# Chapter Thirty-Three

"When I see a hidden action brought to light, I worship the god of Truth."

— *Edna St. Vincent Millay*

Smith knelt and rolled back one of the room's carpets, revealing a trap door. He opened it, and a musty odor crept into the posh office. Gardner stood and motioned Lizzie toward the opening. She glanced at Smith, well aware of the knife in his pocket, then at the office door and estimated her chances of outrunning him. *Slim*, she decided, *even with that limp*. For all she knew, he'd locked the office door, and any attempt to escape would be for naught. *Best to play along until an opportunity presents itself.*

"Where are we going?" she asked, stalling for time.

"The tunnel where your cousin has hidden my statue," Gardner answered.

"I've already told you. Jacob's probably moved her by now. Besides, I couldn't find my way through that maze. It's like the catacombs down there."

"I know the way, Miss Crane," Gardner said. "My family has made use of these tunnels since they were built."

"Jeepers creepers, is all of Salem connected via these stinking, rat-infested burrows?"

"Much of this area near the harbor is. Now, please, don't make trouble.

You should never have involved yourself in this matter in the first place. It's none of your business. Just show us where the statue is, and I'll let you go." Gardner glanced at her feet and chuckled coldly. "Too bad another pair of your shoes will get ruined."

The man in the green cap grabbed her arm and pulled her toward the trap door. Afraid he might push her down the stairs if she refused to go willingly, she stared into the hole that his flashlight beam illuminated. She stepped down into the dark, moldy corridor where for more than a century, all kinds of illicit trade, including human, had moved in secret. Mr. Smith descended behind her, followed by Matthew Gardner.

"Turn right and walk about fifty feet, then take a left," Gardner directed.

Lizzie did as told, careful not to slip on the wet brick floor. The stench of stagnant brackish water, vermin waste, and the detritus of untold decades of debauchery assaulted her senses. When she paused, gagging, trying not to throw up, Smith pressed his palm between her shoulder blades and pushed her on. A rat as big as a cat darted in front of her, and she balked. Her heel caught on the uneven floor. She tripped and fell to her knees. He grabbed her arm and jerked her upright.

The men's footsteps squished behind her on the wet bricks as she stumbled along the passageway. After several more turns, she lost track of where she was. The tunnel seemed to twist around itself like a pretzel, without the sun's light or any landmarks to guide her. At times, the ceiling was so low she had to bend over to keep from banging her head. The crypt-like quarters—cramped, dark, and slimy with mold—made her shudder, and she struggled to stave off a rising swell of panic.

"Turn left, about twenty feet ahead," Gardner said from behind her.

A narrow brick hallway opened ahead of her, and Lizzie entered it. Despite her disorientation, she sensed she was moving into familiar territory, although she couldn't say why. It looked the same as the rest of the tunnels she'd trudged through. Yet something about it triggered a memory. *This is where I first laid eyes on the goddess,* she realized. Smith's light shone on the dark-stained wall where the door to the secret vault hung agape.

Beside it stood Jacob Watkins.

He held a nine-inch-long fishing gaff in his meaty hand, its double-barbed point glinting menacingly in the flashlight's beam. "You want the lady? Come and get her."

Confused, Smith appeared to be measuring his knife against Watkins's gaff. He turned to Gardner as if seeking instruction, but Gardner seemed equally uncertain. *They didn't expect this,* Lizzie realized. *They'd hoped to come down here, snatch the statue, and sneak her back out, without anyone being the wiser.*

"I was right about you, Cousin," Watkins sneered at Lizzie. "You were working for him all along to steal the statue from me."

"No, they dragged me here at knifepoint," she said, thinking *if it comes to a fight, at least he should know Smith is armed too.*

Watkins slapped the back of the gaff against his left palm. "Matthew Gardner, you like to call yourself a gentleman. A pillar of the community. Yet you kidnap my cousin and bring your henchman down here to steal property from me. Property my father risked his life for. What kind of a man does that? Not an honorable one, that's for sure."

Smith's shoulders twitched slightly. He shifted his weight so his good leg bore most of it. Then he pulled his knife from his pocket and lunged at Watkins. As her cousin raised his fishing gaff, Lizzie dashed toward the wooden ladder that led into Misery Tavern's ladies' room.

She'd climbed only three steps when a hand clasped her ankle and dragged her back into the fetid tunnel. She fell against Matthew Gardner, and they both tumbled to the floor. While he struggled to regain his balance, Lizzie stood and pulled off her right shoe. She slammed its heel into his left temple. Gardner yelped and stumbled backward, his arms flailing as he hit the brick floor again.

Ignoring the grunts and groans of the men below her, Lizzie dashed up the ladder. She threw herself against the secret door at the back of the utility closet. It didn't budge. She shoved again, harder, but the door remained stuck. Desperately, she hammered on it with her fists and shouted, hoping someone might hear her.

She heard a creak and turned to see Matthew Gardner climbing the ladder below her. Blood trickled from his temple. He reached for her ankle, and Lizzie kicked him. Her heel glanced off his cheek as she pounded on the hidden closet door again.

"Help! Somebody, please! Open the door!"

Hooking her elbows around one of the ladder's rungs for support, Lizzie flailed at Gardner with both feet. She landed a solid blow under his chin, then another on his forehead. He grabbed for her foot. And missed. As he fell back, a rectangle of light opened in the dark wall behind her.

A woman's voice called out, "What the hell's goin' on down there?"

# Chapter Thirty-Four

"How did I escape? With difficulty. How did I plan this moment? With pleasure."

— *Alexandre Dumas, The Count of Monte Cristo*

A pair of strong hands dragged Lizzie through the tiny door in the back of the closet. She flopped onto the grimy ladies' room floor and sat there trying to catch her breath. Two women who looked like versions of the same person, but with twenty years separating them, stared down at her.

"What the hell?" the older one said.

"Call the cops," Lizzie said.

"Are you hurt?" the younger one asked, appraising Lizzie's torn dress, shredded stockings, and ruined shoes.

"I don't think so. But three men are fighting down there. They have weapons. Someone could get killed."

The women grasped Lizzie's arms and pulled her to her feet. "Can you stand?" the older one asked.

"I'm okay, but I need to get away from here."

"I've got a motorcar. I can give you a lift," said the younger one, who appeared to be about Lizzie's age.

"Thanks, I'd really appreciate that."

"Mom, how 'bout you ring the cops while I drive this lady home?"

The younger woman snatched her coat from the back of a chair as she and Lizzie dashed through the pub. They hurried down the street to a rusted old auto that looked like it should be drawn by a horse. Its owner cranked the motor to life, then the two of them climbed up onto the bench seat. *She probably thinks I'm a prostitute,* Lizzie thought.

"Those men fighting over you?" the woman asked.

"Not in the usual sense," Lizzie answered. "They're actually fighting over another lady. I just got caught in the middle."

The woman shifted into gear. "Where to?"

Lizzie told her the address, and the driver whistled. "What's a lady from Chestnut Street doing in a joint like Misery?"

"It's a long story...."

The young woman laughed. "It always is."

They rumbled down Derby Street in the open auto with the cold wind off the harbor whipping at their hair and clothing. A single schooner bobbed on the black ocean, lanterns twinkling on its bow.

They drove past the train station and south onto Chestnut Street. As they pulled up in front of the Gardners' mansion, Lizzie said, "Thanks again for rescuing me. I wish I could pay you for your trouble, but I seem to have lost my purse in the scuffle."

The driver shook her head. "Wouldn't hear of it. You see a sister in trouble, you gotta help. Simple as that." She studied Lizzie with genuine concern on her face. "You sure you're okay?"

"I know, I look a fright. But I'm all in one piece." Lizzie opened the passenger door and climbed down from the car. "Please thank your mother for me too. I don't want to think what might've happened to me if you hadn't shown up in the nick of time."

The young woman waved and called, "Fare thee well," then made a U-turn and headed back toward the pub.

* * *

A light shone above the door to the carriage house apartment. Sid's Buick

220

was parked in the driveway. Lizzie hurried past the Gardners' mansion, bolted up the stairs, and knocked on the door.

Bert opened it. Even before he spoke, his expression revealed how dreadful she looked. "Lizzie, what happened to you?" He grabbed her wrist and pulled her inside.

"Matthew Gardner and another man kidnapped me and dragged me down into the tunnels that run beneath the streets of Salem," she said. "Where's Sid?"

"Out looking for you." He handed her a piece of paper on which Sidney had scribbled a quick note to the saxophonist.

> Lizzie's missing. Melody and I have gone with Alan to Cora's house to try to find her. Wait here in case Lizzie shows up.

She considered walking to Cora's house to let her friends know she was okay, but she didn't want them to see her like this. "Did they say when they'd be back?"

"No." Bert studied her torn garments again. "Why did Gardner kidnap you? Did he hurt you?"

Lizzie waved off his questions. "I'll explain later. We have to skedaddle out of here sooner than planned. Gather up your stuff and Sid's too. Load it in the breezer. I'm going to pack my clothes and Melody's. Meet you back here as soon as possible."

"Are we in trouble, Lizzie?" he asked, nervously cracking his knuckles.

"Well, I am, so I guess by association, the rest of you are too." Trying to reassure him, she patted Bert's cheek. "It will all make sense tomorrow. Trust me for now and just do as I say."

Without waiting for his answer, she ran down the outside stairway, around to the mansion's back door, and into the kitchen. Fortunately, only a couple scullery maids remained at this hour, and they kept to their tasks as she darted through. She wondered how long it would take Matthew Gardner to come back here. Long enough to let them get away, she hoped. He had other problems to tend to—he might even have been injured when she kicked him and knocked him off the ladder, or in the scuffle with Jacob.

Pushing those thoughts out of her mind, she let herself into the pleasant bedroom she'd shared with Melody these past twelve days. Steeling herself, she looked at her reflection in the vanity mirror. Her beautiful cashmere coat had survived the ordeal. Although it was smeared with filth, it could be cleaned. However, her lovely evening frock hung in shreds. Her silk stockings had practically disintegrated. Her shoes were beyond repair and, when she yanked them off, she spotted what looked like blood on the right heel.

Tossing the wrecked garments in the wastebasket, she turned on the tap and ran hot water in the tub. Grime from the tunnels streaked her face and legs. The stench and the ignominy of the evening made her stomach churn. While the tub filled, Lizzie pulled evening gowns and flapper dresses, skirts and sweaters and blouses, hats, scarves, and more than a dozen pairs of shoes from the wardrobe. She collected nightgowns, slips, and underwear from dresser drawers and shoved everything into suitcases. She swept jewelry, cosmetics, and an array of other personal items into a tapestry satchel and dragged what she could manage to the door. She set Melody's instrument cases beside the other bags.

Then she slid into the tub and hurriedly scrubbed off the foulness of the past two hours. The bathwater washed away the disgust that had engulfed her, but she still felt anxiety and guilt. *What if I killed Gardner?* she worried. She'd only fought back in self-defense, she hadn't wanted to harm him. *What if he hit his head when he fell, like Nicholas Owens did when Jacob slugged him?*

She recalled Gardner's words. "You should never have involved yourself in this matter. It's none of your business." He was right. She wished she could start all over again from the beginning, wished she didn't know what she knew now. But it was too late for that. Lizzie stepped out of the bathtub and toweled off. She dried her dark hair as best she could, then pulled on underwear, a silk blouse, a calf-length woolen skirt, and matching sweater.

The bedroom door opened, and Melody entered. "Lizzie? Where have you been? We've been so worried about you!"

"Matthew Gardner and another man kidnapped me. They got in a fight with Jacob in the tunnels."

"What are you talking about? What man? What tunnels?"

"I've packed our clothes. Help me carry everything downstairs and put them in the breezer."

She grabbed the handle of a trunk and motioned for Melody to take the other end. Between them, they managed to lug the heavy case down the stairs, out into the clear cold night. Sid and Bert met them beside the Buick.

"Lizzie?" Sid said, confusion contorting his face.

"Where's Alan?"

"At the Hawthorne Hotel. What's going on?"

"We're leaving ahead of schedule. I'll explain when we're out of here."

The urgency in her voice cut through their questions. While the men loaded the luggage into Sidney's car, Lizzie and Melody went back for the rest of their belongings. They gathered up everything of importance and left behind what no longer mattered.

"I feel like a refugee, and I don't even know what I'm fleeing from," Bert said as he climbed into the backseat beside Melody, whose feet were propped up on a suitcase.

"Where to now, Lizzie?" Sidney asked.

"The Hawthorne. It's too late to start for New York now. We can leave in the morning."

"This is all so dramatic, like something out of a novel," Melody said as Sidney drove into the center of town.

"It's not glamorous, Mel. It's really quite awful," Lizzie said. "And things might get worse. I'm sorry to drag all of you into this. I never meant to cause such a balled-up mess."

Sidney tapped his fingers on the steering wheel, as if he hoped to get a response from it the way he did when he played piano keys. "Cora told us some of what's been going on. Why didn't you let me know what you were up to, Bearcat?"

"I didn't want to worry you," she admitted. Now that they were safely out of the Gardners' home, her fear began to subside. "It's a long story."

"By the way," Sidney said, "Peabody's at the hotel. He's been frantic about you too."

Lizzie felt relief wrap around her like a warm blanket. *He's waiting for me.*

# Chapter Thirty-Five

"He looked at her the way all women want to be looked at by a man."

— *F. Scott Fitzgerald, The Great Gatsby*

Alan stood as Lizzie entered the hotel. His dark eyes burned like beacons, guiding her to safety. She broke away from her friends and crossed the lobby to be gathered in, like a foundering ship, by his strong arms. While Sidney arranged for rooms with the desk clerk, Alan stroked her hair, still damp from her bath. "Stay with me tonight, Lizzie. Let me take care of you."

"Yes." She pressed her cheek against the soft lambswool of his lapel, listening to the steady, reassuring beat of his heart.

Sidney handed room keys to Melody and Bert. He glanced at Lizzie, then at Alan, and back again at Lizzie. "I'd like to leave at eight tomorrow morning. Let's meet here in the lobby then. All right by you, Bearcat?"

"Whatever you say-ski."

"Okay-ski."

"I need to get a few things from the breezer."

"I'll come with you," Sidney said, and she understood he didn't want to let her go outside alone.

He opened the Buick's trunk and waited while she unpacked a daytime frock, underwear, cosmetics. A sensuous silk nightgown. Smoke from his cigarette spiraled up into the chilly night air, the ash glowing like a bright red eye in the darkness.

"I may have been wrong about Peabody," he said. "He seems like a stand-up fella. And I think he really cares about you."

It was as close to an apology as she was ever likely to get. Lizzie threw her arms around her longtime friend and kissed his cheek. "Thank you, Sid."

"Still, I hope you won't throw caution to the wind." He puffed out a cloud of smoke and looked away, as if making eye contact with her was too difficult. "We need you, Lizzie. Much as I want you to be happy, I'm selfish too. The Troubadours are my life. I can't bear to think you might leave us to get married, have kids, all that stuff."

"I think you're letting your imagination run away like a wild horse. It's one night. A bit of fun after a lot of chaos."

"Which by the way, you haven't explained yet. You hustled us out of the Gardners' house like the hounds of hell were at our heels, and I still don't know why. Bert said you showed up at the apartment looking like you'd been ravished."

"It will take some time to tell the whole tale, and I'd rather not keep Alan waiting any longer. In the morning," she promised, pressing her fingers to his lips. "Patience, please?"

She owed him an explanation, certainly, but right now she wanted to think about other things. For the moment, at least, she felt safe, and she longed to hold onto that feeling. By tomorrow evening, two hundred miles would separate her from the Gardners, Watkins, Smith, and whoever else had it in for her. Then her life could return to normal.

Sidney slammed the Buick's trunk shut and reached for the grip into which she'd folded her garments. Reluctantly he said, "Okay, Bearcat. I'll give you 'til the morning. I don't want to put a damper on your amorous evening."

"Sid, you're my best friend in the whole world, and I love you dearly. The Troubadours are my life too, you know. Music, performing, that's all I've ever wanted to do." In her mind's eye, Lizzie saw her once-pretty mother, overworked, despairing, worn thin from raising seven children and washing other people's dirty laundry to make ends meet. Any hopes Polly Crane might once have held when she came from Ireland to the new world now lay buried under the crushing burden of poverty and everyday toil. "A husband and kids aren't on my agenda. Never have been."

He took her arm and led her back to the hotel. "Famous last words."

\* \* \*

By the time they'd settled in for the night, the hotel's kitchen was officially closed. But Alan convinced a member of the staff to deliver roast beef with mashed potatoes, winter squash, Parker House rolls, and apple pie to their room. Food meant to provide not only sustenance, but comfort too.

They ate at a table for two beside a window that overlooked Salem Common. Alan poured rich, deep purple Cabernet Franc into their glasses. "This supper isn't as glamorous as I'd planned."

"It's perfect," Lizzie said. "Thank you, Alan, for rescuing me. Again."

"Don't think of me as your knight in shining armor. You don't need someone to rescue you, just someone to believe in you."

"Maybe it's the same thing."

He touched his wineglass to hers. "To you, Lizzie. I was so worried about you. If you feel up to it, would you please tell me everything?"

For the next half-hour, as they ate and sipped the delicious wine Alan had brought up from his cellar on Beacon Hill, she spun out the story of the Quan Yin statue from beginning to end. *This is hardly the sort of talk a woman uses to seduce a lover,* she realized. *Still, he deserves to hear the whole of it.*

"What if Gardner gets the police to pinch me for assault?" she asked. "I kicked him pretty hard."

"Unlikely. Then he'd have to explain abducting you, which would open the subject of who actually owns the statue, Nicholas Owens's death, and a lot of other things Matthew wouldn't want investigated." He laid his hand over hers. "By the way, I know Dr. Cushing. You're aware of my family's ties to the Peabody Museum, aren't you?"

"I know that your relative, George Peabody, funded it."

"I'll have a word with Cushing tomorrow. Maybe there's hope for the goddess yet."

* * *

Alan trailed a line of kisses from her ear, along her neck, her collarbone, and then down between her breasts. "I've been fantasizing about this since the first time I saw you onstage."

"I saw you first."

"Oh?"

"I was watching from the third floor of the Winslows' mansion when you came to Ipswich last summer. I knew right away there was something special about you."

He eased the straps of her nightgown down over her shoulders and watched it slide to the floor. "I fear we've wasted a good deal of time, dear Lizzie."

"Then we must make up for it now."

# Chapter Thirty-Six

"What fun it had been, having an admirer even for that little while. No wonder people liked admirers. They seemed, in some strange way, to make one come alive."

— *Elizabeth von Arnim, The Enchanted April*

"You're looking chipper this morning, Bearcat," Sidney said.

"Never better," she answered, sensing in his tone a mix of envy, curiosity, and happiness for her happiness. An aura of bliss emanated from her like a heady perfume, and she glowed with the inner beauty that only love can awaken.

"You've had breakfast?" he asked. "Everything's copacetic?"

"Yes."

"Well, then…."

He handed his car key to a porter and instructed him to carry the rest of their bags out to the Buick while he settled up with the desk clerk.

Melody held out her hand to Alan. "I hope we'll see more of you."

"I'm sure you will."

Bert shook Alan's hand, too, then stepped back and glanced shyly at Lizzie. When she caught his eye, he blushed and looked away, unsure how to react to the fact that she'd unabashedly spent the night with her lover and everyone, including the hotel staff, knew about it.

229

"All right, boys and girls. New York City, here we come," Sid said, a staged cheerfulness in his voice.

As Melody and Bert followed the porter out to the Buick, Sidney leaned close to Alan—close enough that Lizzie couldn't hear him—and whispered, "Don't hurt her." Then he trailed the others outside, leaving the lovers to say their goodbyes.

* * *

They drove to the antiquarian shop to collect Lizzie's jade statue of the goddess Quan Yin. The elderly shopkeeper carefully wrapped it in cotton wool, then in layers of crumpled newspaper, and nestled it in a cardboard box.

"I must admit, I'm going to miss the lady," he said, giving his snowy beard a tug.

"She'll have a good home," Lizzie promised and handed him the balance of what she owed. "Thanks for keeping the goddess safe for me."

"My pleasure, miss. May she bring you peace and joy."

Next, they drove to Cora Delaney's home. While Melody and Bert waited in the car, the housekeeper guided Lizzie and Sidney into the parlor, then climbed the staircase with its mahogany banister to let Cora know she had guests. After a few minutes, the card reader entered the comfortable living room.

"Lizzie, I've been worried about you ever since Sid and the others showed up here last night. What a relief it is to see you now, safe and sound." Cora appraised Lizzie from head to foot. "Despite your friends' concerns, you don't look any the worse for wear, I must say."

"Fortunately. Still, it was quite a fright, and I've ruined our chances of getting a recommendation from Matthew Gardner. I hope it won't affect your relationship with the Gardners. The story's too long to tell now, but I'll write when I get home. I just wanted to thank you for all you've done for me—for us—during our stay here. I can never repay you for your generosity. I think you may be my guardian angel."

Cora laughed. "I certainly hope not. I'd rather not have that responsibility."

"Please thank Karl for his help too. I'm sorry to have missed saying goodbye to him."

"I will, and you're most welcome."

She wished she were alone with Cora now, so she could describe the events that had led up to this moment and ask her friend for future guidance. Instead, Lizzie said, "The card reading you did for me on New Year's Eve was remarkably accurate. On all counts. Perhaps we might talk about it sometime?"

The housekeeper still stood patiently at the doorway to the parlor. When she caught Cora's eye, she asked, "Shall I bring tea, ma'am?"

"Thanks, but we can't stay," Sidney said, cutting off the possibility of a more lengthy conversation. "Bert and Melody are waiting for us in the car. We're heading back to New York this morning. We've got a long drive ahead of us."

Cora nodded. "Please let me know that you've arrived safe and sound."

"I will," Lizzie said. She hugged Cora, holding on to her friend as if she feared she might never see her again. "Cora, would you consider coming to visit me in New York? You could take the train, and I could show you the sights...."

"I'll think about it. Safe travels."

\* \* \*

They stopped for lunch at a roadside cafe in Connecticut. After they'd finished eating, the women excused themselves and went to the ladies' room.

"The love charm really worked," Melody said as she washed her hands in the chipped porcelain sink. "Alan is smitten with you."

"Maybe," Lizzie hedged.

This, she knew well enough, was the most perilous point in a hoped-for romance. A suitor might shower the object of his affection with attention, gifts, and pretty words until he got what he wanted, but soon afterwards he'd lose interest and charge off in search of a new conquest. Men like Alan

Peabody, who could have any women they wanted, were the most likely to discard their lovers once the prize was won, the mystery revealed.

"I'm sure of it," Melody insisted.

Lizzie stared at her reflection in the cloudy mirror above the sink and ran a comb through her dark hair. "How can you be sure? You've had, what, one romance in your life?"

"Two, but the first was in high school, and it didn't last long," Melody admitted as she powdered her nose. "You love Alan, don't you?"

"He thrills me. When I'm with him, I feel like champagne's flowing through my veins, but I'm not sure that's the same thing as love."

"What was it like, um, being intimate with a man?"

"Physically, you mean?" Lizzie asked. "You do know the fundamentals, don't you? What goes where? The birds and bees and all that?"

"Of course. But what's it *feel* like?"

"Jeepers, creepers, Mel. I can't describe it. You'll just have to find out for yourself."

Melody let out an exasperated sigh. "No one ever tells you these things."

"That's because it's impossible to describe." Not wanting to dismiss her younger friend's request out of hand, Lizzie tried to think of some sort of explanation. "It's different every time. For each person. Each couple. In each situation. An experienced man who's sensitive to a woman's needs, who's attentive and patient, and caring, can give her a great deal of pleasure. If he loves her, all the better." She dropped her comb back into her purse and pulled out a tube of lipstick. "Are you thinking of sleeping with Douglas?"

"Not until we're married. But I don't want to seem like a complete dunce on my wedding night."

"Poor little bunny, Douglas would probably find your innocence endearing and enjoy being your teacher." She traced a red Cupid's bow on her lips, then blotted her mouth with a tissue. "I promise to answer your questions to the best of my ability when we get back to New York. Now let's get a wiggle on. We've got miles to go before we sleep."

\* \* \*

Couples going out to dinner, to clubs, or the theater were hurrying along the frigid streets of Greenwich Village by the time Sidney pulled up to Lizzie's apartment building near the Cherry Lane Theatre. She located the super, who helped Bert unload her luggage, and tipped the robust man to haul it upstairs to her flat.

"Welcome back, miss," he said, pocketing the money.

She hurried around to the driver's side and leaned in through the Buick's open window to give Sid a quick hug. "Thanks for being my dear friend."

He shrugged. "I can't be anything else-ski."

"Sleep well-ski. Talk to you in the morning."

Lizzie waved to her friends as they drove away. Then she took the elevator—an ornate cage of interwoven metal bars that attempted an elegance far beyond that of this lower Manhattan neighborhood—up to the third floor. She opened the door to her apartment to let the super bring in her luggage and stepped on a telegram lying on the floor. She picked up the yellow piece of paper and read Alan's words:

> Dear Lizzie,
>   I can't stop thinking about you. I'll be in New York on Valentine's Day. If you're available, may I take you to dinner and a Broadway play? Please let me know which one you'd like to see so I may arrange for tickets. Until then, I will treasure memories of our time together.
>   With great affection,
>   Alan

She read the telegram twice, letting her own memories of his touch, his kiss, the sense of safety and comfort she'd felt lying in his arms flood her mind and body.

The super cleared his throat. "Will you be needing anything else, miss?"

Jarred back to the present, Lizzie shook her head. "No, thanks. A good night to you."

She unpacked what she needed for the night—the rest could wait until tomorrow—and ran hot water for a bath. While she waited for the tub to fill, she stepped out onto the fire escape and gazed up at the moon. Tonight it hung in the sky over Manhattan, half illuminated, half in darkness. It seemed an apt symbol for her life: half glowing with hope and possibilities, half still hidden in secret.

* * *

A week later, a letter arrived from Cora. Eagerly Lizzie slit it open and pulled out a sheet of thick paper that smelled faintly of lavender, along with a clipping from *The Salem Evening News*.

She unfolded Cora's short letter and read it.

> Dear Lizzie,
>
> Enclosed, please find an article from the newspaper that may be of interest. I can't help wondering about its connection with you. When you have time to write, I hope you'll reveal the entire story.
>
> My fondest wishes for happiness in your relationship with Alan. The cards were right (as usual).
>
> Your friend,
>
> Cora

Next, she read the newspaper article, a small write-up in the police reports dated January 8, 1926.

> *Two local men were taken to the hospital yesterday evening after being injured in a fight. The men were released after treatment, and no charges were pressed. Matthew Gardner and Jacob Watkins, both Salem businessmen, stated the fight ensued over a financial matter.*

The snippet was annoying in its brevity and raised more questions than it answered. Had Gardner been injured when he fell after she kicked him?

234

What happened to the mysterious "Mr. Smith"—the article made no mention of the man in the green plaid cap. And what about the Quan Yin statue? Had Jacob moved her to a safer location? Sold her to someone with deeper pockets than Gardner? Or had Smith made off with her during the turmoil? As Lizzie slid the clipping back into the envelope, she hoped Alan had managed to contact Dr. Cushing at the Peabody Museum to discuss options for the goddess's future—if any still existed.

*  *  *

Lizzie lifted the Bakelite earpiece of the telephone in her tiny living room and heard Sidney's voice on the other end of the line. "Get dressed, Bearcat. We're going out to celebrate."

"What's the occasion?" she asked.

"I just talked to Isaac Roman. We're definitely on for his spring equinox party. It's only a three-day stint—March 19, 20, and 21—but the dough's ducky. He's going to wire a deposit tomorrow. With any luck, it will be almost warm when we get there."

Lizzie would have clapped her hands if she hadn't been holding the receiver in one of them. "That's swell, Sid!"

"Now you have an excuse to shop for new clothes. Everyone in Salem has already seen your entire wardrobe," he teased her.

"I definitely need new shoes."

"I'll pick you up in an hour."

*So we're going back to Salem*, she mused. *I hope I don't run into Jacob, the Gardners, or the man in the green plaid cap ever again.* Even from this distance, the thought gave her shivers. *On the other hand, I might find out what's happened to the Quan Yin statue. Maybe I'll get to visit her in Isaac Roman's private gallery.*

# Chapter Thirty-Seven

"Happiness is a work of art. Handle with care."

— *Edith Wharton*

As the day of Alan's arrival neared, Lizzie fretted about what he'd think of her modest three-room apartment in a section of the Village favored by artists and other bohemian types. Ordinarily, she spent so little time here that its appearance didn't matter much to her. Now she worried he'd see beneath the glamorous façade she showed to the world as an entertainer and discover the uneducated daughter of poor Irish immigrants.

She spent all day Friday sweeping, scrubbing, dusting, polishing, washing windows, and organizing her belongings neatly into closets, cabinets, and shelves, trying to put the best face on things. She bought new sheets and a fluffy down comforter at Macy's. She put French lavender soap in the bathroom. She arranged a vase full of red and yellow tulips—forced to bloom early in a greenhouse somewhere in New Jersey—and set them on the table.

"Okay, Quan Yin, bring me good luck," she petitioned the graceful jade goddess, who now sat on her bedroom dressing table.

Saturday afternoon, Lizzie took the subway to Penn Station to meet Alan's train from Boston. *If only the weather wasn't so dreadful,* she rued. The temperature hovered just above freezing, and a wet, wind-driven snow fell on the city, making everything gray and soggy. But no amount of dismal weather could dampen her spirits. When Alan stepped from the train, she ran down the platform to greet him. He swept her into his arms, lifting her feet off the pavement, and spun her around in circles until she laughed out loud.

"How was your trip?" she asked after he put her down.

"Uneventful, thankfully."

"How's your mother?"

"Still holding her own. It's hard to believe she's lasted this long. She has a strong will, though, and seems determined to stick around for a while yet."

"That's good news."

He instructed a porter to collect his luggage and follow them out to the street. There he hailed a taxi and helped Lizzie climb inside. After tipping the porter, who loaded his bags into the cab's trunk, Alan brushed wet snow from his overcoat, shook off his fedora, and slid into the backseat next to her.

As they motored down Seventh Avenue, he took her hand. "It's good to see you, Lizzie. How have you been?"

"Copacetic," she answered. "Much better now that you're here."

He peeled off her glove and pressed her bare palm to his lips.

\* \* \*

Alan declined the drink she offered and pulled her against him, kissing her with an urgency that made her dizzy.

"I've thought of nothing else during the entire trip from Boston," he said as he unbuttoned her silk blouse.

With his help, she eased out of her skirt and undergarments. He rolled off her stockings with deliberate slowness, trailing a line of kisses down her legs. While he removed his own clothing, she watched brazenly. Then she threw back the down comforter, exposing the new sheets, and invited him into her bed.

\* \* \*

"You're the most beautiful woman here and I'm proud to be your escort tonight," Alan said as he guided Lizzie down the aisle of the Ambassador Theatre to their seats in the orchestra section.

She'd taken off her black velvet opera cape to showcase the new scarlet evening gown she'd bought for this occasion. Its strapless bodice revealed her ivory shoulders, the ruched skirt hugged her curves, and the dramatic train cascaded from her right hip to the floor like a waterfall of rich red wine. It had cost a fortune, but the look in Alan's eyes made it worth the price.

She'd wanted to see the stage production of F. Scott Fitzgerald's popular new novel, *The Great Gatsby,* which had opened only twelve days ago. But after the curtain fell, she second-guessed herself. *I should've chosen something lighter and more romantic. I hope this won't put a crimp in our evening.*

Alan draped her velvet cloak around her bare shoulders and brushed a kiss on the back of her neck. "Where would you like to go for supper? I made reservations at the Waldorf Hotel, Delmonico's, and Fitzgerald's favorite, the Plaza."

"They're all magnificent," Lizzie said, "but would you mind terribly if we went somewhere quieter and, well, less ostentatious?"

"I know just the place."

\* \* \*

Alan flagged down a cab, and they rode through the snow-splattered night to a restaurant not far from Lizzie's apartment, although she'd never heard of it before. They walked down a flight of stone steps, and he opened a door that led into a room barely twenty by twenty feet, with stucco walls and a beamed ceiling. So many candles burned in sconces that she felt like she'd interrupted a religious rite. A plump woman invited them in with a broad grin and showed them to one of only three tables, all unoccupied.

He introduced Lizzie, and, as their hostess and Alan exchanged pleasantries, she realized that he'd been here many times before. Their easy banter had the comfortable familiarity of people who've known one another a long time. After a few minutes, the plump woman excused herself and returned bearing two glasses of sun-colored wine to their table in blatant defiance of the Volstead Act.

Alan lifted his glass to Lizzie and toasted, "To us."

She sipped the delicate wine that resonated with the promise of golden days ahead while they sheltered in this warm, intimate cellar on this cold New York night.

"What is this place?" she asked.

"Some friends of mine own it," he said and laid his hand over hers. "Lizzie, I have some good news for you. At least, I think you'll find it good news."

"Good news is always welcome. What is it?"

"The Peabody Museum has acquired the Quan Yin statue Howard Watkins rescued from *Peregrine* when she sank."

"Really? That's wonderful! Thank you, Alan! What happened?"

Before he could answer, the plump woman brought a platter of baked haddock to their table and spooned the delicate white fish onto their plates, along with spears of asparagus.

"After I spoke with Dr. Cushing, he contacted your cousin and suggested the museum might be interested in the statue. Cushing asked him to show it to a few members of the museum's staff, and Watkins agreed. They found her every bit as beguiling as you'd promised."

"They bought her from Jacob?"

"Not exactly. As it turns out, the company that insured *Peregrine* had paid William Gardner for the loss of his ship and her cargo more than fifty years ago. Therefore they owned whatever goods survived the wreck, including the statue. The insurance company agreed to donate Quan Yin to the museum—it's good publicity for them and probably a nice tax write off too. The indemnity club that covered the remainder of Gardner's losses has long since ceased to exist."

Lizzie took a bite of her fish. *Karl Blume was right,* she thought, recalling the attorney's explanation of the arrangements the owners of clipper ships made to protect themselves against financial losses.

"So Matthew Gardner couldn't claim he owned the statue," she said.

"No, but neither could Jacob Watkins. She didn't qualify as jetsam, and in a court of law, she might be considered stolen."

"How did the museum convince Jacob to part with the goddess?"

"When he presented her to Cushing and his colleagues, various matters involving suspicious activities came up, including the death of the thief Nickolas Owens whom your cousin sent to his Maker, unintentional as it may have been." He paused to eat some of his haddock and an asparagus spear before continuing. "There were also questions about where Howard Watkins got the money to set up Misery Tavern and whether Jacob was moving alcohol through the tunnels. He was in no position to argue."

"Will Jacob go to prison for manslaughter?"

"I don't know. The police are still investigating him and his activities."

Lizzie recalled her meeting with Dr. Cushing. From the man's attitude, she'd gotten the impression that the museum wouldn't involve itself in anything shady or even controversial. When she mentioned it to Alan, he laughed.

"If you study history, you'll find museums aren't always as upstanding as they pretend to be. Self-interest has a way of influencing even the most high-minded."

The plump woman approached their table and cleared away their dishes. She replaced them with plates that held medallions of rosy-red beef and honey-glazed carrots, then glanced at Alan. When he nodded, she removed their wine glasses and brought two new glasses filled with what looked like melted rubies.

As Lizzie cut into a tender slice of beef, she pondered the events surrounding the Quan Yin statue. "Neither Jacob nor Matthew Gardner ever actually owned the lady, and now she's lost to both of them. I bet they're both furious. But their loss is Salem's gain." She couldn't keep from smiling at the irony of it all.

"The museum did agree to pay Jacob what they called a 'storage fee' for housing the statue all these years, but I'm sure it was only a fraction of what he'd hoped to get from selling her."

"I'll be able to visit her again the next time I'm in Salem," Lizzie said, her eyes dancing with delight. "How can I ever thank you, Alan?"

"Seeing you happy is thanks enough."

\* \* \*

After they'd arrived back at her apartment and changed out of their evening clothes, Alan opened one of his bags and withdrew a box wrapped in blue paper. He handed it to her. "I brought you a present."

"Another present? You've given me so much already," Lizzie protested.

"Open it."

She fingered the initials on the golden seal that fastened the paper: AGP. "What does the G stand for?"

"Grey. It's my mother's maiden name."

Carefully she broke the seal and unwrapped the box. Inside sat a statue of the Buddha about the size of an apple carved out of cinnabar with a round belly and a jolly expression on his face. Lizzie placed the glossy red figure on her dressing table beside the jade goddess.

"Do you know Quan Yin is sometimes considered the Buddha's feminine counterpart?"

He nodded. "I think you may have told me that."

"Thank you, Alan. He's magnificent. What a lovely gift."

"He'll keep your goddess company when you're away." Taking her in his arms, he said, "I have to go back to Boston in the morning. Can you get away for a few days and come with me?"

"Yes, I'd like that very much. I've never been to Boston."

"Then I'll have the pleasure of showing you around my city."

He kissed her, stroking her body through her silk nightgown. When he reached to switch off the bedside light, Lizzie stopped him.

"One moment." She stepped to her dressing table and turned the statues of Quan Yin and the Buddha around so they faced away from the bed. "Now we can leave the light on."

\* \* \*

Wet snow streaked the windows as the train pulled out of Penn Station, heading north to Boston. Still only half-awake, Lizzie rested her head against Alan's shoulder. She wasn't used to being up and about this early, and they hadn't gone to sleep until nearly 2:00.

*Maybe I'm still dreaming,* she thought as she felt him squeeze her hand. *This is too good to be true. I feel like Cinderella.*

The train's whistle jarred her back to reality. *I'll have to telephone Sid when we get to Boston so he doesn't think I've eloped with Alan.* She sat up and gazed out the window into the pewter-gray dawn. *Two hundred miles isn't such a long way, after all.*

# A Note from the Author

This is a work of fiction, though it contains real places and events that actually happened. Except in the case of historic fact, any resemblance to actual persons, living or dead, is purely coincidental. When real people or situations are presented, it is in a fictional context. For example, artist Edward Hopper visited Salem and painted in Gloucester, Massachusetts in the mid-1920s, but he never met the characters in this book (at least to my knowledge). The Peabody Essex Museum was originally established in 1799 and was named for its benefactor George Peabody. However, Dr. Cushing is a product of my imagination, and bears no resemblance to anyone associated with this esteemed institution. Alan Peabody, too, lives only in my mind and has no known relationship to the noted philanthropist.

Many of the other places mentioned here are real, including the House of the Seven Gables, the Custom House, and the Hawthorne Hotel. The smuggling tunnels, built in the early 1800s and financed by some of Salem's most prominent citizens, are mostly closed today. The Peirce-Nichols House on Chestnut Street inspired the Gardners' mansion, although the Gardner family never lived there. Misery Tavern isn't real, but the islands are. Unfortunately, some of the places that existed at the time this story takes place, such as the impressive train station, have since been demolished.

I have endeavored to convey events, people, products, technology, music, literature, entertainments, social norms, fashion, food, and other details accurately, in keeping with the period. When it comes to matters of clothing, I'm indebted to Debbie Sessions of Vintage Dancer for her extensive knowledge of everything from hats to undergarments. I hope you'll find this information intriguing and that it will enrich your enjoyment of the story.

Salem has been one of the most fascinating and beautiful cities in America for nearly four centuries. I consider myself fortunate to have lived there for eight years, and hope that if you've never seen it, you get a chance to visit soon.

# Acknowledgements

I am deeply grateful to Level Best Books and the Dames of Detection—Verena Rose, Shawn Reilly Simmons, and Harriette Sackler—for making this, the third in my Lizzie Crane series, available to readers who love historical mysteries. I also want to thank my fellow Level Besties for generously offering encouragement, tips, advice, and other assistance—you really are the best.

Many thanks to my writing group and all the rest of you who read early drafts of this book and offered much-needed guidance, especially fellow crime writers Kate Flora, Susan Oleksiw, and Paula Munier. Thanks to Martha Mitchell, too, who hated my original ending and coerced me to write a better one. Y'all caught my mistakes, polished my prose, and made me look better than I would have without your input.

# About the Author

Skye Alexander is the author of nearly fifty fiction and nonfiction books. Her stories have appeared in anthologies internationally, and her work has been translated into more than a dozen languages. In 2003, she cofounded Level Best Books with fellow crime writers Kate Flora and Susan Oleksiw. After living in Massachusetts for more than thirty years, Skye now makes her home in the heart of Texas.

AUTHOR WEBSITE:
 www.skyealexander.com

# Also by Skye Alexander

The Lizzie Crane series:
    *Never Try to Catch a Falling Knife*
    *What the Walls Know*
    *The Goddess of Shipwrecked Sailors*
    *Running in the Shadows*